A WISH SO WANTED

THIEVES OF ZAREEN

Z.R. ABADDI

To our future children,

We love you.

Z & R

CHAPTER
ONE

The first light of dawn crept over the horizon, casting a soft, golden hue over the city of Zareen. It was an hour when the world seemed to hold its breath, caught between the stillness of night and the bustle of day.

Nisha sat atop the camel, feeling the gentle sway of the beast beneath her as it moved with a slow, measured pace through the streets. She had always thought that camels were majestic, beautiful creatures. But now, with a white-knuckled grip of the pommel, she knew better; the sundamned creatures were terrifying, and far too high off the ground.

She glanced toward Sher beside her, riding his own camel. It had been a tough morning. King Razhan had sent a team to treat them, stitching together cuts and spreading salve on their wounds with unbelievable proficiency. They didn't have to spend long on Nisha, as the only thing that needed attention was her leg, which got caught in a barbed wire net during her attempt to steal the lamp. Sher, however, demanded most of their time, his body a canvas of cuts after being shoved into a pit of glass-sharded sand. He'd forced her to betray him, but that didn't help the guilt gnawing away at her.

Nisha stared while the healers had worked, fixated by the cuts that laced his skin. Before her, Sher's skin had been perfectly smooth. But now the scarred tapestry of his skin told the truth. The moment she entered Sher's life was when the glass shards began cutting.

He had to be in a world of pain, but you wouldn't know it by looking at him. His back was straight, his chin held high, and his stony, golden gaze was fixed firmly to the west, as though he could see the Angel in the far distance.

Nisha sighed, loosing a tense breath as she looked away from him.

The quiet of the morning did nothing to put her at ease. It was unsettling because Zareen was never this quiet. This time of the morning, the merchants were usually setting up their stalls, laughing and shouting with friends and enemies. But now, as they made their way through the empty streets, there was nothing. No shouting, no soft murmur of a forming morning crowd, no sound but the clop of their camels walking over the smoothed stone pathway.

It felt *wrong* to leave like this.

She glanced back over her shoulder at the Peak District, to where the white marble mansions towered. She could still sense her daughter, sleeping soundly in her soft bed.

All these years, she'd hated the Bloodlined family that stole her to raise as their own. But maybe it had been the best thing for her because in trying to take Auri back, in trying to claim all the years that had been taken from them, Nisha had done the one thing she'd sworn she would never do.

She'd put her daughter in danger.

What kind of mother did that? The thought clawed at her. And yet, as much as she wished she could, there was no reversing what she had done.

The only way to protect Auri now was to do as King Razhan said: bring him back a tear from the Angel in the West. Otherwise, he would put her daughter in the ground.

She faced forward just as they passed through the gates to the Glass District. The smoothed stone pathway gave way to soft sand, riddled with glass shards, sharp enough to cut a bare foot to ribbons.

A simple, raw anger burned in the pit of her stomach, growing hotter with each pounding heartbeat. Razhan thought he had her under his thumb now. He was mistaken.

Perhaps once he would have understood the kind of place she came from and the kind of person she had to be. After all, Razhan had once been a thie—

Nisha frowned as her mind went completely blank. It was strange. The thought was on the tip of her tongue. She hated forgetting things. With a sigh and a shake of her head, she moved on. It didn't matter. Her point remained the same. Stuck up in his golden domed palace, the King was too far removed from the horrors of where she came from to know that street rats are most dangerous when they're cornered.

They passed through the Glass District, Sher's hand resting on the pommel of a sword sheathed away at his side. But Nisha was more relaxed. She knew her people well enough to know that nobody, not even an ember-dusted fool would dare interfere with them. After all, they were riding camels branded with the King's own mark. Interfering with them meant interfering with the King's business, and a pair of camels saddled with anything less than their weight in pure gold wasn't worth risking the King's wrath.

The only thing of value was her rose quartz necklace, and it was tucked safely away. She knew it wouldn't be smart to wear jewelry into the desert, where the heat could brand her with it, but she wasn't ready to leave it behind. It meant too much now.

When they finally reached the outermost edge of Zareen, they came to a stop, as if they both realized that this was it. This was where everything they knew came to an end and where the danger ahead began.

Nisha stared at the endless sea of golden sand.

"I've never left Zareen," she said, breaking the silence that had lingered since the moment they'd awoken in each other's arms. "It's an awful place. But ... it's really the only place I've ever known, you know?"

Sher was quiet for a minute, then he answered in a soft voice.

"It's home."

Nisha drew a deep breath. She'd never really thought of it like that. Yet, as she looked back at Zareen and took it in, she was struck by its beauty—from the slums of the Glass District to the golden-domed palace surrounded by its thousand spires, boxed in by the towering sandstone walls, all under the shadow of the Angel's throne atop the red, flat-topped mountain.

Her eyes welled with tears.

Home.

Nisha cleared her throat, dried her eyes, then drew her hood closer and lifted her scarf to shield her face from the desert sun.

"Six months. That's all we've got, Sher, and we're wasting time gawking at this shithole. So let's get going. The city will still be here when we get back."

With a tap of her foot, her camel lurched forward, taking the first steps into the endless deserts of Sundara.

CHAPTER

TWO

Nisha thought she knew the desert. She thought she understood its harshness and cruelty. But she was wrong; she knew *nothing*.

On the first day of traveling, the relentless sun bore down on them with a cruelty unlike anything Nisha had ever experienced. Its unyielding heat sapped the very life from her body. Despite her attempts to shield herself, the heat attacked through her clothing, scorched her skin, and made it impossible to speak.

As her camel plodded behind Sher's, the silence between them grew. Every time she tried to start a conversation, her mouth felt lined with cotton, and her throat grew parched and raw with each swallow.

Without conversation, time passed slowly as Nisha kept pace behind Sher. At times, in the wavering heat and pounding silence of the desert, she thought she lost him. He seemed to move like a mirage, a distant figure swaying with the rhythm of his camel. But she trusted her camel to follow his lead and dedicated her energy to two things: staying atop the sundamned beast and fighting off the demons in her mind.

Desert guides always said that the most dangerous thing about the desert wasn't the brutal heat of the sun or even the lack of water or food. It was the threat to a person's sanity. The harshness of the desert and the dull monotony of golden sand stretching as far as the eye could see made it easy for the mind to crack. It drove a soul to madness, to hallucinations that pulled a traveler from safe paths to get lost amongst the endless sand. It could even drive them to attack their own friends and family, convinced they were being plotted against.

Nisha stared at Sher's back. A cold chill traveled down her spine. It was difficult enough for her out here, with the hounds of madness barking at the gates of her mind, screaming about what an awful mother she was, about what kind of *scum* she was. But he was the one whose mother died while he was out helping her. He was the one who'd been betrayed, despite asking her to do it.

What would she do if he went mad out here, and he blamed her?

Her mouth went dry at the thought. Her daughter's life was at stake. Maybe she should be wary of trusting him. Maybe she should—

Nisha cursed under her breath. What in the sundamned hells was she thinking? This was *Sher*. This was the man who'd given up his chance at the magic lamp for her, to help her save her daughter. If she couldn't trust him, then she was as good as dead, and so was Auri.

She forced herself to close her eyes, ignoring the

sense of nausea washing over her. A memory played in the ensuing darkness, and everything around her faded away: the heat, the nausea, the thirst, and the hunger.

The only thing she became aware of was his warm hands cupping her face. His thumbs wiping away the fat tears rolling down her cheeks, his soft lips pressing against hers.

Nisha released a heavy sigh and opened her eyes, surprised to find that the sun had fallen in its high arc across the sky. How long had passed since she had closed her eyes?

Sher's camel slowed to a halt, and a few minutes later, Nisha pulled up beside him. He locked eyes with her, her heart skipping a beat at the intensity in his golden gaze. But it was a fleeting feeling. Something flashed across his eyes before he looked away at the horizon.

"It's time to make camp," he said in a haggard voice.

"What's wrong?" she asked.

"Nothing."

"You're hurting."

"I am fine. We can set up here," he said, starting to dismount with less grace than usual.

"But—"

"I said I'm fine!" His shout rang across the emptiness of the desert.

Nisha stayed mounted, staring at his blood-stained saddle. "Your salve—"

"—was useless in the heat," he snarled.

Sher turned away from her and busied himself with the camp. Nisha quietly dismounted, her own body aching from the day's ride. The desert around them began to change, the open blue sky darkening to deep crimson. Strokes of purple and orange brushed across the sunset.

For a moment, Nisha stared at the beauty of it, at how the colors of the falling sun danced along the sands. It was breathtaking. She'd never seen anything like it. But she couldn't fully lose herself in the sight, not with Sher in pain.

She looked back over her shoulder at Sher. He stood next to the kneeling camels, retrieving the dried strips of meat and water. There was a certain jerkiness to his movement that betrayed how much he was struggling to move.

Nisha sighed as he brought her two strips of meat.

"We'll have to ration these. I'm not sure how far west the desert stretches, so it's best to be careful."

"Sher."

"What?"

"Let me help you."

"I—"

"Stop being a sundamned fool. Let me *help*."

He hesitated, but with a resigned sigh, nodded. Gingerly, he removed his cloak and shirt, wincing as he tore it away from the dried, clotted blood.

Nisha retrieved the jar of salve from the camel's pack and knelt down next to him. She opened the jar, and the scent of herbs filled the air, mingling with the cool evening breeze. Her fingers brushed against the warmth of his skin, and she felt him tense.

The silence returned as the light continued to fade.

Before, the silence had been maddening, insufferable. But now, it was different. It was strangely ... nice.

Strange. She had learned to be wary of silence because in the Glass District, it always meant something bad was about to happen; some poor soul would suffer at the hands of black-hearted men, their dark eyes filled with darker intentions. But out here, silence with Sher meant something else. It wasn't just companionship; it was something ... more.

She ran her fingers over him, applying salve to each and every cut. Her touch was as gentle as only a thief's could be. His neck, shoulders, arms. Then down his back, before working her hands around his torso, her fingers brushing against the hardness of his abs.

She knew what it was like to be cut by the glass shards. Everyone who'd grown up in the Glass District did. But to be cut to such an extent, she couldn't even begin to imagine the pain.

And he'd endured it for her.

"I'm sorry," she whispered.

The words felt alien coming from her lips. She couldn't remember the last time she apologized to anybody. Any time she'd ever done something to someone in the Glass District, they usually deserved it. But Sher didn't deserve what she'd done to him.

She looked up into his eyes, only to find a depth of emotion there that she wasn't prepared for. She saw it now, the love he had for her. But there was something beside it. Was that fear?

"I was supposed to die, you know," he said in a raspy voice. "I wasn't supposed to feel this."

"Feel what?"

He stared into her eyes, and she saw a depth to the fear there that scared her. She didn't understand it.

"What are you afraid of?" she asked again.

He shook his head and, with a heavy grunt, pushed himself to his feet. He held his hands out for the salve.

"I'll apply the rest myself."

Nisha felt a tightness in her chest, an emotion she couldn't quite place. She held up the jar, and without another word, he took it from her and left.

She sighed and watched the last rays of sunlight disappear beneath the horizon. She drew her knees to her chest and watched as the stars emerged, spreading across the sky like grains of sand in the desert. They shone almost as brightly as the moon itself.

Nisha sat there for a while, her mind empty and numb. It was only when Sher returned that she realized how much she was shivering from the cold night.

"I set the bedrolls down between the camels. They'll keep you warm."

"What about you?"

He looked out over the rolling sand dunes.

"I'll keep watch for a while."

Her brows furrowed as she looked up into his eyes. "Keep watch? We're in the desert, Sher. There's nothing out here. No people, no creatures. It's just us."

"Until it's not. You should get your rest. I'll get you when it's your turn."

She sighed, stood, and dusted the sand off herself. With one last look at him, she left and settled herself into the bedroll. True to his word, the goatskin material and the camels on either side of her staved off the cold chill.

She closed her eyes. She was exhausted and should've been able to go to sleep without a second thought. Yet, as she lay there, sleep eluded her. She shifted restlessly, trying to find a comfortable position, trying to find a way out of her head. But it was no use. The cold seeped in, not from outside, but from within.

Then, after what felt like hours, just as she began to drift off, she sensed him.

Sher.

He stood over her, looking down at her from beneath a sea of stars with those eyes that made her heart ache. His presence melted her worries away.

The darkness pressed in, and those three magic words he had whispered to her before appeared in her mind.

I love you.

Her breathing deepened.

I love ...

His hand touched hers.

I ...

At long last, sleep took her.

CHAPTER
THREE

The second day was even worse than the first. Somehow, the sun was hotter, beating down on them as if it were angry that they dared to cross the desert.

Her lips dried and cracked beneath the scarf wrapping her face, making it painful to even open her mouth. She glanced up at the open blue sky, searching for clouds, but there were none. Any hope she had of momentary relief from the cursed sun evaporated.

With a heavy sigh, she turned her gaze back to the man riding ahead of her. He had lied to her last night. He hadn't come to wake her. Instead, he'd stayed awake the entire night, keeping watch over her. He couldn't have gotten a single minute of sleep. It was obvious in the droop of his shoulders.

Nisha pushed forward, driving her camel to catch up to Sher.

"Let me lead," she said, wincing as her dry throat throbbed in pain.

He shook his head, not even looking at her as he answered, "Not today."

"What are you doing, Sher?" Nisha pressed, her eyes watering from the excruciating pain in her throat. "Why are you being like this?"

"I'm guiding us west," he said as he reached down, grabbed his ration of water, and passed it to her. "Drink. It's dangerous to be dehydrated out here."

Nisha glared at him, leaving his hand outstretched. "Dehydrated? How are you going to talk that kind of shit to me when you didn't even *sleep* last night?"

She coughed violently, her body shaking as she held her hand up to her mouth. It felt as though someone had force-fed her a handful of sand, with the way that her throat tightened around every word.

With a frustrated growl, she snatched his water from him and took a sip. The water was hot and nasty, but still, the pain relief it brought gave her the chance to say what she needed.

"I'm taking the lead from you, and if I hear you say a single word, I'll kick you off your camel. Now tie yourself down to your sundamned camel, close your eyes, and get what rest you can."

She shoved the water back into his arms and pushed her camel forward.

His voice called from behind, "Do you even know which way is west?"

"Of course I do!" she shouted back.

"Then why're you headed north?"

She cursed him under her breath as she brought her camel to a halt. "Which way is west, you smug bastard?"

He hid his smile behind his face covering. "Keep the sun on your right. Once I get whatever rest I need, I'll take back over."

Nisha didn't say another word as she nudged her camel into motion. Sun on the right. Where did he learn a trick like that? She knew he had visited Sandspire before. He had mentioned it the first day she met him, when she had gone to steal the painting from him. But she had always imagined him riding in the comfort of a palanquin, with a hired guide leading him and other Bloodlineds safely through the desert.

Focusing on the simple task of keeping the sun on her right, her mind began to wander. There was a lot about Sher that surprised her. It wasn't just his trick of navigating the desert. He was a skilled thief. She'd seen him in action, and his touch was almost as good as hers.

But how?

The only reason she knew how to steal as well as she did was because her survival depended on it. And it wasn't easy learning. She had seen what the other orphans did right and, more importantly, the things they did wrong that led to them swinging at the gallows or their hands on the chopping blocks. It took years to perfect her craft, years filled with close calls and narrow escapes. Before her fingers grew quick and strong enough to dance into pockets and take what was hers; before she could draw someone's gaze away with the slightest gesture or distraction; before she learned the hardest trick of all: how to steal and be forgettable.

It was impossible for a Bloodlined who grew up in luxury to be a great thief. They didn't have the *hunger* driving them, the need for survival. They already had everything you could want: wealth, power, status, even the Angel's own blood running through their veins. And yet, here was Sher, a man who had managed to steal from her with an ease that suggested a lifetime of practice. The fact that he managed it still left the taste of salt in her mouth.

There was far more to Sher than his simple Blood-lined heritage. She could still remember how easily he had slain the Peddler and his men. Without any second thought, he'd driven his sword into them, painted the walls and floors with their blood. And when those intense gold eyes bore down on her, she knew that he was prepared to do the same to her.

A chill ran down her spine as she remembered his voice as he stood over her, demanding to know if she had kept the key from him. She'd known then that he was fully prepared to put her down just as easily as he had done the Peddler.

Nisha understood why he did that now; his mother's fate rested on whether he got that key or not. But still ... the *ease* he'd done it with. Even the way that he left Zulmar for her, chained against the wall. She'd never seen fear in Zulmar's eyes until that moment, and he was not an easy man to break.

She should have been frightened by the darkness hidden behind the veil of his precious soul. But strangely, she wasn't. Instead, she wondered what had happened to him.

As she stewed over that thought, her camel began to

act up, its steady pace turning erratic. It grunted and shook its head back and forth.

Nisha cursed and pulled gently at the reins, trying to calm the camel down. But the camel only grew more agitated, and a bad feeling began to build in her gut.

She looked up and saw the horizon darkening, a shadow spreading across the sky that hadn't been there moments before. At first, a flicker of excitement sparked within her. Clouds. Maybe rain was coming—something to look forward to in this sundamned desert. Her heart lightened at the thought of cool, refreshing rain washing away the day's heat and dust.

But as she watched, the dark line grew denser and wider, moving towards them with unnatural speed. Her initial thrill dissolved into a cold realization. No rain clouds could move that quickly.

The air grew heavy, charged with static, as a low rumble disturbed the silence of the desert. The sides of Nisha's cloak began to flap in the building wind.

As a street rat from the Glass District, she had heard every bone-chilling sound imaginable: death rattles, haunting cold screams, and the soft squelches of eaten flesh. But none of those sounds frightened Nisha as much as what she heard then.

A distant growl that echoed in the bones of the earth.

"Sher!" Nisha called out, her voice tight with sudden fear.

His eyes jolted open at the sound of her voice. In an instant, his gaze locked onto the horizon.

"Sandstorm!"

Nisha snapped her head back to the horizon, horror

and awe holding her captive as she watched the sand-storm blanket the open blue sky.

The camel suddenly knelt down, nearly rocking Nisha off her saddle as it made itself small against the sand dune. The camel closed its eyes, its mouth, and lowered its head. She looked back at Sher to see that his camel was doing the same.

"Stay where you are!" Sher shouted over the rising wind. "I'm coming."

"What do I do?" Nisha screamed back, her heart pounding in her chest. A shadow passed over her, and the sun's heat instantly evaporated. Goosebumps ran over her skin as she looked back and saw the sandstorm blotting out the sun. Her mouth dropped at how small it made the desert seem.

Sher raced from his camel to hers, stumbling as the sands shifted beneath his feet. He staggered and tripped, sliding down the side of the sand dune with a frustrated, pain-filled roar.

Without a second thought, Nisha scrambled off the saddle and ran toward him, the violent winds battering her back and forth. The growl grew until it morphed into a howl that slammed against her ears and bones. It was loud enough that she was unable to make out what Sher screamed to her.

The wind picked up, ripping her scarf from around her face and neck. Grains of sand stung against the back of her neck as she ran. She staggered down the slope of sand, but managed to reach him in time before he slid too far. She helped pull him back onto safe footing, and together, they ran back toward the camel.

The behemoth towered over them, howling with unmatched fury. The grains of sand flying through the air struck hard enough that she could feel her skin getting nicked in places, with thin lines of blood running down her face. She coughed, struggling to breathe through the sand and dust in the air.

The moment they reached her camel, they buried themselves against its side. Sher reached up, untied one side of the blanket fixed to the saddle, and pulled it over them both. The wind threatened to tear it from him, but he held on with a white-knuckled grip. Nisha latched onto the other side of the blanket, holding it down so they were locked in a cocoon. She locked eyes with him, his golden gaze glowing in the darkness.

Then the sandstorm hit.

A sudden gust of wind slammed into them so hard that the camel groaned next to them. Every breath she took was filled with dust. She clung to her side of the blanket, knowing that if she let it escape her grasp, that would be it. They would die a horrible death, with the swirling sands clogging their throat and stripping their skin from their bones.

Muscles straining, she loosed a scream into the endless howl of the sandstorm. Together, they fought for their survival, the long seconds stretching into minutes, and the minutes into what seemed like hours.

It was only when the awful howl began to soften that Nisha dared to hope that they would survive. The relentless battering of the sand against the blanket slowed, the winds dying down to a mere whisper compared to the monstrous howls that had engulfed them moments before.

With muscles aching from the tension and her hands cramped from gripping the blanket, Nisha exchanged a look with Sher.

Was it over?

He gave a cautious nod. They slowly lifted the blanket, sand cascading off like water, and together, they stood. The sandstorm was gone, its only trace a distant line on the horizon. The furious howl that raged against the world had been replaced by a calm and eerie silence.

Nisha's eyes widened as she looked up. Above them, the sky unfolded in a breathtaking display of colors she had never seen. The sun, now low on the horizon, painted the sky in shades of purple, pink, and gold. It was as if the heavens themselves were celebrating their survival.

She drew in a deep breath. The air was cool and fresh; nothing like the hot, sandy wind that had consumed them. She turned to Sher and saw him looking back at her.

With shaking arms, he pulled her into his embrace.

Adrenaline and relief still coursed through her veins. She closed her eyes and pressed herself into his chest.. Her heart began to finally slow. He tightened his hold around her, and she felt the strangest sense of *belonging*, of being exactly where she was meant to be.

She didn't care that he was covered in sand dust, because in that moment, nothing else mattered except that they were alive and together.

Nisha wasn't sure how long they stayed like that, but

when he pulled back and looked into her eyes, she wondered what he would say beneath that quiet, stunning sky.

Would he say those three magic words again? The ones that she so desperately craved to hear?

He opened his mouth.

Her breath hitched.

"Why didn't you listen to me?" he asked. "Next time I tell you to do something, *just* do it!"

Nisha's mouth parted as her heart twinged in pain. She stepped back from him.

"What're you talking about?"

"What am I talking about? You nearly *died*. I told you to stay where you were, but you didn't listen. You came for me."

Nisha didn't back down. She stared up at him, her brows furrowing as her own anger set in. "*That's* what you're mad about? That I came for you? Of course I came for you. You fell like the clumsy idiot you are, and if it weren't for me, you would have died!"

He stood over her, shaking with absolute rage. Then he released a shout that shattered the emerging peace of the desert and walked away.

Nisha remained where she was, watching him stumble away to his camel, his movements slow and painful from the reopened wounds. She felt empty and numb, cold except for where his hand had gripped her arm. His warm touch had branded her and left her hurting. Not in any sort of physical pain, but a pain that reached far deeper than her skin.

She turned away from him and busied herself with

checking on the supplies attached to her camel. Besides the fact that sand covered everything, it seemed like everything was okay. Except …

She frowned. The strap that held her water skin hung freely, its end snapped and torn. She looked around the base of the still-kneeling camel, in case it had simply fallen down, but it was nowhere to be found.

Sapped of what energy was left in her, she fell to her knees. A sudden wave of thirst washed over her, and she could do nothing but run her tongue over her cracked lips.

She ran her hand through the sundamned sand. It wasn't there either. Her water skin was gone.

Doing everything she could to not break down, Nisha pulled her goatskin bedroll off the camel, shook off the sand, and lay it out. Hunger bit at her, demanding she eat. But in that moment, she could care less about the demands of her stomach. She was familiar with hunger and starvation. The pain she felt now was nothing compared to what she'd known in the past.

She crawled into her bedroll and stared up at the emerging stars. It was truly beautiful. A single tear slipped from the corner of her eye and rolled down her cheek. Of all the doubts that she had in being able to save Auri, she had never once thought that crossing the desert would be where she failed.

A frustrated shout drew her attention to Sher, who was attempting to drag his camel toward hers. But the beast wouldn't move, content to stay exactly where it was.

She turned over, closed her eyes, and went to sleep.

CHAPTER
FOUR

The dream consumed Nisha, the void wrapping around her with a cold, dark embrace. She turned and searched for some hint of the light, but she saw nothing.

"Hello?" she called out.

Silence answered her.

Frowning, she took a step forward and heard the distinct clink of iron. A numbness crept over her as she knelt down and felt a band of iron clasped around her ankle. The chains connected to it were thick and heavy.

What in the sundamned hells?

She tried to pull her foot free, but it was no use. She frowned and grabbed hold of the chain, following it through the darkness. Besides the clink of iron, she could only hear her own heavy breathing. Her feet grew weary as she continued through the darkness, but she did not stop. She had to know what she was chained to.

The chain grew tauter in her hands. She was getting closer.

Then a soft howl passed through the darkness. She froze,

still haunted by the memory of the sandstorm. The howl didn't grow louder, though. Not until she took another step forward, and another.

Nisha's heart pounded in her chest as she moved forward. The darkness seemed to press in on her, thick and suffocating. Still, she pushed on until finally she saw them—two points of light flickering in the dark. Golden, intense, familiar. Sher's eyes pierced the darkness, staring off into the distance with an intensity that stole her breath away. As she drew nearer, the howling grew louder, more furious.

Nisha stopped just feet away from Sher. The glow of his eyes revealed enough of his face for her to realize that the deafening howl was coming from his gaping mouth. His gaze was tormented, filled with rage, coldness, despair, and deep, unending grief.

She could feel it all, vibrating through the chain. The depth of his pain frightened her.

"Sher," she called out, her voice barely audible over the howl. "What's happening? What is this?"

But he didn't answer. He couldn't. The howling seemed to consume him, coming from him and through him, a tempest of his own making.

Nisha took a step closer. She reached out, her hand trembling, and grabbed his shoulder. The moment she touched him, the howl came to a stop and his gaze snapped to hers.

Her breath caught as a wave of fear washed over her. She watched him stand, his movements slow and terrifying. And before she could retreat, his hand wrapped around her throat.

She gasped in shock and horror.

"You did this," he seethed.

His voice was cold, heartless. It was every nightmare of

hers come to life. Nisha struggled to breathe. Her feet kicked as he lifted her.

Then a second voice came through the darkness, every bit as awful as Sher's.

"You did this."

Nisha wheezed, the edges of her vision pulsing with a deep, different kind of darkness. She followed the sound of the voice to a second set of eyes appearing in the darkness. They were a deep shade of brown, and these eyes she knew better than even her own.

Auri.

Her silhouette stood next to Sher, her face passive and calm as she watched Nisha choke in his grasp. Nisha's eyes rolled as she struggled, despair creeping into her bones as the only two people she ever loved watched her slowly die.

"You did this," they said again, this time their voices running together.

Tears spilled down Nisha's cheeks. As the last of her breaths came, she let loose a howl of her own, letting it shake the darkness.

But that didn't stop the pulsing edges of her vision from taking over. The golden glow of Sher's eyes began to fade. Her heartbeat thudded against her chest. She felt it slowing, beat by beat, until at long last, she—

"Nisha!" Sher's voice cut through the dream.

Nisha jerked awake, gasping and wheezing for air. It was dark, but she could still feel hands on her. Desperate to be free, she fought.

She heard him curse as she delivered a punch with full force. He staggered back, and she drew her knees up to her chest and wrapped her arms around herself.

Deep breaths.

Cool air made its way into her lungs. She didn't want to close her eyes, for fear of returning to the nightmare. So instead, she raised her gaze to the night sky.

Breath by breath, she calmed down. It was just a bad dream. But it felt *so* real. She could still feel the ghost of his touch around her throat. When she touched a finger to her neck, there was nothing there.

"Are you okay?"

She looked to the side and saw Sher kneeling nearby, an angry red bruise starting to form along his cheekbone. She looked into his eyes and saw no hint of the malice that had been in her dream. Only concern.

She sighed deeply, feeling the tension leave her body. "Yeah, I'm okay. Just a nightmare."

"I know," he said. "You were screaming."

"Go back to sleep. I'll be fine."

"Go back to sleep?"

He sat next to her. She noticed that he left a small gap between them.

"I couldn't sleep anyways."

Nisha grunted in response. That was nothing new. He was probably keeping watch again, though she had no idea for what.

He reached for his side and pulled out his water skin. He offered it to her with a soft smile.

"I noticed yours got lost."

Nisha's face burned. She didn't want to take it from

him, but she was aware of how thirsty and dehydrated she was. With an ugly snarl, she snatched the water skin from him and drank deeply before passing it back.

"How bad is it that mine got lost?" she asked.

His slow sigh told her everything she needed to know. It was bad.

"Don't worry," he said. "We're two stubborn bastards from the greatest city in the desert. We'll figure it out."

She glanced at him. He cared about her; she could see it in the way he looked at her. So why was he treating her so coldly?

She looked away.

"Want to tell me about the nightmare?" he asked.

"Not really."

A second passed, then he answered. "Okay."

They sat there in silence, both of them staring up at the canvas of stars painted above them. Moonlight shone down on them with an ethereal light that was straight out of one of Fatima's tales.

She eyed Sher from the corner of her eye.

How was it possible that something so beautiful could be hidden behind something so cruel?

"I dreamt I was chained to you. You were howling, just like the sandstorm. And when I tried to help you, you grabbed me by the throat. You were choking me."

She looked away.

"Then Auri came and watched. The whole sundamned time, both of you were saying, 'You did this.'"

A moment passed.

"Damn."

"Yeah."

"I hope you know I wouldn't ever lay a hand on you like that."

"I know. Because if you did, I'd gut you and leave you here for the sun to dry out."

He chuckled, but she knew he wasn't laughing because he thought she was joking. He was laughing because he knew that she was serious.

When his laughter fell to silence, his voice took on a deeper note. "You didn't do this. None of it. You know that, right?"

She frowned, "I'm not so sure about that. Auri *is* in danger. That's all my fault."

"You're wrong. It's the fault of one man, and one man only. King Razhan. You shouldn't ever put yourself to blame because that bastard chose to threaten your daughter."

She nodded quietly. He was right, and she knew it. Still, she couldn't help feeling the way she did, knowing the part she played in it.

"One more thing."

She turned to him.

"I ... I'm sorry. I shouldn't have shouted at you. You were right. You *did* save me, and I ... well, you were right."

"Yeah, I was. I didn't mean to hit you, but you deserve that bruise."

He grimaced, gingerly touching a finger to his cheek-bone. There was a slight swell to it now. "I probably did."

He hesitated, then asked, "Are we on good terms now?"

She let the silence hang for a minute, letting him stew in the tension of his own making. When she felt he suffered enough, she sighed, "Yeah, we're good."

Nisha shifted, drawing her knees closer to her chest as the silence enveloped them once more. It was a comfortable silence, filled with the soft sounds of the desert night and the occasional brush of wind against their skin. She let her gaze wander back to the stars, amazed by how bright they were. This was one thing she would miss when it was all said and done. Back in Zareen, the stars were beautiful, but they never had the same kind of glow that she saw now.

After a while, curiosity got the better of her. She glanced at Sher, who was still looking up at the sky, his expression thoughtful.

"Sher," she began, her voice softer now, as the earlier tension between them dissipated.

"Yeah?"

"Truth for a truth?"

The corner of his lips lifted into a gentle smile. "Sure."

"How'd you get to be such a good thief? I mean, you grew up in the lap of luxury. Probably had some nannies feeding you with silver spoons or some bullshit like that."

"Don't be stupid. Our spoons were made of gold."

"Are you serious?"

He chuckled, his smooth deep voice sending shivers through her body. She had forgotten how much she loved the sound of his laughter.

"Of course I'm not serious. Gold's a soft metal. It'll bend if you use it on a regular basis."

"The fact that you know that, I don't even know what to say."

He turned his head to look at her, his golden eyes reflecting the moonlight. He seemed to consider her question for a moment before saying, "My story's not as exciting as you might think. I didn't have some master thief come teach me his ways or anything like that."

"Tell me."

He gave her a silent nod before his voice softened to a level that she had to strain to hear. "It started when my father got sick."

Nisha straightened and leaned in. He had never spoken about his father.

"Growing up, I always thought he was invincible. I was convinced that even the sun would burn out before he grew weak. I mean, he was the strongest man I knew. I looked up to him."

A quiet moment passed.

"I remember the first night I heard him cry. He was screaming, and was in such pain that he begged for my mother to end his suffering. But the next morning, he looked normal, except for some redness in his eyes. I thought maybe I had dreamt it."

He paused, his fingers absentmindedly sifting through the sand. "But then, it continued. Night after night, his screams haunted me. I couldn't stand it, listening to my father break like that. Think what you want, but when it got dark, I snuck out. I needed the peace.

"Soon, his pain carried through the nights into the days. And eventually, I found myself spending more time outdoors than at home, walking the streets of the Peak and Market Districts. I just needed to escape, you know?

"That's when I first saw her," Sher continued, his gaze drifting back to the stars. "A girl in the Market District. I watched her slip a loaf of bread from a stall, then an apple from another. The way she moved, it was like magic. So fluid, so fast. But it was her smile, Nisha, after she'd made her escape, that caught me. It was... euphoric. She had this look of pure joy."

Nisha remained silent. She knew the joy he meant. For Glass District orphans, there was a thrill that came through thieving, through knowing you'd have a full belly even just for that one night.

"I wanted to feel that," Sher admitted. "So, I started small. Whenever I attended balls and dinners with other Bloodlined on behalf of my father, I stole. Nothing of any real value, but still, for the first time in a long while, I felt *happy*. So I kept at it."

"And you got good?" Nisha asked, a smirk playing on her lips.

"I got very good," he said. "I loved it. Not for anything I took, but for the feeling of being alive, of being someone else. When I was ready, I tried my hand in the Market District. I spent every waking hour practicing, until I got so good, I could slip coins out of any purse I saw. Nobody ever suspected me of it either."

"Then something changed," she said, noting the shift in his tone.

Sher nodded as his face fell, "A man I stole some coin

from blamed this young boy who was minding his own business. They had his hand to the block faster than I could believe. I stepped in, handed him his coins with a few extra and said he dropped them. He believed me. After all, I'm Bloodlined. But I realized that if I was just a second late, or if I wasn't Bloodlined, that boy would've lost his hand."

"So you stopped?"

"Not exactly," a small grin played across his lips. "I started targeting thieves."

Nisha shoved him, thinking of how he'd swapped her purse with a rock-filled one. He laughed, but his laughter was short-lived.

He continued, "My father died not long after that. And then my mother fell ill. Everything changed. I had responsibilities, expectations. Things that took me away from it all, except for those rare days and nights where I could escape."

Nisha reached out, laying a hand on his. "Sher, I—"

"I think it was fate."

She paused.

"If my father had never gotten sick, I never would've gone down the path I did. I never would've become a thief. And ... I never would've met you."

Her breath caught as he pressed his hand over hers and looked into her eyes.

"What a sad life that would've been," he said.

He pressed his lips to her fingers. A swarm of butterflies fluttered in her stomach. Even after he stood, she could still feel the ghost of his lips on her skin.

"Good night, Nisha," he said.

He turned away without even asking her for the truth she owed him. She was about to call out after him, but then she heard something else: a whisper so soft that it should've been lost to the desert breeze.

"If only fate didn't have to destroy my family so that I could have you."

CHAPTER
FIVE

Sher led the way through the desert, his figure outlined against the rising sun, the silhouette of a man carrying the weight of the world on his shoulders.

He was breaking, as if something was tearing him apart. She knew that whatever the reason, it went beyond the grief and helplessness he felt about his mother's death.

Days had passed, and every morning was the same. He'd wake her and have her drink from his rationed water, his silence draped around him like a thick, impenetrable cloak. Once she was done, he'd give her the cold shoulder while he prepared the camels. When they were ready, he'd mount up and start off, expecting her to follow.

She wouldn't hear more than a few sentences from him until night fell, with its full moon and heart-aching stars. It was only then that his hard shell would soften, and he'd speak to her. He'd share memories from the past while they stared up at the heavens, and she would do the same.

She'd shown him the raking scars on her forearm from when an ironmonger nearly caught her. He'd touched them softly, brushing his fingers over her skin in a way that left her heart racing and hoping that he'd kiss her, pull her close. But he never did.

And when the morning sun rose, so did his walls.

Her gaze clung to Sher's back. He was holding back. But why?

The rest of the morning passed in silence, the only sounds the soft shuffle of sand underfoot and the occasional grunt from their camels. Nisha felt the weight of the sun bearing down on her, and the heat began to build; a slow, oppressive force that sucked the moisture from every breath and left their clothes clinging to their skin.

Nisha cursed beneath her breath as she realized that this day was going to be hotter than any they had faced so far.

As the sun climbed higher, Sher finally halted their progress. He dismounted, wincing at the soreness of his healing wounds.

"What's going on?" she asked, her camel stopping next to his.

His camel let out a soft grunt and lowered itself down to the sand. Her camel did the same.

He lowered the cloth covering his face and squinted up at the sun, "Day's getting too hot for the camels. We'll rest, conserve our strength. When the sun's past its peak, then we can go."

Nisha nodded, her throat too dry for words. She started to dismount, pausing in surprise as he offered her his hand. His touch was gentle, and when their eyes met, it felt like the desert around them faded away.

With his help and a grimace, she hopped off the camel. He stabilized her as she started to stumble, her legs shaky from the long ride. A flicker of gratitude passed through her.

He turned away and withdrew a handful of sticks and a blanket that had been packed away. Stabbing the sticks into the ground and stretching the blanket between them, they soon had some shade to rest under.

Nisha and Sher crawled into it, sighing with relief to be out from under the sun. Hearing their sighs of relief, the camels turned and looked, seeing the shade. They grunted and moved to squeeze next to them.

A stream of curses spilled from Nisha's lips as she attempted to shove them away. It seemed the sundamned beast didn't care for her response, as it let out a fart that left her eyes watering and struggling to breathe.

Sher could not help but chuckle to her side. Nisha flipped him a finger, and his chuckles settled into a deep, humored smile. It was refreshing to see after a long day of coldness from him.

He offered her the water skin.

She took it gratefully, her throat feeling almost torturously dry and her lips cracked from the day's heat. She was so thirsty that she failed to realize how little water was left until she'd tipped the last drops into her mouth.

It took a moment for the realization to settle, but when it did, she looked at him in horror.

"Before you waste your breath, yes, that was the last of it. And no, I do not know if there's water nearby."

Nisha's pulse raced. They wouldn't last long without water. "So, what are we supposed to do?"

Sher's expression hardened, the playful light in his eyes fading into a steelier resolve.

"We'll find water," he said. "But for now, there's nothing we can do. The cooler it gets, the easier it will be to move."

Still reeling from the abrupt shift from relief to desperation, she struggled to digest his words. "Just like that? We're in the middle of a desert, Sher. Water doesn't just appear out of thin air."

He glanced toward the horizon, his gaze scanning the endless dunes that surrounded them. "No, it doesn't. But panicking won't make it appear faster. As soon as the sun starts to fall, I'll go look for some. You stay here, conserve your energy. If there's water out there, I'll find it."

"There's no way I'm letting you go by yourself. I—"

"You'll do what I tell you," he said with a cold edge to his voice. "Because if you don't, then I can't protect you, and I—"

"You think I need you to *protect* me?" she interrupted in disbelief. "Did you wake up and suddenly forget who I am? Where I come from? I'm not your soft little princess, Sher. I'm a street rat. I learned how to defend myself a long time ago."

"None of that matters."

"It doesn't matter?"

"No! It doesn't. Because if I don't take control, if I leave you to the hands of fate, then I'll lose you too. And *that* is not something I'm going to let happen."

The burning coals of her anger began to dissipate. That's what it was all about. He was afraid of her dying, of being left alone in the world with nothing and no one.

"Sher ..."

"Enough. We're supposed to be resting. It's this sort of thing that will get us killed."

She hesitated, wanting to push into the heart of the problem. But he was right. She could feel the energy sapping from her in the heat of their argument.

With an explosive breath, she agreed. "Fine."

Without another word, he settled down, folding one arm behind his head and closing his eyes. He was tense, she could tell. But eventually, his body relaxed and his breathing deepened, leaving him between that realm of sleep and consciousness.

Nisha couldn't bring herself to do it, though. Sitting there, lost in her thoughts, her gaze wandered to the horizon. The heat made the air dance, distorting the view, but amidst the shimmering waves, she thought she saw something—or someone. Was it another trick of the desert? A mirage born from her desperation? It wouldn't be the first time she thought she saw something, only to realize she'd been made a fool.

But as the figure drew closer, it solidified into the unmistakable shape of a man. One thing set him apart from any mirage she'd seen before—the distinct sound of a singing voice, just loud enough to reach her ears.

Nisha grinned to herself. He was coming from the west. He could tell them how far they were from getting out of this sundamned desert. He might even be able to tell them where to find water.

"Sher," she whispered, as if the man in the distance could hear her if she spoke any louder.

He didn't stir.

Nisha gently nudged his leg, but still, he didn't wake.

With a sigh, she decided it might be best to let him rest. After all, it wasn't like she was going far. Her camel watched, curious and bored, as she pushed herself to her feet and stepped out into the sun.

She started toward the figure, her hood pulled to protect her from the brutal heat of the sun. It was only after she reached the peak of the closest dune that she yelled and waved for him.

The man's rich voice halted abruptly. His surprise was evident even from a distance as he turned and paused, as if questioning whether she was a mirage or really there. She never thought she'd be so happy to see someone she didn't know. She started down the dune toward him. The closer she grew, the more she was able to make out of him, and she quickly realized that there was nothing ordinary about him.

His skin was like alabaster, so pale that she wondered if he'd ever been exposed to the sun. And although he wasn't Bloodlined, his eyes were a shocking shade of blue.

The differences didn't stop there. His clothing was unlike anything she'd ever seen before; it was a second skin of fabric that shimmered subtly under the sunlight, hugging him from neck to foot. Muted shades of gray and blue wove through it in a way that reminded Nisha of veins.

She noted the small bag slung over his shoulder before her gaze locked onto something even more interesting: a strange ring with a fitted ruby that gave off an air of power.

His reaction to her stare was quick; a subtle shift of his body not to shield the ring, but the bag. The thief in Nisha stirred, and she couldn't help but wonder ... what was in the bag?

"Hello," she said.

He cocked his head. Just as she began to wonder if he understood her, he responded.

"Hello," he said back his voice an echo of the song he'd been singing.

"You look like you're a long way from home," she said.

"I am."

"Where are you coming from?"

He didn't answer. Instead, he glanced past her toward their makeshift camp. There was something about the way he studied it that set her on edge. But she forced herself to relax. He was just a strange man from a foreign land.

"I am searching for a city called Zaren."

"You mean Zareen? I'm from there, and if that's where you're headed, then you've got a long way left to go."

He turned his attention back to her in surprise. "You

are from there? Why do your eyes not glow, if you are from the city of glowing eyes?"

"Because I'm not Bloodlined," she said. She paused and frowned. "You don't got Bloodlined where you're from?"

His expression shifted. "No, we do not."

A bad feeling began in her gut. Her nerves screamed at her to turn around and walk away, but she couldn't. Not yet.

"Look, as interesting as this conversation is, we're out of water. We're headed the way you came from, and—"

"Nisha!" Sher's shout drew her attention, and she turned to see him riding the camels hard, kicking up a cloud of sand behind him. Even from this distance, his golden gaze shone like a pair of twin suns.

The stranger's bag dropped to the ground behind her, landing with a soft thud that made her tense up. When she faced him again, the dark intent in his gaze chilled her. It was a look she knew all too well from the Glass District's shadowed alleys—a predator's gaze.

Nisha's instincts, honed in the unforgiving streets of the Glass District, screamed at her to move.

She rolled to the side just as the man's hand flicked out, his ring glowing. Ethereal light appeared, materializing in the form of a massive spear that hurtled toward her.

The spear missed her by inches and slammed into the sand with a harsh thud before dissipating into wisps of light just as quickly as it had appeared.

She came up in a crouch, her heart hammering

against her ribs. Another construct of light appeared above her, this time in the shape of a massive hammer.

The man's brow furrowed as he twisted his fingers, and the hammer slammed down.

Nisha let out a panic-filled shout as she scrambled forward. The hammer smashed into the sand behind her, raining grains over her. But the stranger didn't pause for even a moment. A flurry of arrows began to form above his head.

She grabbed a fistful of sand and slung it at his eyes.

The man stumbled back just as the arrows formed, his ringed hand pointing in a different direction from her.

The arrows fired through the air.

"Sher, watch out!"

Her warning came too late; the arrows were already upon him. Sher rolled off his saddle just as they struck. The camels, burdened and slower to react, collapsed beneath the rain of arrows. Their blood began to stream down the side of the dune like small rivers.

As the air filled with the distinct smell and taste of discharged energy, Nisha stared. Ice-cold numbness spread over her heart. She waited for Sher to appear, to stand up from the collapsed heap of camels, but he didn't.

A sudden surge of violence pumped through her veins. She turned to face the stranger.

"I'm going to fucking kill you."

The man advanced, his expression one of grim determination. He summoned another construct, a blade of pure light.

"You will have no such luck," he said, just before he lunged at her.

She slid under the attack and rammed her fist up into his groin, folding him over before following up with a fist to his jaw.

He fell to the ground with a heavy grunt.

She jumped on top of him and, keeping his sword hand pinned, ground a fistful of burning sand into his face. He roared, and an explosive blast of light threw her back from him.

Nisha landed a dozen feet away, her body aching like she'd just fallen from a two-story mansion.

He pushed himself up and stood over her, his face contorted in pure rage.

"You do not fight with honor."

Nisha spat blood to the side. "Honor? You have no idea where I come from."

"Then perhaps you will find your honor in the under realm," he said, pointing his finger at her. But nothing happened. His eyes widened as he realized his ring was gone.

Nisha bared her teeth and revealed the ring nestled in her palm. She had managed to slip it off his finger just as the magic had blown her back.

She slid it onto her finger, feeling a strange presence press against the edge of her mind. But before she could figure out how to use the ring, he jumped on her.

Fists pummeled her face, rocking her head from side to side. She didn't feel the pain, but she saw her blood spatter the sand around her. Her vision began to dull, and she realized she had messed up. She'd let herself get overconfident, thinking him useless without his ring and forgetting he was still a man. He was still stronger and heavier than her, and with him on top of her, there was nothing she could do.

Once again, she was helpless, and this time, she would die.

When he was done with her, leaving her too weak to move, he stood and held the ring up to the sun. He smiled to himself and slid it back onto his finger.

"Goodbye, sand dweller."

He pointed the ring at her.

A sword plunged through his chest with a sickening thud. His mouth gaped wide with shock and pain as he stared down at his own blood running down his body.

Sher's face appeared over his shoulder, his eyes filled with a wrath she'd never seen before. A roar split the air as he drove the sword deeper into the stranger's chest and lifted him.

The man gasped, a strangled noise escaping his lips. Then, with a final, forceful twist, Sher yanked the blade free, and the man's body went limp, collapsing into the sand

Sher didn't waste a moment. He dropped to his knees beside Nisha, his hands hovering over her as if afraid to touch her, to cause more pain.

"Nisha?" His voice shook with fear.

Nisha coughed, the taste of iron sharp in her broken mouth. It was hard to breathe, her vision pulsing in tune to the pounding in her head. She had made a mistake, and the desert was not the kind of place you could make a mistake.

A tear slipped from her eye, stinging as it slid down to mix with her blood.

"Go back," she rasped. "Save Auri. Don't let Razhan—"

Darkness took her.

CHAPTER
SIX

The sound of running water trickled into Nisha's consciousness, pulling her from the void. She cracked her eyes open. Instead of a sea of endless golden sand, she was surrounded by vibrant green underbrush and countless palm trees that reached for the open blue sky.

For a moment, she lay still, disoriented. The sight of so much green was alien enough that she half-expected the cool, verdant shades around her to dissolve into the harsh, sun-blasted reality she was used to. But as it persisted, she started to wonder.

Was she dead?

The whisper of a thought disappeared the second she tried to sit up, met with a sharp lance of pain that coursed through her body. No, she was very much alive. She had a hard time imagining that the dead felt pain like this.

A moan escaped her lips as she lay back down. A wave of dizziness washed over her, causing everything to spin.

The sound of running footsteps, and a moment later, Sher appeared at her side, his silhouette framed by the soft light filtering through the leaves above.

He knelt next to her, holding their water skin. She expected it to be empty, but to her surprise, water touched her lips. She drank deeply, mouthful after mouthful. He pulled the cup back with a soft chuckle.

"Drink too much, you'll end up regretting it," he said, his voice a soothing balm to her pounding head. "Trust me. I made the same mistake."

He was solid, real, and *alive*. Relief flickered in her chest. But there was a weariness to his eyes. He lifted her head gently to the cup again, allowing her to take a few more sips.

"You scared me. I thought I'd come too late."

Nisha drew back and tried to speak, tried to tell him that she thought he was dead. But it was impossible. Her eyes watered with pain, and he began to shush her.

"Lay back, and for Angel's sake, don't talk. You're in rough shape."

She sighed and did as he said. She didn't need him to tell her what shape she was in. She could feel it, and having been beaten this badly a handful of times in her life already, she knew what it would look like. Back then, she couldn't simply lie back. She'd had to move, had to find coins and food to steal to pay her dues to the Peddler and to eat.

But now, things were different. She wasn't alone anymore. She had him to take care of her. Which was good, because the stranger had been thorough in breaking her.

It seemed that Sher understood what she wanted to say, because he answered.

"The camels took the brunt of the arrows," he said. "I tried to come faster, but the camel fell back onto me. I had to dig my way out of the sand just to make it to you."

Nisha tried to convey that it wasn't his fault. She'd made the mistake of approaching the man by herself. She should've known better. The desert wouldn't suddenly make friends out of strangers. People were people, and out in the harshness of the desert, it would only bring out their worst.

"Don't know what you were thinking, taking him on like you did," he said. "I ... I thought I lost you. I cannot lose you. You know that? I can't."

She nodded, then winced as pain wracked her.

"Head's pounding?"

She grunted.

"I'll be back," he said. "I'll get you a wet cloth."

She watched as he disappeared back into the oasis. A pocket of life surrounded her, palms and grasses swaying gently in a cool, calming breeze. Birds chirped and flitted from branch to branch, a strange sight after being isolated in the desert for so long. She'd never been one to cry at something like that, but it was beautiful. Despite herself, a tear escaped her.

The tear stung as it slid down her cheek. Carefully, she raised a finger to her face, feeling the extent of the damage the stranger had caused.

Her fingertip traced the tender skin, flinching as it brushed against swollen areas and cuts. It wasn't the physical pain that bothered her as much as the flash of vulnerability that cut deeper. It reminded her of the last time she'd been left this way, broken with the seeds of a child left in her.

She'd made herself a promise back then: never to let a man gain control over her again. And yet, she'd failed; this time, her near encounter with death would have cost Auri her life.

What kind of mother made mistakes like she did? What kind of mother would allow herself to fall prey to a stranger so easily? Nisha ground her teeth in frustration as she tried to fight back the dark thoughts.

Sher returned, his footsteps soft on the grass, holding a torn piece of cloth that was damp with cool water. Gently, he dabbed at her face, the coolness soothing against her bruised skin. She sighed as the sharp edge of pain softened.

"You must be wondering how we got here," he said. He brushed a strand of her short hair away from her forehead. "With the camels dead, I had to carry you. I don't know how long I walked. It must have been half a day before I saw this place."

He paused, then added with a dark laugh, "I nearly ignored it. Thought it was just a mirage, a figment of my imagination."

Nisha stared into his eyes, captured by their golden glow. She couldn't imagine how difficult it must have been to carry her so far, without even a drop of water left in their water skin. This man loved her more than life itself. She could feel it in the way he cared for her. So why had he been acting so strange lately, after everything they'd been through?

He noticed her staring, and he gave her a sad smile.

"You need to rest," he murmured, his voice low and steady. "We're safe here. For now."

Nisha wanted to argue, to insist that they needed to go. The days were numbered, each as precious as the very water that touched her now. But the truth was, her body needed healing, and she knew she wouldn't make it far.

He took her hand in his, raised it to his lips, and she felt the brush of his whisper across her fingertips. "I promise, nobody will touch you ever again."

She closed her eyes and allowed herself to relax, to lean into the comfort of him, and into the comfort of the oasis.

It wasn't long before Nisha found herself drifting off to sleep. At first, she resisted, not wanting to give in to the darkness for fear of what might come. But in the end, she found herself too weak. Sleep took her anyway.

And this time, she was glad for it. When sleep did take her, the nightmares did not come. Instead, there was only the beautiful, sweet nothing, accompanied by the ghost of Sher's kiss on her head.

CHAPTER
SEVEN

Light invaded the darkness, slowly pulling Nisha back into the realm of consciousness. When she opened her eyes, she saw a ray of moonlight filtering through the leaves overhead, shining straight down onto her. She wasn't sure if she'd ever seen a moon so bright.

Pushing herself up, Nisha fought against a wave of dizziness. The pain had dulled in her sleep, and despite the brief dizziness, it was more manageable now.

A blanket of warmth wrapped around her, bringing a small smile to her lips. All her life, she'd never experienced warmth like this except for her time at the Matchmaker. Caught between the desert chill that would make her bones ache at night and the blazing hot sun that did its best to kill her, she'd nearly forgotten that there was a middle ground.

She rose to her feet, her body groaning in protest. She wasn't going to stay down now; she wanted to see more of the oasis.

The brush parted before her, the ground soft and covered in a lush carpet of grass that tickled her bare feet. It was quiet, except for the whisper of the gentle breeze and the soft trickle of running water.

Nisha followed the sound deeper into the oasis. The moonlight guided her, painting the world in an ethereal silver glow.

When she broke through the last of the vegetation, she found a lake, its surface glowing with the reflection of the moon. It turned the water into a pool of liquid light so beautiful that she could not help but wonder how something like this could exist in the harshness of the desert.

Then Nisha saw him standing in its waters.

Sher stood with his back to her, shirtless, the contours of his muscles bathed in moonlight. The cuts he'd taken from the glass shards of the trap she'd pushed him into were nearly healed, now etched into his skin as countless fine, pink scars.

A sharp pang of guilt tightened in her chest. She'd done that to him. She wanted to say something, but she was left breathless by the sight of him, his outstretched arms trailing along the surface of the water, creating small ripples. For the first time, he looked so relaxed, like this magical place was able to wash away all of his worries.

"Beautiful, isn't it?"

Nisha jumped at the sudden sound of his voice. "How'd you know I was here?"

It hurt to speak, but she was tired of the quiet.

Sher turned, his expression softening as he caught sight of her. Her gaze danced down his torso, from his powerful shoulders to his sleek abs, which were also covered in scars.

"You're losing your touch," he said. "A deaf man could've heard you with the way you stomped through the oasis."

Her heart lightened at the joke. He sounded like himself, before everything happened.

Despite the ache in her face, she grinned. "Careful, or I'll steal your clothes again. Leave you wandering the desert shirtless."

She took his laugh as an invitation to join him by the water's edge. The ground was soft and wet where she sat, but it didn't bother her at all. She removed her leather sandals and slid her feet into the water, sighing at the cool relief it brought.

"I still can't believe you did that, you know," he chuckled. "Stole my clothes, left me penniless to pay Farrakhan, and slipped me the rose quartz necklace all in one go."

"You deserved it."

"For what?"

"For actually thinking you were the best thief in Zareen. You needed to be humbled."

He grinned back at her and started toward her, the water edging lower with every step he took. The moonlight reflected off the water, casting fleeting, silvered patterns across his bare stomach. Her gaze roamed from the fine hairs soaked on his chest down to the suggestive lines of his hips. Every step revealed more, making her heart pound and her pulse race.

She realized that he wasn't just shirtless. He was naked, and all that kept her from seeing the rest of him was the silver moonlight dancing on the water.

Her skin burned, and her heart jumped into her throat. Her eyes flicked back up to his; the glow of them seemed more prominent than ever. There was an intensity in them that captured her, holding her hostage in a way that she never wanted to be let go.

"And you were the one to humble me, huh?" His voice was husky, as if he too knew how little separated him from her. He stopped just a step away, the water now lapping at the very lowest part of his waist. "I suppose I should thank you, then."

She suddenly became conscious of him, of how alone they were, and of every curve, every vein, every scar of this beautiful man. She swallowed as the tension grew taut, threatening to snap at any moment.

"Why would you thank me after what I did to you?" she asked, her voice strangely thick.

He glanced down at his own body, his fingers brushing against one of the larger scars across his ribcage. Then he looked back up at her, his gaze softening.

"You think you did this?"

"I was the one who pushed you."

He sighed, his warm breath crossing the distance between them. "This isn't your fault. You did what I told you to."

"It is my fault. We could've found another way. I ... I

just had my eyes on myself, on the sundamned lamp," she said, drawing her knees up to her chest and squeezing her eyes shut to fight back the tears.

She hated this. It was like she was anchored to the slums, and everybody she dared to reach for, she dragged down into her hellscape. The guilt ate her alive. All she wanted was to be a decent person, but no matter how hard she tried, she only ever seemed to make things worse.

His hand touched hers, and she looked up to meet his eyes.

"That's not true. You had your eyes on your daughter. You have a heart like nobody I've ever met before, and that's why I lo—"

Her breath caught. She didn't realize how badly she craved to hear him say those words again.

Finish the words.

Please.

He looked down and sighed. He let the words hang, unfinished, as he extended his hand toward her. The gesture was an invitation, a bridge over the turmoil of emotions churning between them. But she wasn't sure where it led.

"I can't swim," she said.

"Do you trust me?"

For a moment, she hesitated, frozen by fear of the water. She'd never been around this much of it. Even though the water was calm, the idea of being trapped in it terrified her. But the sincerity in his eyes drew her in, and convinced her to put her hand in his. His skin sparked against hers and stole her breath. Somehow, her heart pounded even harder.

With a gentle tug, he drew her closer, guiding her into the water. It was colder than she thought it would be, but she hardly noticed as the warmth of his hands held her above the water, close to his chest.

His body was hard against hers in a way that felt *good*. This was a strength she could trust in, that would always be here for her. She leaned her head against his chest and breathed him in.

Back in Zareen, he had always smelled so good—a special mix of saffron, leather, and amber. But out here in the desert, there was only one note that left parts of her aching for him. It was the pure, unique scent of him.

"Lean back," he said, his voice soft and gentle.

She hesitated.

"I have you."

She swallowed in an effort to conquer her fear and leaned back, her arms shaking as the water lapped up into her hair.

Then her ears dipped beneath the water. She placed one hand on his shoulder, imagining the waters splashing up over her face, threatening to drown her.

Except, they never did. Not even as Sher stepped further back into the lake, his hand sliding down to the small of her back, holding her core up so that she did not dip below the water.

The tension that had held her so tightly began to unfurl. She breathed out and closed her eyes, submitting to the weightlessness, to the muted world around her. This was what it meant to be at peace. It reminded her of that void she escaped to when she slept, where there was blissful nothing.

When she opened her eyes, she found Sher staring down at her, his golden gaze so intense it was like everything else ceased to exist. Held so close to his chest, she could feel his breathing was different now. Tighter, faster.

Nisha lifted her head up, the water dripping from her hair back into the lake. "What are you thinking?"

"I'm thinking you're the most beautiful person I've ever seen."

Butterflies fluttered in her stomach. Her heart skipped a beat as she asked, "Then why haven't you kissed me yet?"

His breathing raced faster. He wanted to. She could feel it. But something was holding him back.

"Because I'm afraid."

There it was again. The fear seemed to coil around him so tightly now, it was suffocating him.

"What're you so afraid of?" she asked.

He was quiet. For a long moment, she wondered if he would draw back, just as he did the last time. But then he answered, his words no louder than a breath.

"I'm afraid of loving you the way I do," he whispered.

Her heart shattered. "But why?"

"Because if I lose you, then … it'll ruin me."

Nisha looked deep into his eyes and felt herself swallowed by the depths of his fears. He was trying to grasp for control in a world that seemed so damned determined to break him. Fate made him helpless as he failed to save his mother, and again, he'd been helpless as Nisha had been beaten within an inch of her life.

Everything made sense now; his coldness, his outbursts. It was all fear and worry, mounted upon the grief he still felt in losing his mother.

Nisha didn't know what to say. It wasn't like there was some magic phrase she could say that would suddenly heal him and put him at peace, that would reassure him they could survive this together, no matter what came their way. Because as wonderful as words were, they paled in the face of reality. They were out in the desert, headed toward a place they knew nothing about. There would be more dangers, more threats to their lives.

No, words weren't good enough.

"Will you let me kiss you?" she asked.

His breath hitched as he blinked in surprise. Then, without a word, he nodded.

She traced her hand from his bare shoulder up his neck to his chin, pausing to rest her thumb against his lips. Then, with deliberate slowness, she leaned in to press her lips against his.

At first, his hesitation built a wall of fear between them. But then, just as slowly, he began to kiss her back, his hesitation melting away as he surrendered.

He turned her in the water so she could lock her legs above his waist, leaving his hands free to run over her. One hand ran up to the back of her neck, and he deepened the kiss with a burning intensity that seared through her.

She bit gently into his lip, drawing a deep groan from

him. Conscious of his nakedness and threatening to drown in a sea of her own desire, she dug her nails into his back. She wanted more. Needed more.

The water caressed them in gentle waves, drawing her closer until she was flush against him. Her fingers ran through his hair.

"Please," she whispered, her body shuddering with desire.

His tongue darted across her lips and he took the first step toward land, where they could be freed from this sundamned water. His hands came back down to grip her waist.

She tensed as a sharp pain shot through her ribs, stealing her breath and desire away in one fell swoop. He immediately loosened his hold, keeping her above the water. His eyes filled with concern.

"Are you okay?" he asked.

She ground her teeth against each other to try and stave off the nauseating waves of pain.

"What's wrong?"

"My ribs," she gasped.

"Shit. Your ribs might be cracked. I knew I should've bound them," he said, guiding her to the edge of the lake.

"It's fine. I'll be fine. Just ... just stay in the water."

Nisha stumbled up the wet slope with one hand on her ribs. She glanced back at him, aware of how her wet cloak clung to her. She was still breathless, partly from the pain shooting through her ribs and partly from whatever nearly happened between them.

There was something about the way he looked just now, silver moonlight dancing on rippled water and flushed skin. She knew she would remember this image of him forever. And she had a feeling that he was thinking the same of her.

Pain lanced through her ribs again, nearly bowing her over. She cursed and, with one final wave, started back, a stream of quiet curses spewing from her mouth.

The stranger who had spoiled the moment by leaving her with cracked ribs ... he'd met his end too easily.

CHAPTER
EIGHT

Nisha awoke to the soft murmur of the oasis. The sun, barely cresting the horizon, spilled golden light over the greenery around her. She prepared for the shooting pain as she sat up, but to her surprise, all she felt was a bit of stiffness. Her body wasn't nearly as sore as it had been the day before, and her ribs didn't carry any of the shooting pain she'd experienced.

A sound drew her attention to the side, where she saw Sher sitting atop a fallen log, staring at a few items laid out in front of him. He was lost in thought.

"Don't tell me you didn't sleep again," she said, subtly checking to make sure the strip of cloth she'd bound around her ribs was still in place.

His eyes were bloodshot, and he looked exhausted. There was a fresh scratch along the side of his neck. Had she done that? She looked away, fighting off a blush.

"I did try, believe it or not," he said with a heavy sigh. He brought her the water skin and a strip of dried meat.

Nisha took them with a grateful smile. "Bad dreams?"

"You were snoring."

His answer was so unexpected that she laughed. She couldn't help it. He looked absolutely miserable. But then their eyes caught, and she knew that he was still thinking about the night before.

He cleared his throat. "Feeling better?"

"Still stiff and kind of sore, but nothing like yesterday."

He nodded to himself. "I thought I was imagining it before last night. That's why I was in the water. I thought it might help with the cuts."

"Did it?"

He lifted his shirt, and Nisha frowned. She drew closer, running her fingers over his wounds. Strangely enough, the cuts had completely healed over into scars now.

"What in the sundamned hells? No way it should've healed that fast."

"I couldn't help but think the same thing about you."

"Me?"

"You were swollen up like a melon when I first got here. But after a few hours of soaking your head with a wet cloth, the swelling had gone down."

Nisha touched her fingers to her face, shocked to find she didn't flinch away from the pain.

"You think the water here's got something to do with it?"

He shrugged and gestured around them. "It is kind of a magical place, don't you think?"

He was right, Nisha thought as she looked around. This was the desert, and yet, they were sitting in an *oasis*. It didn't make sense to her. How could something so beautiful exist in a golden sea of lifelessness?

Fatima had always said that the world was a magical place, full of wonders that the mind would struggle to comprehend. Of course, Nisha had always thought that was utter shit. But perhaps this was one of those places she was talking about.

She wondered what Auri would think of it.

"I was looking at everything we have," he said, taking his seat. He ripped up a blade of grass and fit it to his mouth before pointing to the items on the ground. "There's not much. I didn't want to weigh myself down too much, since I was carrying you. One water skin— which we can fill up at the lake, but it won't be enough for us both if we have much desert left to cross—and a pack of dried meat. Not much left in there either. Then there's the other stuff: my sword, some thread and needle, a spare cloak, the salve, and of course, what the stranger had."

Nisha looked at the small bag and ring that lay separate from the rest. "What's in the bag?"

"A small orb. I thought it might be a relic, like the one Razhan used that night to teleport us to our chambers. But it doesn't seem to do anything."

"Let me see."

Sher tossed her the bag. Nisha grunted as she caught it. It was heavier than she expected. She pulled out a black orb that seemed to suck up all the light. It was cool to the touch, but to her hands, it felt very ordinary. It didn't carry that same kind of presence that the relics did.

The ring, however, did.

She retrieved the ring, still able to remember the presence pressing against her mind, like a heavy fog slowly encroaching on a field.

"I've never seen magic like what he did," she said, holding the ring up to the light.

The red gem caught the light and threw it back in deep, pulsating hues.

"I would be careful with that," he said.

"Why?"

"Sometimes these relics carry a price to wield them. My father always said, don't pay when you don't know the cost."

He was right. The lamp was proof enough of that; the King himself had paid a steep cost, wishing for eternal life, for wealth and power, and for—

Her mind went blank.

She frowned as a flicker of something—more a sensation than a memory—teased the edges of her consciousness. She tried to focus on that fleeting thought, but it slipped away each time she nearly had it, like water through clenched fingers.

With a sigh of exasperation, she shook her head. It would come back to her later. She was sure of it.

"This is it then," she said, frustration creeping into her voice. "An orb that does nothing, a relic we're afraid to use, and a bunch of shit."

"The sword too, but yeah, that's exactly all we have," he said as he tossed the blade of grass aside.

"Angel's balls."

"I know," he said.

"So our choices are to fill up a single water skin between us and head out into the desert and probably die, or ..."

"Or stay here and hope that someone comes with enough supplies to get us out of the desert."

Nisha buried her face in her hands. "Shit."

"There is a third option."

She looked up. "What's that?"

"You stay here. I'll go out into the desert."

"No."

Sher leaned forward. "Think about it, Nisha. It's a good idea."

"Absolutely not. There's no way."

"You could be safe here to rest and heal, while I go find out what we're up against."

"It's my daughter. I'm the one that put her in danger, the one who brought you into this whole thing. I'm not going to sit here in this oasis, twiddling my Angel-damned thumbs, while you go out there by yourself."

"We don't know what we're headed for. It's better for you to stay behind."

"Why's that?"

"Because you're a *liability*," he snarled, jumping to his feet. "Look what that stranger did to you."

It felt as though a great shadow passed over them. Nisha stood, her expression darkening.

"I made one mistake, and you think I'm a liability?"

He drew a deep breath before shaking his head. "I

think this would be easier if you just let me go and handle the danger on my own."

"Easier for you."

"Yes."

"In case you forgot, Sher, we're in the middle of the sundamned desert. We're supposed to stick together, not separate from one another."

"If you stay here, I'll know exactly where you are."

"You'll know where I am? It was by pure luck that you found this oasis."

He pursed his lips. He knew it was true.

She crossed the distance between them until she was close enough to feel his hot breath on her face.

"I'm not one of your Peak District girls. I'm from the Glass District, and people like me don't sit back and hide because it's a little dangerous. So if you think you can control me, protect me by keeping me where it's *safe*, then you fell for the wrong girl."

His breathing sharpened, his hot breath spilling across her face in waves. He was intimidating, with his height and jet black hair falling down over his face, golden gaze as intense as ever. But she wouldn't back away, wouldn't blink. She would not bend, because the one time she did—when she allowed the monsters to rip her daughter away from her arms—she regretted it forever.

Sher turned and stalked away.

Nisha remained where she was. Her fingernails dug into her palms as she raged inside. She hated that there was a truth to his statement. She *was* a liability out here in the desert.

She was used to a world of dark alleyways filled with rats and shadows, and streets that teemed with people; knife fights that were almost over before they ever began, because nobody from the Glass District fought a fair fight.

She didn't know how to navigate the stars or how to hold her own in an open space where the enemy could see you from miles away.

Sunlight danced off the ruby ring, pulling her attention. A relic like that could change things for her. Help her hold her own against any enemy they came across.

With that ring on her finger, Sher wouldn't have to worry about her, and they could get on with finding the Angel so they could save her daughter.

Suddenly, Sher's warning about whatever price might be associated with the ring didn't seem so bad. That was, if it carried a price to wield it at all.

The ring was heavier than she remembered. The metal was cold as she slowly slid it onto her finger, closing her eyes with a sigh that seemed to echo all around her.

At first, there was nothing. Nothing but the deep blackness behind her eyelids.

Then, she heard it. The discernible sound of a whisper, crawling through the darkness. The hairs along the back of her neck stood as goosebumps riddled her skin.

She waited for the whisper to come closer, to become clearer. She waited for it to become the nightmare she imagined, there to claim her mind for its own.

But it did not come.

The sound remained as it was, the whispered words impossible to make out.

Nisha opened her eyes. How did the ring work? The stranger had been able to summon construct after construct, almost like it was ... imagined.

With a frown, she focused on the memory of the spear hurtling toward her. She fixed it in her imagination, demanding it appear. When she opened her eyes, though, there was no sign of it.

She walked around the space, feeling a little dumb. How could someone simply imagine something and it would just *appear*? There had to be more to it.

Maybe it had something to do with the voice?

She tried again, this time working to draw some connection between the eerie voice and the spear. Nothing happened, except that the voice drew back when she reached out.

"Come on," she growled, shaking the hand with the ring.

The gemstone glinted mockingly in the dim light, as if it were amused by her attempts. Nisha clenched her jaw, her frustration growing.

She pushed her will into it, as if she could bend its nature to her wishes. Without warning, the air around her charged, tension building like static before a storm.

A surge of power coursed through her. It was like the ring was alive, feeding off her emotions, her own desperation. She could feel an energy pulsing at her fingertip.

With a thought that was more of a pleading wish than a demand, she willed the power to manifest. Fragments of light rushed toward her, forming the ethereal

shape of a dagger. The whisper at the edge of consciousness pushed forward, pressing against her mind. But
still, she couldn't make out its words.

She gasped as she stared at the floating dagger. It
was a perfect replica of the one she had back in Zareen,
from the length of it down to the chips that had formed
in the blade over the years. This wasn't a simple
construct. It was something that she pulled from her
own mind.

Just as quickly as it had appeared, it vanished into
motes of light that dissipated into the air. The voice in
her mind softened and fell back.

Her heart raced. She'd done it. She stared down at the
ring. The energy still surged through her, and for the first
time, she felt *powerful*. There wasn't a soul in the Glass
District that wouldn't fear her with this kind of magic at
hand.

A thought came to mind.

Did she even need the Angel's tear now? Couldn't she
just turn back, put an end to King Razhan?

She scoffed and dismissed the thought. The ring
wouldn't protect her from Razhan's assassins, Malzor
and Azaroth. She'd seen how they managed to step out of
thin air, strapped with relics. And even if she managed to
handle them, the King had a vault filled with more relics
than she could count. Who knew what he had up his
sleeves?

With a heavy sigh, she resigned herself to the truth.
The only way out of this, the only way to save her daughter, was by finding that bastard Angel and forcing a tear
from him.

Perhaps it was time to find Sher now. He'd be upset that she put on the ring without him there, but it was better to get it over with. Time was ticking. The sooner they made up, the sooner they could get back to saving Auri.

As she walked past the bag holding the orb, she felt it: an undeniable pull, like the ring and the orb were calling to each other.

With cautious steps, Nisha moved closer to the bag. The ring began to thrum on her finger, its power resonating. As she reached out and moved the folds of the bag away, a faint light began to emanate from the black orb within.

Her eyes jolted wide as her ring hand yanked forward, pulling her toward the orb. She grabbed hold of her own wrist, digging her heels into the dirt.

"Sher!" she called out, her voice urgent.

His steps thundered nearby and he broke into the clearing, his eyes landing on her in an instant. He dashed over and wrapped his hands around her waist, trying to drag her back. But even with their combined efforts, they were only able to stay at a standstill. Wind began to swirl around them, as though angered by their attempt to pull back.

"What happened?" he yelled.

"I don't know!" The wind howled loud enough that she had to yell to be heard over it. "I put on the ring, and I did some magic, and then I was coming to get you but—"

Ethereal light blasted outward from the orb, tendrils of magic wrapping around both her and Sher. Despite their desperate resistance, the ground beneath their feet started to give way.

The light began to pulse in time with their heartbeats.

"Take it off!" Sher shouted, the veins in his neck and arms bulging as he struggled to pull her back.

Nisha tried to slip the ring off her finger, but it wouldn't budge. She looked up in panic as the light from the orb intensified, swirling like an angry storm.

"I can't!"

At last, the ground beneath them gave way.

The ruby slammed against the orb with a soft *clink*. Without warning, the world twisted. They tumbled through light and darkness, through blistering heat and then freezing cold. Their screams echoed all around them, the volume pitching as they were soon enveloped by a blinding luminescence.

Then it all came to a sudden stop.

They slammed into cold, dark stone with such force that it robbed them of their breaths. Her heart racing, Nisha looked over at Sher. He looked back.

They were still alive.

But where were they?

An audible crack broke the silence, and the last echoes of light faded from their vision. Once her eyes adjusted to the dimness of their surroundings, she saw what had cracked: the orb rested in two pieces, as though the magic that had coursed through it had been too much.

Nisha looked around in disbelief. They were in an empty chamber, air tinged with the smell of ancient stone and dust. The ceilings were high and arched, with elaborate carvings running all along the walls, illuminated by pulsing, glowing mineral fragments that cast off a soft blue light. There was something about the space that was *off*. Something that absolutely terrified her.

Sher released his hold on Nisha, steadying himself against the smooth stone floor.

"Where are we?" he asked, his voice echoing slightly in the vast emptiness.

"I... I don't know." Nisha's voice was a whisper of awe and fear.

Then it hit her, what frightened her so much.

"Sher?"

"Yeah?"

"Where's the sun?"

Her whole life, there had been few things that remained constant. The one that prevailed over the others was the fact that the sun would always be there, from dawn till dusk, beating on them with all its cruelty.

And yet, here she was, cold and hollow, like the sun was just a distant memory. It was unnerving. She wasn't so stupid as to think that the sun had gone somewhere, but the real question was ...

Where had *they* gone that the sun didn't shine?

What kind of hell were they in?

Footsteps echoed.

Nisha and Sher stood, their eyes fixed in the direction the sound came from.

The footsteps grew louder, the rhythm a calm,

measured beat against the stone. Every few steps, something tapped against stone.

Then, from the shadowy embrace of the chamber, a figure emerged.

He was old; old enough that his wrinkles had long disappeared, his alabaster skin now drawn taut over the bones of his skull. A long, gray beard interwoven with small colored beads of stone stretched down over his suit, the same veins of gray and blue weaving their way through the fabric. However, they didn't simply shimmer; they pulsed, almost like a heartbeat.

Hunched over a walking stick, the old man stared at them, his gaze lingering on Sher. A ring gleamed from his finger with the light of the fire around them, fitted with a dark sapphire instead of a ruby.

Then he spoke, his voice firm and strong, despite the frailty of his appearance.

"You are not Kaelum."

CHAPTER
NINE

His voice carried a resonance that reminded Nisha of King Razhan. This wasn't just some old man; he knew power.

"Kaelum? Who was he to you?" Sher asked, taking a half step forward and positioning himself slightly in front of Nisha. She wasn't the only one who recognized that the old man carried a hint of danger with him.

"Someone I trusted."

Nisha grimaced.

"He must be dead, for you to be wearing his ring," he said to her. It was impossible to tell what he was thinking.

"He is," she answered, not wanting to say any more. Her heart pounded in the quiet that followed.

Then the old man sighed. "That is unfortunate. I knew that it was likely Kaelum would see an early grave. I will thank you for returning his ring."

Nisha didn't move. Sher hadn't had a chance to grab his sword before they'd been teleported here, wherever *here* was. The ring was their only means of protecting themselves. She wasn't about to give it up so easily.

The old man smiled. "I see. You wish to keep it, but that cannot happen. Only the honored in Salstadir are allowed to wear the ring."

"I don't really give a flying f—"

The dark sapphire glowed, and before Nisha could react, a spark of light looped around the ring and yanked it off her finger, shooting it straight into the old man's waiting hand. He tucked it away before replacing his hand on the walking stick.

Nisha's stomach dropped as the indiscernible whispers disappeared from the edge of her consciousness. Just like that, they were powerless before the old man. And it seemed Sher had the same thought.

"I think we got off on the wrong foot," he said. "I'm Sher. This is Nisha. Who are you?"

"I gave up my name long ago. You may call me the Speaker." He turned and began to walk away, leaning on the walking stick for support. "We shall speak again soon."

"Wait, where are you going?" Nisha called out.

But he didn't answer. Instead, he disappeared into the shadows.

Nisha glanced at Sher. That was it?

Before they could follow him, they heard more footsteps. Guards appeared, each wearing more of the ruby rings.

Nisha and Sher tensed, instinct urging them to fight against the guards and flee. But they both knew that there was no point in resisting. They didn't know where they were or who they were up against, except that these people had relics like they'd never seen before.

"Come with us," the lead guard demanded. The harshness in his stare gave them little wonder what would happen if they didn't comply.

She thought they'd rough her up, same as the guards did back in Zareen. But to her surprise, they didn't. In fact, they didn't even lay a hand on her as they surrounded her and Sher. Perhaps they were wary of who they were too.

The guards led them out into the corridors, which were unlike any Nisha had ever seen. The minerals that cast off light continued to spread throughout the corridors, shadows dancing in the corners.

They followed the maze, so twisted that it was impossible for even her to keep track of, until they came to a section where the passageways narrowed. The earth pressed in on them, threatening to suffocate her. Just when she thought the space might be too tight to pass through, they came to a halt in front of a heavy door, made out of the same blue steel that the guards wore.

One of the guards stepped forward, and a moment later, the door swung open with a heavy groan.

Nisha sighed when she saw the small, barren cell inside.

"Inside," the guard said, motioning for them to enter.

With a resigned glance at each other, they stepped into the cell.

The door clanged shut behind them, the sound reverberating off the stone walls and fading into the distance.

Nisha watched the guards retreat through the small barred window until they disappeared from view.

They were alone now in the dark, save for a sliver of the strange, pulsating light that seeped in from under the door. Nisha walked to the back of the cell, trailing her fingers along the cold, damp wall. It felt like the stone was alive.

"Why is it that we always find ourselves in prisons?" Nisha asked.

"Because we're thieves."

Despite the worry creeping up in her, Nisha smiled. "Maybe."

Sher sat with his back against the wall.

"Kaelum. You ever hear a name like that?" Nisha asked. "Or Sal—Shit, what was it called?"

"Salstadir, and no, I haven't."

She noticed his shoulders were tense, and his voice was clipped, like he was angry.

"You're mad."

"Yes, I'm mad. Why did you have to put on the ring, Nisha? I told you not to do that. I told you what would happen."

Nisha scoffed. "You didn't know that this would happen."

"That's beside the point. I *told* you I'm afraid to lose you. So why'd you do it?" he asked, his nostrils flaring.

"Because I saw what that guy did with the ring. It is power like we've never seen. Maybe with that, you'd trust me, and you wouldn't think of me as a *liability*."

"But the risk—"

"Risk? You think I care about *risks*?"

"I know you don't. But I do!"

Nisha paused and met his gaze, the faint glow from the pulsating minerals casting shadows across his face. Her expression softened, but her voice was firm when she spoke.

"People who worry about risks don't last long in the Glass District. You know why? Because they're always so cautious, so afraid, that they miss out on what it takes to *live*."

Sher's frustration waned. He watched her quietly, his brow still furrowed.

"You spend so much of your time worrying about me, trying to control what I do, trying to protect me from everything, but you're killing me. You're killing *us*."

"I—"

"You're too afraid to even tell me you love me again."

He fell silent.

"Life, love, risk, pain, you can't have any of it if you're not willing to accept it all."

The anger drained from his face, replaced by a deep, complex sorrow. He nodded to himself, but didn't say anything else.

She drew a deep breath and sat down next to him, resting her head back against the wall. A few minutes passed, the silence so deep and cumbersome that she wondered what she could do to break it.

Then she looked at him and smiled. "Think I can break us out of here too?"

He stayed quiet, until finally, "You never told me how you did break out of that cell."

"You really want to know?"

"Go on, tell me."

Nisha raised an eyebrow, a playful smirk forming on her lips. "I seduced the guard."

His golden eyes flashed with fire, and she couldn't help but laugh. Her soft voice filled the despairing silence.

"Calm down, I didn't seduce him, really. Just convinced the idiot to step close enough that I could take his baton. Knocked him flat out with it."

"The baton? What did you do with that?"

"Stripped naked, tied my robe around the window bars, and managed to twist it open using the baton. It was so sundamned cold, I swear my nipples probably would've been sharp enough to cut the bars themselves."

He chuckled, and as the seconds dragged on, laughter bubbled up out of him, filling the empty space around them, shattering the silence.

"You're unbelievable."

"I told you from the start. You've never met a thief like me."

"Actually, at the start, you said you weren't a thief or a beggar and that you were a lady looking for the help of a decent man."

This time, it was Nisha who laughed. It felt good to laugh so hard.

"Funny how things work out," she said.

Another moment of silence passed. This one was different, more companionable. She didn't mind it.

Then she felt his hand on hers. He took her fingers and lifted them to his mouth, pressing his lips softly against them.

"These fingers, they steal my heart."

He brushed a strand of hair away from her face.

"Those eyes, they steal my breath."

He kissed her forehead.

"And this thief, this thief has stolen everything I am."

Then he pressed his lips against hers, and the chill air faded before the fire that burned in her core. She pressed her fingers against his jaw and drew him in again, not wanting to let him go.

But he pulled back. "Just promise me you'll always be careful."

She kissed him again, smiling against his soft lips and the scratch of his stubble.

"I'm always careful. I've got both my hands still, don't I? You'd have some hard luck finding another orphan from the Glass District that does."

"Just promise me."

"Fine." She kissed him once more, then rested her head on his shoulder. The necklace he'd given her was cool against her skin. "I promise."

CHAPTER
TEN

Nisha jerked awake to the distant echo of footsteps. Her hand instinctively went to where she normally kept her dagger when she slept, only for her to remember a moment later where she was.

She glanced over at Sher, who was still sleeping, his head leaning back against the wall. They might both be thieves, but that was the difference between them. He'd grown up with four walls, a roof, and a safe bed to sleep in.

He never had to worry about what the sound of footsteps meant. For him, it probably meant a servant coming with breakfast; for her, it meant something far worse. People who fell into deep sleep never lasted in the Glass District for good reason.

"Sher," she said, nudging him with an elbow.

He woke, looking around with groggy eyes.

"Shit, it wasn't a bad dream then."

"Missing the oasis already, huh?"

He grunted.

The footsteps reached the door, and a moment later, they heard a click. The door swung open with a deep groan, revealing a single guard.

Nisha fought back the urge to attack. Between her and Sher, they could have overwhelmed him. Even though he had a ring, he was alone. It might have been enough for them to escape if they were careful. But none of it mattered. She had learned young that you don't make a move unless you're either forced to or you know what's around you.

And judging by the lack of hostility in the way that the guard openly stared at Sher, this wasn't a case of being forced to make a move. It would be better to scope out the situation before she tried anything.

"What are you staring at?" Sher asked.

"I have never seen anybody like you," the guard said.

"What do you mean?"

"Your eyes ..." The guard cleared his throat, as though he realized he wasn't supposed to be so open with them. "Come with me, please. The Speaker has requested your presence."

Nisha and Sher exchanged a glance, a silent communication passing between them. Was this a trap? Neither could guess the Speaker's intentions, but it seemed Sher held the same thoughts as Nisha; they needed to know more about where they were before they could attempt an escape.

"Fine," Nisha said, standing up. Her muscles ached from the cold floor and the tension that had knotted her body. "Lead the way."

The guard nodded, stepping back to allow them to

exit the cell. As they followed him through the winding passageways, Nisha couldn't help but notice again the veins of minerals that pulsed along the walls, lighting their way. It must have been day now, but without the sun, it was impossible to know. Everything looked the same as when they'd been led to the cell.

Her fingers trailed along the walls, brushing against the cold stone. She would have thought they were inside some massive fortress, except for the minerals embedded in the walls. Those weren't put there. This wasn't something any man could make.

Sher walked beside her, his steps measured, his own eyes darting around, taking in their surroundings. She could tell that he was realizing the same.

The guard led them through a series of turns, each passage looking much like the last, until they arrived at a chamber so large that it reminded Nisha of Razhan's throne room.

All along the sides of the room, pillars stretched upward, arching toward where a massive group of mineral veins converged, casting its light down onto them.

And directly below the cluster of minerals, the Speaker sat in a modest stone chair, cushioned with some fabric. When he saw them, he stood with the help of his walking stick. The guard stopped behind them.

The Speaker didn't say anything. He didn't look at her even once. Instead, he studied Sher, like he'd never seen a Bloodlined before. Something about the way he disregarded Nisha bothered her.

"I see you," she said.

His gaze slowly pivoted to her.

"Not talking to us yesterday, stuffing us in that cell, it was all to prove you have power over us, wasn't it?"

The corner of his lip quirked upward. "You believe that was a display of power?"

Leaning on his walking stick, he made his way down the steps and approached them. He moved so painfully slowly, Nisha wondered if he was doing it intentionally. But then, she'd never seen anyone even remotely close to his age.

"If I wished to prove that I have power over you, I would not have bothered with the cell."

The sapphire ring gleamed with power, almost as if to emphasize his point.

"But I do not believe in needless violence. Of the few things I believe in, one is never being late to a meeting. The timing of your arrival was simply inconvenient, and so you spent your night in our cell, as you call it."

A meeting? They teleported straight into wherever the sundamned hells this was, and he found it *inconvenient timing*?

"Now that we have time for conversation, there are some things I must know. To help keep the peace, you understand."

"We do," Sher said, stepping up next to her and taking her hand in his.

"A man and a woman appear in our sanctum, wearing the ring of a murdered son of Salstadir. How can I be sure that you are not enemies, come to destroy our great society?"

Before Nisha could say anything, Sher answered.

"Because we're not looking for you."

"If not us, then what do you seek?"

He started, but paused, and exchanged glances with Nisha. She nodded.

"We're looking for the Angel."

Nisha waited for the old man to laugh at them, but he didn't. Instead, he asked, "Why?"

"Because my daughter will die if we don't bring back one of his tears."

The old man narrowed his gaze, the skin around his eyes pulling so taut that she could see the veins straining to keep from tearing. He wasn't prepared for her answer.

"And you believe the Angel is here?"

"Well, where is *here*? Is it west of the desert?"

"The desert?"

It occurred to Nisha that, living here so far away from the sun and the outside world, the old man might not even know what a desert was. After all, she hadn't even imagined something like the ocean could exist until she saw Sher's relic painting.

"The desert's an endless sea of sand," she said, unsure of what more to say. Then she added, "And it's hot."

Sher smirked at her side. Saying it was hot was an understatement, and he knew it.

"I see," the Speaker said.

"Look, we're just trying to find the Angel. We didn't come here to attack you. In fact, our being here is a whole sundamned accident. The ring sucked us toward your orb."

At that, the Speaker frowned. "You did not press the gemstone to the orb yourself?"

"No, we tried to stop it. We couldn't pull away."

The Speaker smacked his lips, his eyes falling into contemplative thought. He began to mutter to himself.

She exchanged another glance with Sher. There was something off about all of this.

"I've never heard of Salstadir. You never said where this place was."

"No, you would not have heard of us. Our society is quite protected. None find their way here unless it is ordained."

Ordained?

"You didn't seem surprised by the idea of the Angel," she said.

His eyes flicked up toward her, "That is because I am not."

"Wait." She took a half step forward, hope burgeoning in her pounding heart. "You know about him?"

Maybe he could point them in the right direction.

"I do. And as the Speaker, I represent his wishes to our society."

She gaped. "You mean he's *here*. In Salstadoor?"

"Salstadir. And yes, he is."

A massive burden lifted from her shoulders. Nisha wanted to laugh. Perhaps fate was finally doing them a favor. They deserved it, after all the shit it'd put them through.

"Will you take us to him?" she asked, trying not to think about the fact that she was requesting to meet with the Angel, the very same being who ruled over the Sundara desert for a thousand years, whose throne she'd looked at every day for as long as she could remember. This wasn't just some scab off the side of the street.

The Speaker considered the two of them, and everything they said. Her heart raced against the cage of her chest. If he said no, then she had no idea what she would do. But one thing was for sure. She couldn't sit back and just wait. The clock was ticking. Her daughter's life was at stake.

"I cannot promise that the Angel will grant you audience."

"That's fine. Just take us to him. We'll do the rest," Sher said.

The Speaker gave them a heavy sigh and nodded. "Very well, come with me."

He passed between them without a word, motioning for the guard to follow them.

The old man walked slowly enough that it aggravated her. Knowing that the Angel was so close, it was almost impossible to keep from shoving him to go faster.

She couldn't wait to be done with all of this shit. The sooner she got the Angel's tear, the sooner she and Sher could leave this strange place and make their way back to Zareen.

"The mountains, huh?" Sher asked. Nisha glared at him. Conversation wouldn't help this old man go any faster. "So we're inside what, a massive cave?"

"A cave," the Speaker chuckled to himself. "A cave would be an oversimplification. Salstadir rests at the heart of the mountains, where our souls come to dwell when we pass."

He gestured to the pulsing mineral veins running all along the walls. "Here, you are surrounded by all those that came before us. They share their light with us."

"And your relics?" Nisha said, nodding toward his sapphire ring. "The Angel shared that with you, right?"

He lifted it to the light. "Relics. That is a strange name for such a gift."

"It's what we call them. They're just things left behind when he asc—," she paused, "when he left."

"I see. Do you have many of these relics, then?"

"No," she sighed, trying not to think about the King's vault. Could you count something that had been given as a result of the lamp's wish?

A guard passed ahead of them, moving through an intersection of paths. He glanced toward them, his steps faltering as he noticed Sher's glowing eyes.

"Be on your way," the Speaker said.

The guard dipped his head in obedience and disappeared in a hurry.

The Speaker looked back over his shoulder at them with an apologetic smile. "You will have to forgive my people. You must understand, we have never seen someone such as yourself. Even now, my guards whisper of your arrival."

"You don't have Bloodlined here?" Sher asked.

"If you mean others like yourself, then no. You are the only one of your kind we have seen. Are there many others like you where you come from?"

"I don't know if 'many' is the right word," he said.

Nisha scoffed. "There's enough."

"It sounds as though you speak with rancor."

Rancor? Her eyes narrowed. What was the pale old bastard trying to say?

Next to her, Sher smiled. "You could say we come from different parts of our society. The Bloodlined are, as you would say, honored. The Commonborn aren't."

"This is a foreign concept to me. All within Salstadir are equal."

"Are they, though?" Nisha asked. "Not everybody's got one of those rings, right? You said before that only the honored get to wear them."

"You are an astute listener. Yes, the honored have the rings, but they are no better and no less than those who do not."

"How aren't they better? They get magical fucking rings."

The old man came to an abrupt halt and fixed her with a gaze that sent a chill running down her neck. "I must ask you to refrain from your vulgar language, outsider. Here in Salstadir, we speak to one another with respect."

A retort bubbled up to the tip of her tongue, but a sharp elbow from Sher held her back. He was right. She wasn't in Zareen anymore. Seraphine had taught her that if you wanted to get someone to do what you wanted, you needed to blend into their world. She'd let herself forget.

Nisha gave the old man her best smile. "My apologies, honorable Speaker."

The old man stared at her for a moment longer, as

though he was contemplating if she was sincere or not. Then he nodded and continued to lead them through the passageways.

"The honored are blessed with rings from the Angel so that we may better serve Salstadir. This is how our great society functions. This is how we have achieved eternal peace."

Eternal peace? The idea was laughable, but who was Nisha to comment on it? She wasn't a leader. Besides, this was a different world, with its own history and customs. If everybody was happy and shit didn't roll downhill from these so called honored, then good for them. It didn't matter to her. She wasn't here for them. As soon as she got what she needed from the Angel, it was back home to her daughter.

Hells, she missed Auri.

When was the last time she'd seen her? Too long.

She tried not to think about it as she followed the Speaker through the seemingly endless tunnels. Their journey took them deeper into the mountain, the air growing cooler, and the light from the veins more pronounced, casting an ethereal glow over everything. Eventually, they arrived at a set of stairs that spiraled downward, disappearing into the darkness below.

Instead of making a poor attempt to wobble his way down the steps with bad knees and a shaky grip on a walking stick, the Speaker summoned the power of his ring. Ethereal light gathered beneath him, providing a platform for him to stand on. It traveled slowly down-ward, a new platform forming beneath it every dozen steps as the previous one expired.

As Nisha, Sher, and the guard followed on foot, the air grew heavier with a sense of anticipation. She felt a tingle of magic in the air, like a charge that buzzed against her skin.

Not even a year ago, she'd been slumming in the Glass District, hunting for hard pennies in people's pockets to pay the Peddler. And now, she was about to meet the *Angel*.

That fact hit her like the weight of a hammer when they finally reached the bottom, where a golden gate stood shimmering with blinding magic. It was unlike anything Nisha had ever seen, with wisps of ethereal light emanating from it in waves. She tried to see what was beyond the gate, but the magic was so intense, it was impossible to see through.

The Speaker paused before the gate, turning to face them. "The Angel is ... selective about who is allowed to enter his domain. If you can pass through, then you will gain an audience with him. If not, then you must go back with Fenrik until an audience is granted. Is that understood?"

Nisha nodded, unable to tear her eyes away from the golden gate. There was so much *power* coming through it. She could feel it. This wasn't some dirty trick the Speaker was playing. This was real.

"Fenrik, you know what to do?"

The guard behind them dipped his head. "I do, Speaker."

"Then I will pass through first to receive you on the other side."

His walking stick tapped against the bare stone as he

approached the gate. The magic warped, ethereal wisps of light wrapping themselves around him as though they were eager to welcome him. A moment later, he disappeared from view.

"I'll go first," Sher said.

Nisha grabbed his wrist. "Let me."

He hesitated, but with a reluctant sigh, he agreed and stepped back.

Nisha straightened her back and lifted her chin. She started toward the gate, trying to appear confident despite the fear prickling at the back of her neck.

As she reached the threshold, the ethereal light brightened. A whisper at the edge of her consciousness appeared, impossible to understand but growing in intensity the closer she got.

She took a deep breath, her heart pounding in her chest, and stepped forward. The gate warped, and just as she was about to touch the light and pass through, one of the ethereal wisps lashed toward her.

It struck her with a violent force and sent her flying back. She slammed into the wall with a heavy grunt.

It took her a moment to realize what happened, but when she did, the weight of despair crashed down onto her. The shock of rejection felt like a cold slap to her face.

Nisha ground her teeth and stood, ignoring the pain throbbing in her shoulder. She wasn't going to give up. No matter what, that Angel bastard would let her through the gate.

Before she could move, Fenrik's hand shot out and grabbed her arm.

Her hands curled into fists.

"Take your hand off me, or I'll break it off for you."

The ring on the guard's hand shone softly.

"Nisha," Sher said.

Shaking with murderous rage, she glared at him. He shook his head.

"Don't."

Tears of frustration welled in her eyes, blurring her vision. "I need to save her."

"I know. Let me help. That's what you brought me for, right?"

It was and it wasn't. She brought him because she needed him, needed the love to help keep her standing. But she was supposed to be the one to get what they needed to save her daughter, to undo everything that she'd done. Letting him go in her stead, that didn't make her a better mother.

A tear spilled down her cheek. She wiped it away quickly, embarrassed by the selfishness of her own feelings. What was she thinking? Auri was in *danger*. That mattered more than anything. Besides, it was a fantasy to think that finding the Angel and getting the tear they needed would make her a good mother.

"Go," she rasped.

He nodded and approached the gate with quiet confidence, as though it were unthinkable that the gate would refuse *him*. It was the same determination that had drawn her to him.

The gate warped, ethereal wisps of light gently reaching for him. He stepped into their reach and passed through the gate without issue, disappearing from sight.

She breathed a heavy sigh of relief. She wasn't sure

what would have happened if they'd both been rejected by the Angel.

The guard's voice carried an unexpected note of sympathy. "The Angel has made his decision. It is not your fault."

She couldn't bring herself to look away from the gate, as though there was still some possibility that the Angel would grant her an audience. But she knew it was over. Everything rested on Sher.

Of course, the Angel would only accept a Bloodlined presence. She'd been a fool to think otherwise. After all, everything she knew of the Angel pointed to the fact that he was an awful bastard.

He'd ruled Zareen, took as many women as he wanted and left all his Bloodlined fatherless when he pissed off into the desert, pretending to 'ascend.' What a joke. The Angel reminded her of every black-hearted bastard she knew from the Glass District.

"Let's get out of here."

She tore her gaze away from the gate and the whispers at the edge of her consciousness fell quiet. Fenrik led her up the stairs. She couldn't help but notice how the earth around them swallowed the sound of every step.

"How long will he be in there?" Nisha asked.

"I cannot say for sure, only that when the Speaker goes to visit the Angel, sometimes a full day passes before he returns."

"That long?"

"The Angel has waited thousands upon thousands of

years to bless us with the gift and honor we have. Who are we to complain about a day?"

Nisha didn't know what to say. The Angel hadn't done shit for her, except have a throne that gave her a bit of shade to hide in when she fled the prison.

"With a whole day to spend, where are you taking me?" she asked.

"Out of the sanctum," he said, then smiled and added, "You are going to get to see the great society of Salstadir."

He led her to a final passage that fed through to another gate; this one appearing far more mundane and heavily guarded than the one that Sher and the Speaker had entered through.

The guards stepped aside without a word, allowing them to pass through.

And when she did, her breath caught in her throat.

The sanctum rested at the bottom of a cavern. Looking up, she saw a city of lights cascading up the walls, ethereal magic dancing from the buildings carved into the mountain. And hanging in the space left by the circling city, a massive stalactite glowed, chasing away the darkness and illuminating the heart of the mountain.

She gaped as she took it in. The stalactite alone was larger than King Razhan's palace.

"Is Salstadir not beautiful?" Fenrik asked with a knowing smile. "Come, come see the city of souls."

She followed Fenrik over a tight narrow street carved into the base of the cavern. She couldn't help but notice that they were the only two walking it.

"Where's everybody else?"

"Only the honored are allowed down here, and of them, only those who have business within the Sanctum."

"So nobody comes to see the Angel?"

Fenrik laughed, "Even the Angel would have his patience tested if all in Salstadir were to come seeking an audience. No, that is what he has the Speaker for. Through him, he speaks to us."

They reached the base of a wall, and stepped onto a platform. Chains ran alongside both sides. She realized that they'd built a massive pulley system. Fenrik motioned to a pair of honored soldiers nearby, and with a jolt, the platform began to raise.

As they passed the second level, headed further up to the city, Nisha saw the soldiers powering the pulley system by touching the ruby ring to an orb attached to the mechanisms.

"You will see this throughout Salstadir. Not only are we blessed with the opportunity to serve our people by guarding them, but we help them navigate the city as well."

Nisha's gaze turned to the rest of the cavern. She could see it now: the city was built in a stair-stepped manner, carved into the walls with countless platforms.

"You have guards just standing there at all times?"

"As I said, we are blessed to serve."

She shook her head. It was incredible, the network they'd built. Even if some foreign army ever managed to penetrate this cavern somehow, they'd find it impossible to capture and hold Salstadir, so long as they didn't have access to the relic rings these people had.

A slow grin spread across her face as she heard the first sounds of the city. Laughter, shouting, murmurs of a crowd. These were things that she knew, and after being away from Zareen for so long, it felt like she was seeing some part of home.

They reached the top, and the platform came to a smooth halt. While Fenrik spoke with the guards, Nisha took in the city.

The architecture was a marvel unto itself, buildings carved directly from the mountain's heart, blending seamlessly enough that it was hard to tell where nature ended and human ingenuity began. Vines and lush greenery draped over balconies and wound around the columns.

And the people of Salstadir passed through the streets, dressed in more of the same fabric with gray and blue veins running through it. Their clothing pulsed in tune with the glow of the massive stalactite, as though their very hearts beat together.

But their clothing wasn't as tight and form-fitting as the others she'd seen. There were distinctive styles, fashion modeled in so many different ways from loose flowing robes to tighter pieces that exposed parts of their pale stomachs and shoulders.

In Zareen, only an emberdusted addict would dress like that. The sun would scorch them, leaving a reminder to always be protected. Here, though, away from the cruelty of the sun, that wasn't true. The air was cool and soothing.

It was a strange sight to see. While she'd always known there had to be people beyond the vast deserts of

Sundara, she never realized they would have their own cultures, fashion, and ways of life.

A group of children chasing each other, screaming and laughing with a joy Nisha wasn't sure she ever had, came to an abrupt halt in front of her.

They stared at her with gaping mouths, and she realized just how different she was from these people, from her sand dusted robes to the darkness of her skin. She shifted from one foot to the other. Her whole life, she'd focused on blending into the crowds. It was important for a thief to be forgettable.

But here, that would be impossible.

Fenrik chuckled as he came to stand next to her. He waved the children off, and they reluctantly resumed their games.

"They find you strange," he said.

More people slowed as they noticed Nisha, but unlike the children, they did not openly gawk. Instead, they offered a smile and carried on their way.

"Come, let me show you the markets."

With no small amount of unease, Nisha followed him into the crowd and the markets. When she was on the platform and heard the sounds of the city, she thought that it would bring her closer to something she knew.

She couldn't have been more mistaken.

There was no jostling, no haggling, no merchants trying to shout over one another. It was all very cordial. Their goods were hidden away inside shops built into the rock. People formed lines, each waiting patiently with their coins in hand, and when they arrived to the front, the merchant stated a price that they *willingly* paid.

When Nisha saw that, she could hardly believe her eyes. Those merchant bastards were in the business of making coin, and they only ever had their own best interests at heart. Who in the sundamned hells didn't know that? Why would they pay a merchant's asking price?

"How does Salstadir compare to ... apologies, but where was it you came from?" Fenrik asked.

"I came from a city called Zareen."

"That is a strange name."

"Says the guy who shares the same skin tone as the fucking moon."

Several people nearby glanced at her, frowning.

Fenrik leaned in, "You must be careful with that kind of language in Salstadir."

She grimaced.

"Sorry, force of habit, I guess."

He hesitated, then added, "What is this moon?"

Nisha stopped. The people behind bumped into her, muttering apologies in a way that almost made her miss the violent outbursts typical in Zareen.

"You don't know what the moon is?"

He shook his head. "Should I?"

"How can you not know what the moon is? You've never been outside?"

Again, he shook his head. "Few souls in Salstadir have ever ventured outside."

"What about the sun? You have to know about the sun, right?"

"Ah yes, the son. My brother has two."

Nisha stared at him, unable to process what she was

hearing. "You've got to be shitting me."

"I—"

"What, I can't say that either?"

"I am confused. That is all."

She sighed and continued walking, trying to think about to word things.

"The time we spend awake and the time we sleep are different. Outside this mountain of yours, there's a whole world that's lit by a big ball of fire in the sky."

At this, he started laughing. "A ball of fire?"

"I'm serious," she said. It never hit her how silly it sounded. "And it goes through the sky until it gets to night, which is when the sun goes away, and the moon comes out."

She paused.

"The moon glows white. Kind of like your big rock here. Except ours changes shape throughout the month."

He smirked. "You have a strange sense of humor. My brother will laugh when I share this joke with him."

"It's not—" she sighed, unable to bring herself to finish what she was saying.

As they moved deeper into the city, statues of the Angel began to appear in the streets, his long wings stretching high overhead. The crowd flowed around them, touching their fingers to the springs of water coming forth from his hands.

The city was breathtakingly beautiful, with a sense of harmony pervading everything. Yet, as they continued to explore, she couldn't shake the feeling that something was off. It took her a while to realize that she hadn't seen a single person express anything but pure joy. There were no arguments, no shouting and screaming, no pale faces painted red with rage.

"Fenrik," she said.

"Yes?"

"Why is everyone so ... happy?"

He smiled again. He gestured around them, calling her attention to how *incredible* it all was.

"Would you not be happy if you were so blessed?"

She frowned. She wasn't so sure. There were some Bloodlined in the Peak District who had everything a person could possibly want, and they were still unhappy, grumpy bastards. At the end of the day, no matter how much you were *blessed*, the same issue plagued everybody. They just weren't blessed enough.

But these were different people. Maybe things were different here.

"Come, let us explore this shop. You may enjoy a change of clothing."

In other words, she smelled like shit. She sighed. She should have realized, though there wasn't exactly much she could do about it. Back home, in the Glass District, it didn't matter so much. Everyone stank a bit, after being out under the sun so much. But here, everyone was so *clean*.

"Fine," she said. She never thought she'd miss how direct people were in Zareen.

Nisha followed him into a shop with no sign. The walls inside were lined with neatly organized, folded tops, bottoms, and robes. There were countless different styles, but they were all the same color, all pulsing to the same pace.

"Welcome to Bl—," the merchant stuttered at the sight of her. He cleared his throat and with a glance at Fenrik next to her, he smiled. "Welcome to Blessed Styles. I am Valtor. How may I help you?"

"I guess I need something else to wear," she said.

"Yes, naturally. Is there any particular style you may be interested in?"

"Ah ..." she looked around.

Three other Salstadirians entered the shop. They stared at her.

"Maybe something that will help me blend in."

Valtor was slow in answering.

Nisha looked back at him. His smile was still glued to his face, but his eyes darted from the newcomers to Fenrik, who seemed unaware of the new arrivals. Instead Fenrik was sifting through some clothing at the back.

"Y-yes, I shall find you exactly what you need," Valtor stammered. He hurried away, disappearing into a section behind the counter she couldn't see.

One of the newcomers followed Valtor behind the counter. She frowned and turned to study the other two. The air they carried was far different from the rest of the Salstadirians she'd seen. In place of endless smiles, their faces were stoic and their stares were harsh.

The leader, a man with rather indistinguishable features and a shaved head, stepped forward. A gleaming blade slid from his sleeve into his hand.

The corner of Nisha's lips lifted. Some real life to this sundamned fantasy of a place.

"Finally, something I recognize," she said. She didn't have a blade at hand, but she wasn't worried.

Fenrik was on her side, and he had a relic. The man with the dagger didn't stand much of a chance. "Fenrik, looks like not everybody is as happy as you think."

He turned at the sound of her voice. His smile disappeared at the sight of them.

A muffled scream filled the shop. It was brief. The familiar thud of a body hitting the ground sent chills down her spine as she glanced toward where Valtor had gone.

The newcomer reemerged, holding a blade covered in blood and nodding toward the leader. Fenrik remained absolutely still.

"Uh ... Fenrik?"

He sighed and crossed the shop floor.

Her brow furrowed as she watched him rest his ringed hand on the man's shoulder.

"I trust you remember your instructions?"

"Do not worry. The job will be done as required."

"Good." Fenrik looked back at Nisha and dipped his head. "Goodbye, outsider. By the honor of the Angel, I wish you safe passage over the waters of the under realm."

For once, she was speechless. She watched Fenrik leave the shop, plastering on a disarming smile as though nothing had happened.

This was a setup.

The leader smiled, a dark shadow passing over his face as his blue eyes gleamed with murderous desire.

"So that's how it is," she said, her gaze flicking from man to man. The one who'd killed Valtor was behind her now. A blade slipped into the third man's palm. They were each armed.

It was one thing to be outnumbered in a place you knew like the back of your hand. You could escape down any number of alleys, wait out the danger until you had a chance to get the upper hand. But there wasn't any chance of that here. Even if she knew Salstadir, she didn't have a way to navigate between the platforms.

She was trapped.

Back in the Glass District, threats to her life were an everyday occurrence. That's how it was, living in a place where men with black eyes and blacker hearts ruled. Except this was different. This wasn't just about survival anymore.

Her daughter's fate depended on whether she walked out of this shop.

Her heart hardened. Her gaze sharpened. She took in each man, their blades and their casual stances, letting it all funnel into a single point of focus. She'd never been much of a brawler, but there *was* a reason she lasted as long as she did in the Glass District.

She raised her fists.

"Come on, then. Let's see what you've got."

CHAPTER
ELEVEN

The tension in the room snapped like a taut wire.

The man behind her moved first, thinking Nisha wouldn't expect it. It was a mistake.

She spun, his blade grazing her ribs, and cracked him flush on the jaw. He stumbled back into one of the tables. Stacks of neatly folded clothes fell to the floor.

Before the other two could react, Nisha slammed straight into him. Flesh squelched as she drove his blade into his gut.

He screamed and elbowed her.

Stars exploded.

Instinct made her duck. A blade slashed overhead. She grabbed a fistful of clothes and threw it at the second man who attacked her.

He tripped over her hooked foot and landed with a heavy grunt.

She could taste the adrenaline, metallic and sharp on her tongue, as she drove another punch into the first man. Then, with a burst of energy born from desperation, she lunged toward the blade. He tried to fend her off, but she was too fast. She got a grip on the hilt of the blade.

An iron grip closed around her hand. She tilted her head just in time as he tried to headbutt her, and she heard the sickening crunch of his nose. Hot blood gushed down onto her. His gurgled cry of pain turned her stomach. But still, his grip didn't relent.

Her heart pounded as they struggled. She glanced toward the others.

The leader stalked toward her, a dark grin spreading across his lips. The second man was pushing himself back up to his feet.

She tried to yank back and free the blade, but she couldn't break his grip. Then she drove her knee up into his groin.

The man wheezed for air, giving her enough slack to twist the blade, prompting an ear-splitting scream. She yanked the blade free.

He dropped to the ground like a bag of sand, folding in on himself. His eyes glassed over as blood pumped out of him with every dying heartbeat.

Nisha turned to face the remaining two men.

Her breathing was ragged, every inhale laced with the sharp sting of her rib wound. It occurred to her that if she hadn't gotten into the lake in the oasis, her cracked ribs wouldn't have healed, and the cut would have been enough to do her in. She pushed the thought to the back of her mind as she focused on the leader.

He stared back at her, his grin falling and his brow

rising. Behind him, the second man was clearly shaken by the sight of the body.

"You are more difficult than we were told."

Nisha spat a glob of blood to the side. "Difficult enough for you to piss off?"

The man laughed, "Not nearly. You continue to serve our interests, making our work more convincing."

"You mean you're framing me."

"You are astute."

"I'm experienced. Big difference. Bad news for you."

His grin returned. "Is that so?"

Nisha knew the odds were against her. She'd been lucky enough to catch the first man off guard. These other two would be more cautious now.

But the thought of her daughter buried in a grave of the King's making drew forth a hot and violent rage.

The leader charged forward, his footsteps measured, his blade slicing through the air. Nisha met his blade with hers, and brought her face to his.

There was nothing beautiful about the way they fought. It was no graceful dance. It was ugly, from the way their blades clashed and skipped against each other to the grunts and growls filling the air.

They grappled and rolled, her scrappiness pushing against his strength. Her muscles burned, her bones ached, but she didn't stop. Not even as the other bastard darted in, slicing at her with every open opportunity.

A cut opened up her back, and she loosed a cry of pain before she managed to shove the leader away. He slipped on the blood pooling from the dead man.

Nisha didn't wait to watch him fall. She spun toward

the second man, whose eyes widened with fear as she threw herself at him with reckless abandon.

He stabbed his blade into her shoulder, close to where she'd been struck by an arrow back in Zareen.

She cried out as she staggered into him, dropping her blade. Before he could take advantage, she grabbed a decorative rock resting on the table and slammed it into his temple. He was out cold before he even hit the ground.

Grinding her teeth in eye-watering pain, she turned to face the leader again, only to feel the full weight of him tackling her. The air *whooshed* out of her and she banged her head against the ground.

In an effort to keep up the fight, she clawed at his face, her sand-crusted fingernails digging into his eyes. He shook his head free of them, and worked to drive the blade down into her. It was everything she could do to hold it back.

But still, the blade slowly inched down toward her chest.

"Just *die* already," the man hissed through bloodied teeth.

Her muscles trembled, his strength starting to overcome hers.

She couldn't let this happen. Couldn't let it—

The very tip of the blade scraped against her chest, and a terrified scream escaped her. The man leaned his weight into the blade with a grim smile.

Nisha saw herself reflected in his eyes. She had come a long way from being the starved street rat who stood on the ledge outside her daughter's window. Her pixie cut had grown to her shoulders, her cheeks had filled out, and she'd put on more muscle. She'd grown more capable, but not capable enough. She was going to die. Auri was going to die.

No.

With a gut wrenching scream, she twisted her body so the blade slammed into the space next to her.

His mouth parted in surprise.

She pulled the blade still buried in her shoulder and thrust it straight into his heart. He gaped, stared down at his chest, then slumped down onto her.

She stayed like that for a few minutes, his blood pooling over her while she caught her breath. She winced at her various wounds.

When she was ready, she shoved his body off her with a heavy grunt and surveyed the scene. The shop was wrecked, and the ground was slick with blood. The bodies lay like dolls, as though they'd never been human.

Little Bloodlined boys liked to pretend at fights to the death, their short battles filled with the glory of the rising sun. But that was a lie, as was the fanciful dream of dancing back and forth, crossing blade with graceful maneuvers. She'd seen enough of these things to know that they were always filled with men stumbling back and forth like they were drunk. There were no shouts or declarations. Only guttural grunts, curses, and the occasional whimper.

She knew few men who truly enjoyed the actual act of murder. No, it was the feeling that came afterward that hooked them. The same feeling she felt now.

She had *prevailed.*

They thought they could do her in, and she'd done them first.

Nisha leaned her head back, closed her eyes, and drew in a deep breath of the sweet, blood-tinged air. This air was hers to breathe, not theirs. For a while longer, she stood a chance of saving Auri.

Using her foot, she turned the dead leader over and withdrew the blade. She crossed the room to the man she'd knocked unconscious, crouched over him, and slapped his cheek until he woke.

His eyes cracked open.

Steel touched his neck.

"Do you want to live?"

His gaze flicked down to the blade and back up at her. He slowly nodded.

"Then tell me what you know, or I'll do you like I did your friends. Understand?"

Again, he nodded.

"Good. What's your name?"

"Mirov."

She motioned for him to speak with a flick of the blade.

"We were instructed by the honored to murder you and frame you for attacking a citizen of Salstadir."

"Why?"

He held his hands up. "I do not know."

She pricked the skin of his neck with the blade.

"I promise you, by the Angel's own breath, I do not know!"

She sighed and eased the pressure. "What'd they promise you in return for framing me?"

"Nothing."

"I don't understand. Why do it then, if you get nothing out of it?"

"It was ordered."

Ordered. She frowned. It didn't add up. You don't just order men like these. Not unless you had something you held over them.

A thought popped into her mind. If these men were anything like those that she'd known in the Glass District, she had a slim chance here.

"And Sher?"

"I know nothing about any soul named Sher."

Her lip curled.

"Okay, so who would then?"

"Jorvik."

"This Jorvik, he's the big man? The boss?"

"Y-yes."

The thought took root.

"Tell me where to find him." Her voice was calm, but the blade's touch against his skin made it clear she wouldn't brook any argument. He could obey, or he could die.

The man swallowed hard, his eyes darting around as if looking for an escape that didn't exist. She realized that he was seriously contemplating death, as though it might be better than taking her to see Jorvik.

He seemed to concede. "You will not be able to find him yourself, even if I tell you everything"

"Then take me there."

He swallowed, but conceded.

"If you try anything, I'll go straight to the so called

honored. Let them know about how you and your boys failed to do me in, and how you murdered poor Valtor over there."

"Why would you go to the ones who tried to have you killed?"

"You underestimate what I'd do to spite you. Now come on, find yourself something to change into, and let's get going. Longer we stick around here, the more likely it is some bastard will walk in on us and see all this."

The thought seemed to alarm Mirov enough that he went scrambling to find a set of unstained clothing that would be his size.

She shook her head as she searched for something for herself.

"It would be just my luck, too," she muttered.

CHAPTER
TWELVE

Nisha and Mirov stepped out of the shop, both wearing a new set of clothing, their faces wiped of blood and shrouded by oversized hoods. She'd done her best to bind her wounds with strips torn from other pieces of fabric, but it had been a rushed job. She could still feel blood seeping from them. She'd have to rebind them when she had a chance, but who knew when that would be.

As the adrenaline began to fade, exhaustion seeped into her bones. Each step felt heavier than the last. She ground her teeth in frustration. She wasn't out of this yet, not by a long shot. She needed to keep up her energy.

She glanced at Mirov to make sure he wasn't trying anything, but he seemed to be content with their arrangement. He kept pace beside her, his footsteps a little uneven. She must've concussed him when she knocked him out.

When she looked away, she studied the streets of Salstadir again. They were different now. She saw through the smiles, the peace, and the order of it all. Something very wrong here.

Mirov cursed under his breath as a pair of the honored passed them. They were heading toward Blessed Styles.

"I'm guessing that was arranged?"

He pursed his lips and nodded. "We need to hurry."

"Why?"

He didn't say anything else, instead pushing forward faster toward the nearest platform.

They stepped into a small crowd of Salstadirians. The guards above touched their rings to orbs, and with a jolt, the platform began to rise.

It was only when they reached the top that Nisha got her answer.

A whistle shrilled into the air, loud enough that she had to clamp her hands over her ears. The guards turned toward the sound, as did everyone else they stood with.

Mirov, however, grabbed her arm and pulled her away with a finger to his lips, motioning for her to stay silent.

She glanced back over her shoulder, watching as the guards held their rings to the sky, shooting up a ray of ethereal light to join the hundred other platforms across Salstadir.

Travel was closed.

Her jaw dropped as light streamed from their rings, forming angel wings at their backs. With a running jump, both guards shot into the air.

They began to *fly*.

They weren't the only ones. The air filled with a

flurry of activity as more and more of the guards took to the sky, their wings shimmering with ethereal wisps of light that flickered and danced around them. The magic was still temporary, expiring after a handful of seconds, but every time they expired and dropped the guard through the air, they would summon a new one. It was a strange cycle of flying and falling, a ballet of light and motion that stole her breath away.

She never thought she'd see the day when man began to fly. It was the stuff of dreams, of fantasies so foolish that even emberdusted addicts would be embarrassed to speak them aloud.

A surge of regret passed through her. The relic rings were capable of so much more than she realized. And she'd let the Speaker take it away.

The murmur of the Salstadirians below came to a hushed halt, soft whispers passing through the crowd as they looked up at the guards overhead. The whistle continued to blow, and slowly the crowd began to dissipate into the surrounding shops, leaving the streets clear for investigation.

"Come!" Mirov tugged on her wrist again.

She grimaced and forced herself to tear her gaze away. She suddenly understood why he was so anxious. The guards were flying with unprecedented speed toward Blessed Styles. They'd see what happened there, they'd spread out.

They didn't have long to get away.

The man pulled her off the main path, ducking into a narrow side street filled with modest homes, each identical to the other. They stopped in front of one.

He rapped his knuckles on the door, shifting nervously from foot to foot as they waited. A woman answered the door, glancing down both ways of the street before letting them in.

Stepping in, Nisha paused to let her eyes adjust to the dimness inside. She expected to see the same veins of glowing minerals running through the walls as in the Sanctum. But there were none. Instead, the light came from small, lit candles hanging from the ceilings, their sides decorated with geometric patterns that the flickering flames cast across the smooth stone floor.

"What are you doing?" the woman hissed.

"She is to see Jorvik."

"That was not the plan!"

Mirov shook his head almost apologetically. "The plan has changed."

Mirov motioned for Nisha to follow him deeper into the home.

The space was open, uncluttered, with every piece of furniture there to serve a purpose. In one corner, a piece of stone jutted out from the wall, with one fabric-made chair situated on either side. It took her a moment to realize that was where the woman probably ate.

Something off about the space. It all felt too ... stale. There was nothing out of place, and nothing personal about it at all.

Her eyes caught a small statue of the Angel resting in the corner. Its face was blank, as though it was too precious to see, but the rest of the Angel was carved with great detail, from the feathered wings unfurling from its back to the design etched into the Angel's crown.

Mirov had positioned himself against the wall, digging his fingers into a small gap in one of the wall panels. A second later, a hiss of air echoed through the silence, and the wall panel shifted, revealing a hidden passage.

"Where are the others?" the woman asked.

He didn't answer. Instead, his eyes flicked toward Nisha.

The cold woman's gaze turned on her. Her hand was too still.

"You reach for whatever weapon you have hiding, I'll kill you where you stand," Nisha said. She flashed the tip of the blade, and the woman's eyes widened.

Sundamned hells, when had she turned into a Reaper? She tried not to think about it. There were other ways to persuade people, even women. Seraphine had taught her that much during her training as a Silk Rider.

The blade disappeared.

"Look, I'm just here to have a quick meet with your boss and that's it."

"Why should we trust you?"

"You shouldn't. But it doesn't matter. You have to."

The woman's eyes narrowed. "We have to?"

"Yes, because if you ever want to get out from under the honored's thumb, then you need me."

She glanced toward Mirov, some silent conversation passing between their exchanged looks. It was enough to confirm what Nisha suspected. Someone was holding this group of criminals hostage.

With a heavy sigh, the woman stepped back. Mirov motioned for Nisha to come forward.

She stuck her head through the hole and saw a tight space carved into the rock. A ladder led upward, disappearing in a dark abyss.

"Climb."

Nisha looked back at him in disbelief. "How high?"

"Until you reach the top."

"Yeah, I got that, but how far is that?"

The woman smirked.

Shit. She wasn't sure her shoulder would be up for it.

"Do not fall. I will be below you."

Nisha muttered a curse before squeezing herself into the space and grabbing the iron bars. They were shockingly cold. Her body already ached, and she hadn't even started climbing yet.

She'd done a lot of terrifying things, from walking over glass sharded sands as a child to climbing the side of the red flat-topped mountain in her attempt to escape the guards. But she'd sooner repeat those things than climb these iron bars into the endless darkness.

Still, it was what needed doing. She drew a deep breath, clenched her jaw, and began to climb.

It was hard from the start. The higher she climbed, the more her muscles threatened to give out. She couldn't give in though. She shoved the pain and weakness to the back of her mind and focused on the rhythm of the climb. The darkness enveloped her, a thick blanket that threatened to smother her resolve with its oppressive weight. Yet, with each pull of her arms, each push from her legs, she ascended, determined not to let the void swallow her whole.

Time lost meaning in the dark. The only sounds were

her labored breaths and the occasional scrape of her boots against the ladder. Strangely, Mirov's presence below became a distant assurance, a reminder that she wasn't entirely alone in this abyss.

Finally, her hands found empty air where she expected another rung. Startled, she almost lost her grip, but steadied herself just in time.

She pulled herself up and over the edge.

Torches flared to life, blinding her for an instant. She moved to cover her eyes, but then felt the cold press of steel against her throat and froze.

"Who are you?"

A second, hushed voice whispered, "Her skin. Look, she is an outsider."

She heard Mirov reach the top behind her. Frustratingly, his breathing didn't seem anywhere near as labored as hers.

"She has requested to see Jorvik," Mirov said.

"What happened to Gavrel and Rurik?"

"She sent them to the under realm."

A bark of laughter echoed sharply around them. "Her?"

"Yes."

"You tell me that she defeated the three of you?"

He hesitated, but then nodded. "Yes."

Her eyes adjusted to the light and she saw the man holding the steel to her throat. His head was shaved, and one of his teeth shone with what looked like one of the minerals she'd seen before, embedded in the walls.

"What is your name?"

"Nisha."

"Okay, Nisha. You want to meet Jorvik? Then give me the weapon you hold Mirov hostage with."

She was conscious that all this man would have to do is drive his boot into her chest if he wanted to be rid of her. She'd go tumbling down into the abyss, never to be seen again.

With an ugly snarl, she slid the blade out from her sleeve and placed it in his palm.

He grinned, his glowing tooth mocking her.

"Good. Come."

He led Nisha and Mirov down a side tunnel, leaving the other man to guard the entrance. They passed through a complex network of tunnels. It took her a minute to realize that there were none of the glowing rocks she'd gotten so used to now. Up here, the darkness and chill were kept at bay with torches mounted along the walls.

They passed a few groups of men and women, whose laughter came to a pause at the sight of Nisha. There was no mistaking it. These were rough men and women, the type that would have been more comfortable in the Glass District than anywhere else.

They reached a massive door centered in the stone passageway. The air grew thick, charged with a palpable tension that came from beyond the door.

"Are you prepared?" the man asked.

"Open it," she said.

He smirked,."I was not speaking to you. I was speaking to Mirov."

She looked over her shoulder. Even with his alabaster skin, she could tell his face had paled. He would have to answer for his and his colleagues' failure to frame her death, along with leading her here.

With a loud groan, the door swung open, spilling the sound of howling laughter.

Nisha stepped through, her eye immediately drawn to the ground; it was made of minerals, just transparent enough to reveal the entirety of Salstadir below. The massive stalactite that lit the city swallowed a portion of the view, leading up to the ground itself, where it converged into a massive pillar that ran through to the ceiling of the chamber.

The chamber itself was tight, no bigger than the Peddler's den back in Zareen, with chairs scattered across the room, loosely circling the pillar. They were filled with drunk men and empty bottles. The air stank of piss and sweat.

Nisha found herself disappointed.

This was it? These were the dangerous men who the honored trusted to frame and murder her?

"What toy do you bring my way?"

A booming voice sliced through the laughter, pulling Nisha's focus towards the figure ensconced against the glowing pillar.

Jorvik, the man in command, lounged in an oversized chair that groaned under his considerable bulk. Multiple chins cascaded towards his chest, and his fingers, greasy from feasting, gripped a bottle's neck with possessive strength. Adorned with golden rings that glittered even in the dim light, he seemed to attempt a deliberate display of wealth and power.

But Nisha noticed that, of all the rings he wore, not one was a relic.

She glanced to Jorvik's side, noticing a man who stood relaxed, yet undeniably more alert than any of the others in the chamber. He was well dressed, without so much as a wrinkle in his outfit, and his black hair neatly combed back.

"Now, what is this?" Jorvik hissed.

A hush fell over the motley crew of criminals. Eyes flicked between her and Jorvik, curiosity and anticipation mingling in the air.

Jorvik's gaze fixed on Nisha, assessing her with an intensity that made her skin crawl. He was a man accustomed to being feared and obeyed.

As much as she wanted to walk up to him and force him to tell her what happened to Sher, she couldn't. This wasn't the kind of place she could do that. She'd have to handle it more delicately, and to do that, she needed to call to mind her silk rider lessons. Better to understand Jorvik's fantasies so that she could wield them against him. Luckily, she had a hunch.

"You should be dead," he said.

"Surprise, surprise, you fat bastard."

A collective gasp echoed through the room. Jorvik's eye twitched as he stared at her. Then he burst out laughing, spittle flying left and right. He nudged the men closest to him, pointing at her.

But nobody dared to laugh alongside him. A good thing maybe, because a moment later, his laughter came to a sudden halt.

"Do you have any idea who I am?" he asked, his chins

trembling with rage as he pointed his grubby finger at her.

And there it was. His need to assert power. She could tell by the way his eyes darted from side to side, taking in the reactions of others. His tongue dragged across his bottom lip, licking away the sweat that beaded there.

She audibly sighed. This was too easy. "I'm guessing you're supposed to be the man in charge."

"That is right. I—"

"I said you're *supposed* to be."

He paused, his beady eyes blinking in confusion. "What?"

"Your little minion here told me you were *instructed* to frame me. But when I asked him what you got out of it, you know what he said? Nothing. You get nothing. The only way a man like you would do something like that is if you're downright stupid, or if someone's got your balls in a knot. You don't mark me as someone stupid."

That last part was a lie. But she had to walk a careful line. She had to push him, fan the flames of his rage while stroking his ego.

He sputtered, "I am not stupid."

She didn't say anything. She didn't need to. It was enough for the other men in the room to glance at him. Everyone already probably knew. But it was one thing to know, and another thing to admit it out loud.

"Don't you want to know why I made Mirov bring me here?"

She didn't wait for him to respond.

"I came because I knew you needed my help."

"Help? Why would I need the help of a little thing like you?"

She smiled. "Let's just say that where I come from, nothing and no one was safe from me."

Some careful word play. True enough, and vague enough, for him to wonder.

He leaned forward, his belly rolls pushing out over his knees. "Is that so? And what would you have me do with that information?"

"Use me, of course. It's *wrong* for someone like you to be under another man's thumb. Aim me at your enemy, and I will free you."

A moment of silence followed.

The man standing next to Jorvik studied her with a strangely serious gaze. His head tilted a fraction of an inch.

Then Jorvik burst out into laughter alongside the rest of his men, except for the serious man at his side. Nisha frowned. That wasn't the response she expected.

"You would free me? From the Angel?"

Her heart stopped. The Angel?

His laughter came to a halt as he rose to his feet, grunting with the effort. He stumbled forward a half step.

"Listen carefully, outsider. Through the Speaker, the Angel himself commands us. We make ourselves dishonorable for *him*, we dirty our hands for *him*, and we will soon reap the rewards he has in store for us."

Nisha staggered back. It didn't make sense. None of it did. She'd thought some other faction held power over Jorvik, that someone had their hands on a few honored to do as they wanted. But for it all to be orchestrated by the Angel?

"What happened to Sher?"

"Sher? I know nothing of a man named Sher," he turned his harsh gaze on Mirov. "I sent *three* of you, and still you failed. You disgust me."

Mirov shrank. His knees were trembling.

"Jorvik, I—"

"I have heard enough."

He waved his hand, and the men in the room rushed forward. They tackled her, pinning her down and planting her face painfully against the mineral. She couldn't see what they were doing to Mirov, but she could hear it.

The sound of bone raw fists pummeling flesh, whimpers buried beneath the grunts of exertion, the crack of his skull followed by the squelching of brain matter.

Jorvik's massive feet were all she could see as he strode towards her. He planted his heel on the top of her head, threatening to burst it beneath his weight.

"You are lucky that I do not kill you now. But I do only as my Angel commands. Count your breaths, outsider. There are not many left."

His men dragged her away. She was too numb to scream. She thought she'd had it all figured out, thought that there had to be some other man who'd bought the loyalty of a few honored and had Jorvik under their control. But she'd made the mistake of thinking that this place could be anything like Zareen.

They tossed her into a cell so tight there was not enough space for her to even kneel. The bars pressed against her chest and face, whilst hard stone pressed against her back. She could only watch as the men left her behind.

The door slammed shut and thrust her into an all consuming darkness. This was it. She would die here. There were no other cards to play, no other hopes to bet on. And the only person who could save her had gone to meet the Angel himself.

Somewhere out there, her daughter lived and breathed.

But just as her breaths were running out, so were Auri's.

"I'm sorry," Nisha whispered.

The darkness swallowed her words.

THIRTEEN

After living in the Glass District, Nisha thought she knew what it meant to suffer: to feel hopelessness pressing its boot to her neck, threatening to crush her windpipe. She thought she knew what it meant to feel *pain*, so visceral that it would force even the hardest of men to beg.

But she was wrong. Nothing she'd ever experienced compared to what she felt now, stuck in the suffocating dark of her cell, with striking pain coursing up through her knees. She was trapped in the cramped space between the bars and the stone wall at her back, so tight she could not even sleep.

And without sleep, without any release from the awful torture, she felt the passing of every single minute.

She breathed the thick, stale air. Tears streamed down her cheeks. It was all she could do to fight back the urge to scream for the men to come back and kill her. At least then she'd be freed from the hounds of madness barking at the gates of her mind, reminding her of her failures.

A sound scraped through the dark. Metal against stone. Her heart raced. Had she called out in her delirium? She gripped the bars, trying to pull them apart to no avail.

A sliver of light cut through the darkness, casting long shadows across the walkway in front of her. Footsteps approached, slow and measured.

Her muscles trembled with the effort, but in the end, she was simply too weak. She bit her lip and choked back a sob, her gaze falling to the ground. This was it. This was how things would end.

The footsteps stopped just outside her cell.

"Are you broken?" a disturbingly smooth, low voice asked.

Something about his presence dredged up the last burning coals in her soul, and she raised her eyes to meet those of the man who'd stood next to Jorvik.

He was handsome, with slicked-back hair and pronounced cheekbones and jawline. A shadow of dark stubble grew on his pale white cheeks, but it didn't make him look unkempt. Somehow, it only made him seem more ... dangerous.

He studied her with those stoic, unfeeling eyes. His hands were folded behind his straightened back.

She bared her teeth at him, aware of how crazed she must look.

"Good. There is still life to you."

"Who're you?"

"I am Soren."

"And what in the sundamned hells do you want?"

A sound passed through the darkness again. She'd

spent long enough in the cell to know it was a drip of water somewhere, but it seemed he didn't, as his gaze darted toward the doorway.

She frowned, hope sparking in her chest. "You're not supposed to be here, are you?"

"No, I am not," he said, shifting his focus back to her. "But not all of us share Jorvik's love for the Angel. What is your name?"

"Nisha."

"Then tell me, Nisha, what is it like where you are from?"

"You mean without the Angel?"

She opened her mouth, ready to spin a lie that would draw him in and convince him to let her go. But she hesitated. There was something about him that told her she should be honest.

"Where I come from, it's nothing like Salstadir. The sun'll scorch your skin, the sand'll get in your teeth, and when you wake up, you don't know if you'll make it through the day. It's a place where everybody—even the rich and powerful—wants something. Doesn't matter if it's more coin, power, status, or even just a bit of water. They'll stick their knives in your back to have at it."

"That sounds ... harsh."

"It is. But it's *real*. Our paths and choices aren't dictated to us. You make your own way, and you hope that fate doesn't have some fat, pale bastard standing in your way."

The man watched her, his stoic expression giving way to a flicker of interest. Silence enveloped them, filled only by the distant drip of water and the weight of her words.

"Okay."

"Okay?" Her brow furrowed in confusion.

"Listen to the proposal I have for you and consider it carefully, because if you fail, you will wish that you had stayed here in this cell, waiting for your fat, pale bastard to deliver your fate."

She grasped the bars. "I'm listening."

"The Speaker wears a ring, adorned with a sapphire. You may have seen it."

She froze.

He lifted his chin. "You *have* seen it. Good. Bring me the ring, and I will help you rescue your friend."

She surged against the bars. "Sher?"

"Do we have an agreement?" he asked as he withdrew a key from his pocket. It glinted in the dim light from the doorway. She wasn't sure she'd ever seen anything that looked so sundamned beautiful.

But she hesitated. "How do I know that you'll keep to your word? I mean, if I bring you the ring, then you've got everything you want."

"Because our paths are aligned. When I achieve what I must, then your friend will no longer be in any danger. You and he will be free to go."

"I don't understand. When you achieve what you must? What are you trying to do?"

He smiled, and a dark chill ran down the back of her neck.

"I intend to free us, to remove the boot from our

necks, as you would say. And it is not the boot of the Speaker's. It is that of the Angel's."

He stepped closer to the bars. His shock blue eyes bore into hers. His dark grin inched wider.

"Do you understand now?"

She could hardly breathe.

"I will kill the Angel."

CHAPTER
FOURTEEN

Nisha wasn't sure that she'd ever experienced any sort of pleasure so great as the moment Soren unlocked the cell door. Her knees had given out the instant they'd been released from her weight, and she wasn't sure that they were up to holding her up any longer. Something that was proven true the instant she tried to stand and fell back down.

Soren helped her up, guiding her down the hall toward the door with her arm over his shoulder.

She glanced at him out of the corner of her eye. He wanted to kill the Angel. It was unthinkable. They weren't talking about just some mortal. They were talking about the being responsible for all the magic in the world, who'd lived for a thousand years or more.

Could it even be done?

Soren seemed convinced that it could, so long as he had the Speaker's ring.

Though she wasn't one of the Faithful, the idea of killing the Angel felt *wrong*. But if that's what it took to

save Sher and to get the tear she needed, then, well ...
he'd lived long enough.

They stepped out the door. Her heart raced at the
sudden sight of a man waiting for them, calmed only by
the fact that Soren seemed to expect him.

"Go ahead of us and ensure that we do not have an
unfortunate encounter. We must keep this quiet."

"Yes, Soren." The man dipped his head out of respect
and disappeared down the hallway.

They followed him. Nisha could not help but be
aware of how she was slowing them down. If they got
caught, she imagined only bad things would happen.
Clenching her jaw, she forced herself to carry more of her
own weight, ignoring the painful tingling in her knees.

Voices echoed down the hallway. Nisha strained to
hear.

"—do not want to go that way. Goring peed all up
and down the passage again."

The other two men groaned and said something too
quiet for her to hear, but she suspected that they were
cursing his name. They thanked the man for warning
them, and a few moments later, it was quiet.

The man appeared in the hallway, motioning for
them to continue following him.

It was a painstakingly slow process, with the man
going ahead of them, his raised voice a sign for them to
halt. They'd nearly been caught on three different occa-
sions before they reached a passage that led to a staircase
that spiraled downwards. Its steps were steep and
unwelcoming.

Nisha withdrew her arm from Soren's shoulder and

tested her knees. They still ached, but it seemed they had regained enough strength for her to stand on.

The man waited just at the bend of the staircase.

"Are you coming?"

Soren paused, glancing at her with a look that seemed to gauge her strength.

"It's fine. I've got this."

He motioned for her to go first. With a grimace and a hand against the tight walls, she started down, following the man.

After an age of torture, hobbling down step after step, they arrived at a small chamber. She noticed a massive hole in the ground at the heart of the chamber, light streaming up from it to dance on the ceiling.

"What is this?" Nisha asked, too nervous to stand at the edge of the hole with her still recovering knees.

"This is the well that nourishes us," Soren said as he entered the chamber.

She spotted a large bucket with a long rope tied around its handle. It made sense now how they didn't die of thirst.

He retrieved a small bundle of clothing wrapped in some sort of bag and handed it to Nisha. "You will need this. This is your disguise. You will be playing the part of a Devoted—priestesses who save their appearance only for the Angel himself."

Nisha frowned, "Do they ever actually see the Angel?"

"No, not in this life. This will be a strong disguise for you. I have also included anything you might need to heal your wounds."

She breathed a sigh of relief, thinking of her throbbing shoulder.

"Now, here's what you must do to pass as a Devoted."

The next few minutes passed as Soren taught her the hand signs, the posture, everything that would help frame her as a Devoted to the Salstadirians in the city below. He was calm, collected, but there was an undertone of urgency in his words.

She got the sense that even here, they didn't have long until someone inevitably stumbled upon them. The other man stood guard at the steps.

"The Speaker lives in a home on the first level, just above the Sanctum."

"He doesn't stay in the Sanctum?"

He shook his head. "None live within the Sanctum. Not even him. But make no mistake, his home is as heavily guarded as the Sanctum itself."

"But you've got a way in, right?"

"No, I do not. That task is left to you."

"Thanks," she said, her voice laced with sarcasm.

"Bring me that ring, and I shall save your friend, no matter the cost."

She clenched her jaw and nodded. She had no idea how she was going to break into the Speaker's home, let alone what she was going to do when she saw him. But she was done with failing. Whatever it took to do this, whatever it took to save Sher, she'd do it.

First him, then her daughter.

Soren's expression was unreadable in the dim light, but he seemed satisfied with what he saw in her.

"Brondar," he called out, his soft voice disturbingly loud in the silence.

The man at the steps glanced at him. "Yes?"

"Come here."

Brondar looked once more at the steps, confirming that nobody was coming down, before he crossed the chamber. "What is it?"

Soren's demeanor shifted, his blue eyes going black. Brondar barely had time to register the soft hiss of Soren's blade before it plunged into his neck.

Nisha's mouth parted in shock as she watched Brondar stumble back a step, his hand clutching his throat, blood gushing out from between his fingers. His eyes bulged from his skull.

"Why?" he wheezed.

Soren tilted his head, regarding the man he'd betrayed with unfeeling eyes. He didn't answer. He only watched as Brondar fell to one knee.

Then he drove his boot into Brondar's chest.

Without another sound, Brondar fell back and tumbled through the gaping hole. Nisha counted the seconds before she heard a heavy splash, the sound like a rock smashing against stone.

It had taken him a full thirty seconds.

Her face paled.

"He was the fall man the whole time," she said, working through it all in her mind. "You're framing him for Jorvik, making him think he helped me escape. That's why you brought him, isn't it?"

Soren turned to her, cleaning his blade with a piece of cloth. The corner of his mouth quirked up. "You are clever. That is good. You will need to be in order to retrieve the ring."

His eyes were devoid of emotion, as if he hadn't just murdered a man in cold blood only moments before. He offered her the blade.

Nisha's hands shook as she took it from him. She glanced down at the bloody blade, her mouth suddenly dry.

"I will be here for the next three mornings. You have until then to come. Otherwise, I will assume that you have failed."

She glanced toward the hole, a nervous bead of sweat running from her brow. "How about I take that ladder back down to Salstadir instead?"

"Make sure you do not land flat in the water, or you will die. Good luck."

Before Nisha could fully process his words, Soren's hand shot out, grabbing her by the arm. With a strength that belied his lean frame, he propelled her toward the hole. Her heart lurched, a scream tearing from her throat as she fell, the well's cool air rushing past her.

Plummeting into the darkness, the last thing she saw was Soren's impassive gaze watching her fall. Seconds passed as she tumbled through the air, her scream catching in her throat.

Ten seconds.

She could see Brondar's corpse floating below in a spreading pool of crimson, his legs bent at a wrong angle.

Twenty seconds.

She turned in the air as she struggled to right herself.

The seconds ticked in her mind. Twenty-five, twenty-six, twenty-seven.

At the last possible moment, she pointed her feet and hugged the wrapped bundle of clothing and the dagger to her chest.

Then she hit the water.

Water enveloped her, cold and shockingly clear, swallowing her whole with a roar that drowned out her screams. Water rushed into her open mouth, choking the air from her.

She flailed underwater, doing everything she could to get closer to the surface, all while the water continued to choke her. Her heart pounded in her chest and throat. The edges of her vision pulsed with darkness, pressing in with every passing heartbeat.

A scream was lodged deep inside her as bubbles of precious air escaped through her mouth and nose. She kicked and kicked until, at long last, she broke through the surface of the water.

She gasped for air before submerging again. Panic coursed through her veins as she struggled repeatedly to break the surface. Just when she thought she might succumb to the depths, something solid brushed the tip of her foot. Hope surged. She flailed her arms and legs, desperately reaching for the solid ground.

Moments later, she hauled herself onto the edge, the stone surface hard and jagged, but damn it all if she had never seen anything so beautiful. She collapsed onto her back, exhausted, her hair sticking to her face.

Who could have known that so much water could be so awful?

Her mind turned back to the painting of the ocean and its rolling waves and the way the tide pushed and pulled. She understood now that the ocean shared much with the desert. Get stuck out there, and death was coming for you.

When she had her breath back, she sat up, surprised by the weight of her exhaustion. She was in a large cave, the waters illuminated by minerals in the walls. Far above, the hole she'd been pushed through was invisible, blending into the dark stone. Anyone visiting here wouldn't know it existed.

Brondar's body bumped up against the edge of the water. The crimson continued to spread, dark and ominous. Next to him, her wrapped bundle of clothing floated.

Nisha shivered, her clothes clinging to her skin as she carefully retrieved the bundle. With trembling hands, she unwrapped the bundle Soren had given her.

Besides some strange healing paste and bindings, there was a long flowing robe with matching gloves, stark white against the dim glow of the mineral-lit cave. A gray threaded design of angel wings had been sewn into the back. As for the veil, it was also white, but the face was made from countless tiny, interlocked chips of glowing minerals.

She stripped off her wet clothes, the air chilling her to the bone. Aware that someone could enter the cave at any moment, she quickly applied the paste to her wounds and bandaged them. Then she dressed in the Devoted's garb. The fabric was soft, lighter, and warmer than she expected, but it caught around her legs. She grimaced, realizing it would be impossible to run in. If the honored suspected her, she was as good as dead.

She draped the veil over her face, taking a moment to adjust to the minerals' glow. With one last look at the floating body, she turned and headed toward the narrow path leading away from the well, the stones worn smooth by countless footsteps.

She was exhausted. In the past day alone, she'd survived murder, imprisonment, and near drowning. Her body cried out for rest, but she couldn't stop thinking about what Sher might be enduring.

She summoned the resolve to take the first step. She could sleep later, once Sher and Auri were safe. For now, they needed her.

CHAPTER
FIFTEEN

Dressed as a Devoted, Nisha's experience walking through the streets of Salstadir was far different this time around. People didn't stop to gawk at her, nor did their conversations go soft whenever she approached. Instead, they simply dipped their heads in respect and touched their fingers to their foreheads.

And in return, she did just as Soren instructed: she folded her gloved hands over her heart and whispered back in a low voice, "May the Angel grant you his favor."

The words felt poisonous, knowing that the Angel held Sher captive.

When she first saw Salstadir, she was stunned by its beauty. But now, she saw through it. She noticed the way people's backs straightened and their smiles widened forcibly whenever one of the honored was near. Everyone moved with a carefulness born of fear rather than genuine contentment. The laughter she heard was hollow, almost rehearsed.

As she moved deeper into the city, descending from

the busy sixth level to the second, the presence of honored increased, and the artificial joy became more pronounced.

She noticed how the honored, with their ruby rings of power, eyed people sharply, their calm expressions betraying nothing. Their presence created palpable tension in the air.

How had she missed this before?

She sighed, knowing the answer. She had been so swept away by the city's beauty that she failed to see the insidious undercurrent infecting its streets.

She missed the ugliness of the Glass District, where the place's true nature was more than clear by its glass sharded sands and the ways that men's eyes gleamed with dark intentions. There was never anybody who'd been confused about what exactly the Glass District was.

The only thing worse than hell was a hell made pretty.

As she descended the final platform to the second level, Nisha felt a simmering anger. These people were prisoners in a gilded cage and didn't even know it.

She turned her sight to the Speaker's home in the distance. Architecturally, it looked about the same as every other home on this level. But there was no mistaking about whose home it was by the sheer number of honored guards surrounding it.

When she reached the bottom, she moved toward the house, the crowd parting easily. Her hurried footsteps were clumsy, not as graceful as she wished. The sundamned fabric kept clinging to her legs.

Nisha stopped a short distance away, trying to come

up with a plan to break in. Back in Zareen, she'd just go around the back, climb up and break a window. That wasn't an option here. The Speaker's home was flat against the rock, with no way inside except the front door.

She grimaced. This wasn't going to be easy.

One of the honored patrolling out front paused, his gaze locking onto her. She froze, panic rolling through her. Then he dipped his head and touched his fingers to his forehead. Relief washed over her. She crossed her hand over her heart, and he continued patrolling. Her gaze followed him.

He was more relaxed than the other guards. That much was evident in how he slouched when he walked. But the question was, was he relaxed enough as a *man*?

It was one thing to be a Silk Rider dressed in a luxurious black robe. It was another to be a Silk Rider dressed a sundamned Devoted. She chewed her lip, her fingers anxiously brushing against the dagger hilt. She couldn't afford to mess this up. One shout, and the other guards would come running.

Taking a deep breath, she buried that thought. The only way that this would work was if she carried herself with the utmost confidence. Anything less, she'd spark his suspicion.

Nisha straightened her back and walked toward the man, weaving a path directly to him.

The man noticed her, his eyes glinting with confusion, not quite suspicion. This wasn't normal behavior for a Devoted.

"Blessed Devoted, is there something I can help you

with?" he asked, touching his fingers to his forehead again.

This time, she didn't cross her hands over her heart. She crossed them over his.

His eyes widened.

"May the Angel grant you his favor," she whispered, her hands lingering a moment too long.

He stammered, "You too."

She stood there, head tilted up toward his. Then she leaned in, her voice low and conspiratorial. She couldn't afford for him to detect the difference in her accent. "I must confess something."

He glanced at the other guards, then back at her.

"To me?"

"Yes, you," she said, rolling her eyes behind the veil.

"Okay …"

She stepped closer. His gulp of nervousness was audible. It was clear that this was not normal behavior at all for a Devoted.

"I … noticed you. I wonder if you might help me."

His smile faltered as he blinked. She smirked. His mind was turning toward her suggestion, but he was convincing himself he must be mistaken. A Devoted coming on to him? Unthinkable.

"Of course, Sister. I am happy to assist a Devoted with any of her needs."

"*Any* of my needs?"

His alabaster skin flushed deep red.

"I-I am not sure what you are suggesting. Can you—"

"For Angel's sake, I need a man to do what only a man can do," she said.

He coughed, staring at her with wide, disbelieving eyes, glancing toward the other guards again. Sundamned hells, her voice had risen enough to risk revealing her accent.

Instead, he leaned in, "I thought that the Devoted do not ... participate in—"

"You are honored, are you not?" she interrupted, getting enough of his accent to fake. If the fool hadn't been completely distracted by the thought of what she was proposing, then he might have noticed how poor the accent was.

"I am."

"And I am Devoted."

"You are."

"These things happen on occasion. But they are never spoken of. Do you understand?"

This time, he didn't hesitate.

"I understand," he said with a self-satisfied smirk. "Tell me where you will be, and I will find you when I am finished here."

She shook her head, "I do not have long. Is there some place ... quiet?"

Judging by the look on his face, it was clear he wasn't ready to give up the opportunity. He half turned towards the Speaker's home, silent as he considered the risk. Nisha couldn't stop herself from grinning. Didn't matter if you were from Zareen or Salstadir, all men were the same.

Cocks over thoughts.

"Come with me," he said.

One of the guards raised an eyebrow as they

approached. He dipped his head toward her and touched his finger to his forehead in respect. She muttered her response softly, but his attention was on the man she was with.

"What are you doing, Vargus?"

"This Devoted has business with the Speaker," Vargus said from beside her.

The guard frowned, "The Speaker is not present. You know this."

"I do, but would you make a Devoted stand outside, waiting in discomfort?"

"Hmm ... I suppose not."

"Think how it must displease the Angel."

The guard's eyes flicked toward her. She could tell he was conflicted. They weren't supposed to let others into the Speaker's home, but then again, it couldn't have been very common for one of the Devoted to come knocking.

"Okay, you may take her to the front room. I will be gone soon, but I trust you will stay with her at all times. Otherwise, we risk displeasing the Speaker as well."

Vargus smiled, "On my honor."

It was everything Nisha could do to not snort in laughter.

The other guard stepped aside, and Vargus and Nisha entered the Speaker's home together. The front door clicked shut behind them.

Nisha was enveloped by an opulence that almost took her breath away. The air was thick, perfumed with a dusty scent reminiscent of old books. It was the kind of scent that spoke of long years spent in isolation.

She slowly took in the finely woven carpet and the

paintings and tapestries lining the walls. It was far more luxurious than she had imagined.

In a hushed voice, Vargus motioned for her to follow. "This way."

They moved through the hallway, shadows dancing against the light of glowing sconces mounted on the walls. An empty room with several chairs rested to the right; she assumed it was the waiting room where she was supposed to be taken.

They stepped through to another hall. Vargus stopped in front of a doorway with a big smile on his face.

"In here," he said.

Nisha glanced inside. It was an empty bedroom, devoid of the luxury the rest of the home carried. Dust hung in the air, as if no one had stepped inside in ages.

He must have noticed her silence, because he added, "The Speaker had family once. They are with the Angel now."

She nodded, not saying anything. Her eyes turned back down to the end of the hallway, where there was one other door. There was a lock fitted to its handle.

Vargus frowned.

"What's that?" she asked.

He didn't answer.

"What?"

"Your silence concerns me, Sister. It is unlike a Devoted to withhold their blessings on those that have passed through to the under realm."

Shit. Soren hadn't prepared her for this.

"Yes, of course. Um, may their souls rest easy?"

He tensed. She'd messed up.

"You are not Devoted."

He drew in a deep breath, but before he could raise his ring, Nisha buried her dagger in his chest.

It happened so fast he seemed surprised. He stumbled back against the doorframe, staring at the dagger protruding from his chest.

"Why?" he gasped.

Nisha grimaced. He seemed genuinely sad at her betrayal. Then he dropped to the floor with a dull thud, his chin resting against his chest.

This wasn't good. The last thing she needed was the old man coming home to find blood spattered across the entryway to his dead family member's room.

She worked fast, dragging Vargus into the room with no small effort, and rolled him into a rug to soak his blood. Somehow, that made it only harder to move him somewhere hidden from the doorway. By the time she was done, she was out of breath and drenched in sweat.

The door clicked shut behind her.

Time was ticking now until the Speaker came back. She made her way to the locked door. It was a simple tumble lock. Easy enough to pick, if she had the right tools. Unfortunately though, she didn't, and there was nothing around her that she could see that would serve as a decent set of picks.

With a sigh of frustration, she stepped back and forced herself to turn away. She'd come to take the Speaker's ring, not to uncover whatever secret lay behind the locked door.

A distant voice reached her, followed by soft foot-steps echoing ominously through the dimly lit corridors.

Her heart pounded. She ducked into a room that appeared to be a study and scanned for a hiding spot. Books lined the walls, and a large, ornate desk sat in the middle, cluttered with papers and strange stones. But it was the massive bed in the adjoining room, shrouded in shadows, that caught her eye.

Without a second thought, she dashed toward it, crouched to check the space beneath, and squeezed herself under. It was tight, but it would have to do. Her body pressed against the cool floor, she pulled the deco-rative bed skirt down to conceal herself.

Her heart raced as she lay in the dark, cramped space, trying to calm her breathing. The muffled footsteps grew louder until the door creaked open.

A woman's voice hummed a sweet tune, filling the oppressive silence. Nisha heard the gentle sweep of a brush against the floor and breathed a sigh of relief.

It wasn't another guard, just a maid.

For a moment, she panicked, wondering if the maid would stumble upon Vargus's body in the other room. But she remembered how dusty and abandoned the room felt. The maid must have been instructed to leave it alone. Vargus's body was safe for now.

Nisha closed her eyes, listening to the woman's voice until she finished sweeping. She waited for the door to click shut.

She waited a little longer, knowing it was best to be patient in case the woman turned back.

And then she—

CHAPTER
SIXTEEN

She cursed under her breath, realizing she'd fallen asleep. Her body felt stiff, muscles and joints aching for movement. But she couldn't move. Someone was in the room. The maid again?

A deep, weary sigh filled the air.

She froze.

A cane tapped against stone, its rhythm a calm, measured beat as the Speaker crossed the room.

She wiggled into a position to see through the tiny gap between the bed skirting and the floor. The Speaker's chair creaked as he sat at his desk, resting his cane against the side.

It was hard to tell how long he sat there, doming his fingers and staring off, completely lost in thought. The dark sapphire on his ring gleamed with power. She knew if he realized she was here, he could reduce her to pulp in an instant.

Nisha stared at the ring, hoping he'd take it off and leave the room. It was a fool's hope. Something that precious and powerful would be worn at all times.

It felt like an hour before the old man seemed to have had enough. He pushed himself to his feet and began removing his suit.

A sagging, wrinkled ass convinced her that she was safe to look away for a few moments as the Speaker changed and made his way toward the bed.

The light in the room snuffed out.

He could not have been more than skin and bones, yet when he lay down, the bed pressed down on her enough that she had only an inch of space to breathe and move. She'd never been claustrophobic, but at this moment, she felt like she was suffocating.

It was only when the old man's soft snores filled the silence that she felt safe enough to squirm her way out from underneath the bed.

Her knees creaked painfully loud as she stood and stared down at him. He looked old enough when he was awake, his wrinkles long gone and his alabaster skin drawn taut over the bones of his skull. However, when he was asleep, he looked positively *ancient*.

The dark sapphire gleamed even in the darkness, and he was just pale enough for her to see the outline of his form. It occurred to her that she didn't have to simply steal the ring; she could drive her dagger straight into his heart and put the old man to eternal rest.

After all, her dagger was already bloodied. What was one body more?

Her hand hovered over the dagger's hilt, trembling, but a sudden flicker of conscience stilled her movement.

There would be a difference between this body and the others that lay in her past. Every time she'd killed, she had done so out of an innate need to *survive*. Not to make things easier on herself.

With a deep, steadying breath, she pulled herself back from the darkness.

She wasn't here to kill. She was here to steal, to take what was needed to save the man she loved. Murdering an old man in his sleep, no matter how despicable, wasn't part of the plan.

She exhaled slowly, shifting her focus to the ring that sparkled maliciously, as if it knew her intent. Moving like a shadow, she reached out, her fingers inches from the precious stone on his finger.

As her fingertips grazed the cool metal, the Speaker stirred, a murmur escaping his lips. Nisha froze, her breath caught in her throat. Seconds stretched into an eternity as she waited, praying he wouldn't awaken.

The room remained silent, save for the steady rhythm of his breathing returning to its soft, uneven patterns. She tried again, her movements deliberate and painstakingly slow.

The ring was stubborn, clinging to the Speaker's finger as if it had never been taken off. Nisha held her breath, twisting and pulling with a gentleness mastered from a lifetime of practice. Finally, with a slight pop, the ring slid free, cool and heavy in her palm.

A wave of relief washed over her, quickly replaced by the surge of adrenaline. She had it, but she wasn't safe yet.

She slipped the ring into her pocket and exited the

room, careful to not make so much as a whisper of
sound.

The only way out was through the front door. She'd
have to hope the honored guards positioned outside
wouldn't find it strange to see one of the Devoted leaving
the Speaker's house so late.

Just as she was about to head for the front door, the
locked door appeared in her mind. Again, the insatiable
need to know what lay behind it tugged at her. The
Speaker's ring was cold against her skin through the
fabric of her pocket. Every instinct screamed at her to
leave. She had what she'd come for.

And yet, knowing she had a way in now, she couldn't
resist turning down the dimly lit corridor toward the
locked room. Promising herself she'd work fast, she
approached the door.

The dark sapphire caught the dim light as she withdrew it. The moment she slid it onto her finger, she was
met with an eerie voice at the edge of her mind. It was
stronger, much stronger, but still impossible to discern.

She pushed the voice away and willed the ring's
power to create what she needed. Ethereal light flowed
from the sapphire, and a moment later, she had a pair of
picks in hand.

The lock was quick work. She pushed the door open
just as the construct broke apart, the light fading into
nothing. Her breathing was tight as she stepped into the
dark room.

The room was starkly different from the rest of the
Speaker's luxurious home. It was a bedroom, but one
that screamed of imprisonment. The air was stale and

heavy. A single candle burned on a nightstand, casting long shadows across the room.

A woman chained to the bedpost lifted her head as Nisha entered.

As Nisha's eyes adjusted to the dim light, the features of the woman became clearer. The room felt colder, the air thicker as she took in the sight. The woman was gaunt, with pockmarked, dark skin stretched over sharp bones. Her hair was a mass of unkempt, greying curls, and her hollowed cheeks spoke of years of malnutrition and emberdust.

But it was her brown eyes that stopped Nisha dead in her tracks.

Nisha's heart hammered in her chest as she took a hesitant step forward. She knew those eyes. They had haunted her through a thousand nightmares, accompanied by the last words had ever been said to her.

Finally, I'm free of you.

A whisper escaped Nisha's lips. "Mother?"

CHAPTER
SEVENTEEN

She hated how much she sounded like the little girl who had been abandoned all those years ago.

"Nisha?" Her mother's voice pierced through years of silence, clear and unmarred, so different from the slurred words Nisha remembered. "Is it really you beneath that veil?"

Finally, I'm free of you.

A storm raged within Nisha, torn between the urge to repay abandonment with abandonment and a desperate longing for the warmth of a mother's embrace that she had always dreamt of but never known.

The conflict swirled, a tangle of buried desires wrestling with deep-seated bitterness. How was this possible? How could her mother be *here*, a world away from the Glass District where Nisha had been left to fend for herself?

Emberdust addicts never lived long. Her mother should be *dead*. Yet, here she was, more specter than flesh.

"My sweet little girl," her mother whispered.

"What are you doing here?"

Her mother flinched at the stone cold voice.

Her mother stammered, "It's a long story."

Nisha pursed her lips. There wasn't time for a long story. She glanced over her shoulder. She should go, leave her behind. But her sundamned conscience bit into her and rooted her feet.

Her whole life, she'd vowed to be better than her mother, to be someone Auri deserved. If she left now, that dream was as good as dead, and she would fall into the endless cycle of trauma that the Glass District inflicted on its victims.

With a frustrated growl, she stepped forward and shattered the chains. Her mother rubbed her wrists and breathed a deep sigh of relief, like she too had known how close she'd come to being left behind.

"Come on," Nisha said.

Her mother stood and immediately fell to her knees. Nisha seethed as she stared down at her mother, rage coursing through her veins. This was the woman who'd left her to die in the slums, whose cruelty had cut her more deeply than the glass sharded sands ever could.

How dare she be so *weak*.

Where was the monster who had haunted her nightmares?

Nisha yanked her mother to her feet. Her mother reached out for her, but she was already gone. She had already turned and left the room. A moment later, she felt her mother following closely behind. At least she was smart enough to keep silent. Despite the lush carpet muffling their footsteps, she knew even a whispered word might be enough to betray them in the silence.

The rich carpet muffled their footsteps. It was all Nisha could do to not turn back and rage at her mother, to dig into her and find out how in the sundamned hells she was here of all places. She busied herself by studying the dark shadows, ensuring they were headed down the right path.

It struck Nisha how much smaller her mother seemed. In all her nightmares, her mother had towered over her, breaking her with cruel words. But now, she barely reached Nisha's shoulder. For a moment, Nisha thought perhaps her mother had shrunk over the years. Old people did that sometimes. But when Nisha looked back and met the eyes of the cruel woman who'd left her, she knew it wasn't true. It was Nisha who had changed. She had grown taller and harder under the cruelty of the Glass District.

Her heart pounded in her chest, and it wasn't just because of the threat of the maid stumbling upon them. Nisha reached the front door and glanced over her shoulder, meeting the dark brown eyes that pierced through the darkness.

It was impossible to discern the look in those eyes. Was it love? Pain? Nisha wasn't sure. She felt numb.

"Whatever you do, keep quiet," Nisha said as she removed the ring from her hand and slid it into her sleeve. Better to keep it close in case everything went to hell.

Her mother simply nodded, watching the ring disappear.

Nisha pulled the door open, and together, they stepped into the Salstadirian night.

The honored guards turned and looked at them as one. Nisha's heart leapt into her throat, threatening to choke her with every breath. If she hadn't been wearing the veil, she was sure the guards would have seen her face was nearly as pale as theirs.

Nisha drew a deep, shuddering breath and pushed forward. It took all her self-control not to look back at her mother. She could only trust that her mother wouldn't do or say something stupid enough to give them away.

But her mother had grown up in the same place she had. If her history was any indication, her mother could be as good a False Facer as anyone.

Nisha walked between the guards, her blood racing. She waited for them to say something, to demand she halt and surrender the ring she'd stolen from the old man. But to her surprise, they did not. Instead, they nodded their heads in deference to her as one of the Devoted, touching their fingers to their foreheads out of respect, and carried on patrolling.

It didn't matter that she had entered the Speaker's home alone and emerged with an outsider in tow. It could have been that this was a different shift than the one she had passed when entering. But she didn't think so. There might be a history of men and women coming and going from the Speaker's home.

Nisha released a heavy breath as they passed the last of the patrolling guards.

They continued towards Salstadir. It was quiet, with

not a soul to be seen. It would have been beautiful if not for her mother's presence. Nisha could feel her mother's eyes boring into her back and wondered what her mother felt.

Her mother stepped up alongside her. "It has been a long—"

The words echoed into the silence around them. Nisha glanced over her shoulder and saw one of the guards looking their way. Nisha motioned for her mother to stay silent.

"This isn't the time to talk," Nisha whispered, her voice harsher than it needed to be. But she didn't care. They needed to be far from the Speaker's home because when he woke, all hell would break loose.

They reached the nearest platform that would take them to the next level. Where the honored guards were usually stationed, there was only empty space. It was unmanned.

Before, Nisha would have thought nothing of it. But now she could only think about how it gave more control to the Speaker. Without any way to navigate between the city levels, the citizens could do nothing but submit to the Speaker and the Angel.

Without the sapphire ring glowing on her hand, Nisha too would have been at the Speaker's mercy.

With a careful glance around, Nisha removed the ring from her pocket and slid it onto her finger. The dark sapphire gleamed brighter in the light of the glowing stalactite overhead.

Nisha's mother stared at her, studying her closely.

She ignored her and pressed the ring to the orb. Ethereal light flowed across the chains at the side, and the platform began to rise.

The sounds the platform made as they rose to the next level were nerve-racking. The rattle of the chains raised every hair on the back of her neck. But there was nothing she could do except wait and hope there were no honored guards nearby to question the sound of the rising platform.

When they reached the top, Nisha moved forward, her mother soundlessly following. With every step away from the Speaker's home, she expected to hear the sudden shrill of a whistle. She expected to see a sudden flush of light coursing overhead as honored guards took to the skies, falling and flying all at once with ethereal angel wings summoned to their backs.

But there was none of that. It seemed strange how easily they'd gotten away. As a thief, Nisha knew she had to check herself: just because you'd gotten away didn't mean you were safe.

Soren had instructed her to come to the well in the morning. It was still night, judging by the empty streets. But there was no telling how much longer until morning; at least, no way Nisha could understand.

She frowned. She never thought there'd be a day she missed the sun, but damn it, she did.

With a sigh, she led her mother down an adjacent street, her mind racing. It wouldn't be safe to take her to the safe house. Jorvik would know by now that she'd been broken out of the cell, and he would almost certainly have his men looking for her.

She might be dressed safely as a Devoted, but her

mother wasn't, and she was clearly an outsider. So where was safe to lay low?

She eyed one of the closed shops. It looked familiar. It took a moment to jog her memory, but she realized they weren't far from where she'd fought for her life.

She glanced back at her mother, noting how her mother's clothing hung on her like an empty sack. She couldn't be more than skin and bones at this point. Even if no one had realized yet that she'd stolen both the ring and her mother from the Speaker's home, it wouldn't be long until they did.

Nisha set her jaw and turned back to the main road, quietly guiding her mother to Blessed Styles.

"Where are we going?" her mother asked, her voice raising a chill across Nisha's arms. It was unnerving enough to see her and know she was real, but hearing her voice after all these years was another thing entirely.

"Someplace we can lay low," Nisha said. "We'll get you a change of clothes too. Can't have you walking around like that."

"You know these streets well," her mother commented as they continued towards Blessed Styles.

Nisha scoffed but didn't respond. It was important for a thief to know their way around the streets, to form a quick memory of escape routes. Of course, these streets were far simpler than the maze of Zareen.

Nisha led her mother to the door, finding it blocked off and locked. The honored had made it clear that a crime had occurred here and that going any further wasn't allowed.

Nisha supposed that for the people of Salstadir, it

would have been enough to deter them. People here weren't accustomed to breaking the rules, not with the Speaker's foot on their necks. But Nisha hadn't grown up with the same habits. Breaking the law was practically in her blood after growing up in the Glass District.

Her mother peered over her shoulder as Nisha tried to push the door open.

"Do you need help?"

Nisha froze, the muscles in her jaw flexing in frustration. She couldn't help but snarl, "You're asking me if I need help *now*?"

Her mother fell silent.

With her mother silenced, Nisha slipped on the ring and faced the door again. She pictured a small hooked bar and soon the ethereal light formed it in her hands. She maneuvered the bar into place.

A moment later, a loud crack echoed down the street. Nisha slipped through the entrance, holding it open for her mother.

She shut the door and turned to survey the scene with a grimace. She had nearly forgotten how rough she and Mirov had left it.

The blood had dried, leaving dark, ominous stains where she'd killed the two men. The shelving was destroyed and clothing scattered across the floor. In the corner, she saw her tossed desert robes. There wasn't much here that was salvageable. Blessed Styles had been cursed the instant she'd crossed its threshold.

"What happened here?" her mother asked.

"Some bastards tried to kill me."

Her mother frowned. "I don't understand."

Nisha reached for one of the few clean sets of clothes and, hoping it was the right size, tossed it to her mother. She began searching for another set for herself.

The Speaker would soon know that one of the Devoted had entered his home and left with his most prized possession. Staying dressed as a Devoted was a bad idea.

Her mother's gaze roamed across the shop until her eyes fell and lingered on the pools of blood. Nisha realized that if you looked closely, you could still see the faint outlines of the men's bodies.

"You did this?"

"You're surprised?"

"I—"

"Don't tell me you thought the girl you left behind would grow up to be a princess."

Her mother seemed stunned into silence, her expression shifting to horror.

Something about that expression made Nisha's blood boil. She spun on her mother. "What did you think would happen to me?"

Nisha's mother stammered, her mouth working as she tried to respond. But the longer she couldn't find an answer, the hotter Nisha's anger grew.

"Answer me!" Nisha shouted.

"I don't know," her mother finally said softly.

"That figures. You were more concerned with finally being free of me."

Her mother winced. "You remember."

"Of course I remember. I remember it all: how your eyes were clouded with emberdust, how my father was shouting for you to hurry up, and how eager you were to get away."

Her mother swallowed, her gaze falling to the ground.

"Was it worth it?"

"No, not at all."

"Good. That's the least you deserve."

"Nisha, I—"

Nisha slammed her fist into the shelving next to her, breaking it off the wall. Her hand stung, but all she could feel was the pure rage channeling through her. She pointed her finger at her mother.

"You don't get to call me by my name."

"I'm still your mother."

Nisha ripped her veil off, her eyes black as night as her gaze bore into her mother's. But her mother didn't see that. Instead, her expression seemed to lighten as she saw her daughter for the first time.

"You stopped being my mother the day you left me."

Nisha's mother flinched at her harsh words, her lips pursing and her eyes crinkling with tears.

"I'm still your mother, but if you won't see me as that, that's okay. Call me by my name."

Nisha stared blankly at her mother, unable to admit she had forgotten her parents' names over the years. She had been too young to know her by anything other than 'mother.'

Her mother gave her a soft, sad smile and added, "Laila. That's my name."

Nisha couldn't help but think it was a beautiful name. She cleared her throat and looked away. "Yeah, okay. Look, get yourself dressed. We'll lay low here until morning and hope we've got enough time to get where we're going before the Speaker realizes you're missing."

Nisha listened quietly, biting her tongue to force herself to stay silent. She hated that, even as angry as she was, she wanted to hear her mother speak.

"I know this is probably not the time or place, but you grew up to be more beautiful than I ever imagined. In fact, you're the spitting image of my own mother."

Nisha paused in her search for clothes for herself.

"I understand that I failed you," her mother continued. "But you must have so many questions for me."

"I don't," Nisha lied, resuming her search. Frustratingly, everything seemed either stained with blood or torn apart in the struggle.

"You don't have to lie, little Ni—" Laila cleared her throat, stopping herself from saying her name. "You don't have to lie."

"What makes you think I'm lying?"

"Because you were always the most curious little girl. Had to stick your nose into everything."

She glanced over her shoulder and saw a soft smile on her mother's face, as though she was remembering something.

"Alright then," Nisha said, turning toward her mother. "Tell me how and why in the sundamned hells you're *here*."

Her mother sighed and took a seat on one of the table units, testing it to make sure it wouldn't collapse beneath her weight. When she was settled, she answered, "I got lost. Your father and I were supposed to go to Sandspire, but to keep a long story short, we ran out of emberdust and your father sold me to some slave traders we met in the desert. They thought that they could make a fortune by collecting some of us and taking us out west. They were convinced there was untapped wealth here."

She paused, her frown deepening as she continued.

"I'm sure you already know this if you're here, but the journey from the desert to here is a long one, and the slave traders found that out the hard way. It didn't take long for them to turn on each other, spilling blood over rations. But eventually, even that ran out. Food, water, it was all gone.

"I got lucky one night after my slaver left my cage unlocked. I managed to escape into the mountains. He chased after me, but I got away. I was sure I was going to die until I stumbled onto the entrance to Salstadir."

Nisha drew a sharp breath. "You found the entrance here?"

"You didn't?"

Nisha shook her head. "We got in another way. We came across one of the honored out in the desert, and—"

"We?"

Nisha paused, then cursed herself. The last thing she wanted her mother to know about was Sher. "A close friend of mine."

"A man."

Nisha nodded.

Something about that made Laila seem to age as she realized how much of her daughter's life she had missed. For once, Nisha could see herself in her mother. She could only imagine how she would have felt if Auri never got to know her, and if Nisha missed out on every important life development. As it was, ever since the Bloodlined had taken her daughter from her, she had missed out on her daughter's first steps and words.

"As to why I'm here, and why the Speaker was holding me captive, well ... when they took me in, I told them everything I knew about the outside world. But then the Speaker locked me up in that room, keeping me there so that from time to time, he could come and ask more questions. I think he got used to my company. He liked to talk about the city of glowing eyes, as he called it."

"The city of glowing eyes?" The phrase triggered a memory.

"You've heard him say it?"

"Not him, but the honored we met in the desert."

"They were trying to see if it was real, then? The honored brought you here?"

"No, he tried to kill us," Nisha said before looking away. "He came close."

"Bastards."

She cleared her throat. "Anyways, one of the Speaker's orbs teleported us here."

"You touched one of their rings to it, didn't you?"

"Yeah."

"Always the most curious little girl."

Nisha ignored the comment. "So you know how to get out of here then?"

Laila looked up, "I suppose I do."

"Tell me."

"Even if I told you a thousand times over, you wouldn't find it."

Nisha's lip curled. She could hear the ring of truth in her mother's words.

"Fine," she said, holding the ring up and watching the dark gleam of the sapphire in the dim light. Even now, the voice at the edge of her mind pressed against her, insistent and unrelenting. But no matter how closely she listened, the words were indistinguishable. It didn't matter. Once she got this sundamned ring to Soren, the voices would be gone, and she would have the help she needed to get Sher safely out of danger.

"What happened to my father then? Do you know?"

Laila sighed. "He's probably dead. He had rotgut when he sold me. But you're not missing much there. He was not a good person."

"I could say the same about you."

Laila didn't react, but Nisha could tell the words cut her as deep as glass shards. She thought it would make her feel good, but it didn't.

"So this man," Laila said, "is he a good one?"

"He is."

She smiled. "That's good. You deserve that, after … everything."

"It'd be good if the Speaker weren't holding him captive."

"That's why you stole the ring?" Laila's eyes found the ring on Nisha's finger.

Nisha nodded, unsure what to say. The silence stretched between them like a vast chasm, leaving both unsure of how to cross. She felt every second tick by so painfully slow. She was still angry. That was evident in how her fingers dug into her palms. But the trouble was, she didn't know what to do with her anger.

In the Glass District, you scrapped with the person who made you angry. If it came down to it, you stole everything they had and left them scrambling to meet the Peddler's tithe. If they couldn't, he'd strip their roofs from them and leave them to the mercy of the sun. And that was payback enough.

She couldn't do that here. As much as she wanted to, she couldn't just hurt her mother. She didn't want to be that person. And she couldn't leave her behind, not with her mother knowing the only way out of this sundamned place.

She ground her teeth.

"I hope the Glass District wasn't too cruel to you," Laila whispered.

"It was."

Her mother raised her head and stared at Nisha. Nisha stared back, watching as a single tear spilled from her mother's eye and trailed down her cheek. Her anger fell away like the weight of a heavy cloak, leaving in its place a sadness that struck her heart. She was the first to break eye contact.

"I know this isn't worth much now, not after all these years you've been left to fend for yourself. But I am sorry. What I did was selfish, cruel, and downright evil. I'd like to say it was all because of the emberdust, but that'd be a lie, and I'm not going to hurt you anymore. Whatever you want to know, whatever you need from me, just say the word. I know that's not enough, but ... I hope it's something."

A moment of silence passed.

Nisha's hands trembled. In all the dreams and nightmares she'd ever had, she had never imagined her mother apologizing. She hated it, hated that there was still a little girl inside her that clung to those words.

"You're right. It's not enough."

She saw the dagger twist in her mother's heart as her face fell. But in this moment, she didn't care. All she could think about were the years of hunger, of clawing in the glass sharded sands for coin enough to pay the Peddler, defending herself from monsters like Zulmar, and how if her mother had just been around, perhaps she wouldn't have fallen prey to him.

Nisha found another pair of clothes suitable enough for her and stepped into the shadows to dress.

She did her best to ignore the muffled sobs behind her.

CHAPTER
EIGHTEEN

The only sign that morning had come was the sound of voices outside. It started with slow, soft footsteps echoing on the streets outside Blessed Styles. But Nisha wasn't comfortable taking the risk of starting out then.

As more sounds made their way through the barrier, Nisha sat with her hand in her hair. She still hadn't heard a single whistle shrilling through the air. There were no pounding footsteps of guards coming to break down doorways, demanding to investigate every home for signs of the criminal, as Nisha had imagined. Instead, there was just ... normalcy.

That scared her more than having guards hot on her heels.

She glanced toward her mother, now fast asleep with her head resting against the wall. Judging by her gaunt frame and the pits surrounding her eyes, she had to be exhausted. It was smart to get rest. Who knew what was coming up, especially with the fact that the guards weren't after them.

Nisha faced the entrance again, turning her mind back to the problem at hand. There was a possibility that the Speaker woke up and, not wanting the public to know how easily the ring had been stolen, chose to keep it quiet. In fact, she had no way of knowing whether the honored were searching for her and Laila, quietly making their way through the crowd even now.

If that was true, they needed to be on their way. Every moment that passed brought them closer to being found. Besides, who knew how long Soren would wait for them above the well.

Nisha stood and nudged her mother with her foot. "It's time to go."

Laila didn't need to be told twice. She rubbed her eyes and got up to fix the way her outfit hung on her. Nisha watched as she smoothed it out, tucking in the folds of her robe with natural ease. She wondered how long Laila had been stuck in Salstadir.

"It was smart, coming dressed as a Devoted," her mother commented, meeting Nisha's gaze. "Was that your idea?"

"No. Someone else's idea. You'll meet him soon enough."

Laila nodded, content with the answer. "We'll need masks wherever we're going. Otherwise, word will get out about us."

She went behind the counter and retrieved a pair of masks. They were blank, with no eyes or mouths, only tight slits to see through. Laila handed one to Nisha.

"These are masks the Salstadirians wear after someone they love dies. They believe that being faceless honors the Angel and sends blessings to the one they love. We'll get some looks for wearing them without any formal clothing, but well ..." she glanced remorsefully toward the bundle of ruined clothing in the corner. "It's better than everyone seeing our faces."

Nisha had to agree. She took the mask and slid it over her face. "Let's go."

She started toward the entrance, only for her mother to stop her with a hand on her shoulder. "You're forgetting one thing."

"What?"

Her eyes fell to the dark sapphire ring. With a grimace, Nisha removed it. She hated the idea of getting caught by the honored with no means of protection other than a flimsy blade, but it wasn't an option to walk through the streets wearing the Speaker's ring.

They squeezed out of the barrier and joined the forming crowd, Laila staying close behind Nisha.

"Where are we going?" Laila asked, her voice soft enough that only Nisha could hear.

"Up there," she said, motioning to above the stalactite.

Her mother tensed.

"Is that a problem?" Nisha asked.

"It's not safe."

"It is for us." Nisha hoped that was the case, but there wasn't any point in telling her mother anything more.

Passing through the city was one of the most tense situations Nisha had ever experienced. It was subtle, but there were a few more honored in the crowd than before.

Every time one of the honored passed, their scrutinizing gazes fell on them, making her heart feel like it was going to explode out of her chest. But not once were they stopped. It was clear the honored had been instructed to find a Devoted woman, judging by the way every Devoted was pulled to the side.

Just when it seemed they were going to reach the well without any trouble, a man bumped into Nisha. His shoulder hit her jaw, and she tripped, falling to the ground with a heavy grunt that drew the crowd's attention.

As the man apologized profusely, several in the crowd rushed forward to help but paused in surprise as they reached for her.

Nisha realized her mask had been knocked askew, revealing a large strip of brown skin. She cursed as she straightened the mask and stood.

"You are the outsider," the man commented, stumbling over his words.

He was loud enough that several of the Salstadirians passing by paused, glancing their way. But that wasn't what bothered Nisha. It was the fact that they had caused a disturbance in the still forming crowd, enough to draw one of the honored their way.

Nisha glowered at the man as she grabbed a hold of Laila's arm and dragged her forward. She could hear her mother's own curse as she too realized that the honored was following them.

The honored called after them, but they didn't stop. At first, the honored's tone was respectful, as though he simply wanted to check on them. But when they continued to slip away, he grew increasingly agitated, speeding up to catch them.

It was only after they turned the corner and passed a large family that they broke into a run.

Laila was agonizingly slow, but there was nothing Nisha could do to speed her up. After all, her mother had been locked up inside that room for who knows how long.

Nisha reached into her pocket and withdrew the ring. Several onlookers blinked in shock and disbelief as they saw her don the Speaker's ring, but that didn't matter anymore. If the honored caught up to them, it was all over.

They reached the cave, the waters lit by minerals running through the walls. Far above, there was no sign of the hole she'd been pushed through. It blended into the dark stone around it. Anyone who visited here wouldn't even know it ever existed.

Her mother wheezed beside her, ripping off her mask and struggling to catch her breath. She turned to Nisha.

"Did we go the wrong direction?"

Nisha shook her head and closed her eyes, visualizing the angel's wings she had seen the honored summon. A second later, motes of ethereal light bloomed around her, attaching themselves to her back.

She grabbed her mother and shot into the air, shouting in surprise as the wings disappeared faster than she expected. They plunged toward the pool of water, and all she could think about was the darkness beneath the surface and the terrifying sensation of choking.

Her mother gasped breathlessly as they plummeted through the air. Nisha summoned the construct again, the magic sputtering as she lost focus. Just before they hit the water, she succeeded.

They shot up through the air, the wings evaporating again after a few seconds. She was all too aware that if the honored reached the well before they reached the top of the cave, then he'd see them, and that would spell their death.

She could imagine what would come next: he would return with more honored guards, and together they would take back what had been stolen from the Speaker. Blood would be spilled, they would be captured, and her last chance to save Sher would be gone.

She ground her teeth and forced herself to focus. Soren's face appeared with a dark grin.

"You are nearly here."

Nisha continued to summon and resummon the wings, far less graceful in her flight than the honored. Her arms trembled, and her mother began to slip, making it harder to maintain her focus.

But in the end, they reached the top. Soren grabbed hold of her mother before her arms gave out, leaving Nisha free to scramble up. The wings evaporated from her back, leaving nothing but the dark gleam of the sapphire ring.

A second later, she heard the voice of the honored far below. It was muffled, but she could tell he was confused. She would be too. There wasn't any other way out of the cave.

"The ring," Soren said, standing over her.

She glanced up, noticing the blade in his hand.

"Do not even think about using it against me. I will cut your throat before you have a chance to summon the magic."

Slowly, she leaned up until the tip of the blade touched her throat. "I'm not a rat. I could give two shits about the ring, as long as you keep to our deal."

He studied her, then her mother. "Who is this? And what is she doing here?"

"That's my business."

"Is it?"

They stared at each other, tension building. Nisha's heart pounded against her chest. Her breaths were hot and sharp. Then he lowered the blade.

"Very well. The ring, if you will," he said, holding out his hand.

Nisha slid the ring off her finger and placed it in his palm. He lifted it, and for a moment, his stoicism slipped. He seemed genuinely in awe, his hand trembling as he slid the ring onto his finger. He closed his eyes with a deep, self-satisfied sigh.

"The voice of power. I hear it now."

"The Speaker's going to know it is missing," Laila said. "When word gets back to him that a pair of outsiders disappeared in the cave below, the Speaker will know that you've got it."

"Yes, he will. But by then, it will be too late."

Soren turned without another word and started off toward the stairs to the side of the chamber. With a groan, Nisha forced herself up and after him. Laila followed, clearly worried, but unsure of what was going on.

"What's the plan?" Nisha asked as they climbed the stairs.

He did not respond to her, but she got the answer when they reached the top and encountered another man. At first, the man seemed happy to see Soren, but his brow quickly furrowed in confusion at the sight of Nisha and Laila emerging behind him.

He opened his mouth, but a spear of light hurtled through his chest. He collapsed to the ground, his eyes and mouth wide open in surprise. Laila gave Nisha a look, clearly wondering what in the sundamned hells she had gotten her into.

Nisha didn't have time to explain. Soren had already stepped through the man's pooling blood and over his body, continuing down the corridor with bloody footprints trailing after him.

They followed him, stunned into silence as he murdered every person they came across. It didn't matter if they were men or women, their bodies hit the ground all the same.

Nisha began to worry she had made the wrong decision in trusting Soren. It seemed foolish now, thinking back to his statement that he would murder the Angel. If he held such little regard for the Angel, why would he for these people? But there was nothing she could do about it now. She had thrown her lot in with him in the hopes that he would help her save Sher, and now she had to see it through.

Of course, it didn't help that her mother looked at her with worry.

A group of five men turned the corner and froze at the sight of Soren. Soren halted before them, and just as she thought he was about to paint the stone walls with their blood, they began to smile.

"So, it is time?"

"It is," Soren said.

They whooped and drew their blades, racing ahead of them. Soren followed in their direction.

"This was all planned," Nisha muttered.

"There is a split of two factions. Those who believe in the Angel, and those who know him for the corrupt being that he is."

"This is a purge," she whispered.

"It is the only way. What we plan, we cannot achieve with daggers at our backs."

She grimaced but understood. Still, that didn't make it any easier to watch.

Laila nudged her, leaning in to ask, "What is this?"

Worried that her mother might say something that would give Soren the idea that he didn't need them anymore, she shushed her. "Stay quiet."

"This doesn't seem—"

Nisha clamped her hand over her mother's mouth. "There is so much more at stake than you know. Don't fuck this up. I'm telling you, begging you, just stay quiet."

She hadn't told her mother about Auri, but she hoped her mother could see the desperation in her eyes. From the way Laila stared into them, she thought she did. Laila's brows furrowed, but she nodded.

"Is there an issue?" Soren asked.

Nisha glanced toward Soren. He was waiting for them, watching with dark eyes that unnerved her.

"No."

He nodded, then carried forward, stepping over a body slumped half up against the wall.

They reached the massive door in the stone passageway. Soren's men waited, teeth shining in grim smiles that stood out against their alabaster faces. Blood dripped from their blades onto their boots.

Laughter came from beyond the door.

"Open the door," Soren said.

The men dipped their heads in obedience and shoved the door open, spilling out the sound of howling laughter. But the laughter fell into heavy silence the instant the men funneled into the chamber with their weapons ready.

Nisha and Laila followed Soren inside.

Her mother's mouth parted at the sight of the ground, made out of minerals that were just transparent enough to reveal Salstadir far below, along with the massive stalactite that illuminated it.

"What is this?"

Jorvik lounged in his oversized chair, his multiple chins quivering as he stared at Soren and his men. His skin gleamed with a sheen of sweat, like he'd been drinking too much. Judging by the way his fingers gripped the bottle's neck, she guessed he had.

His beady eyes fell upon the dark sapphire on Soren's

hand, and he audibly gasped. The bottle shattered against the ground.

"You wear the Speaker's ring?"

Soren allowed himself a smile. "I do."

"What have you done?"

"It is time for a change, Jorvik. Too long have I stood by and watched you disgrace us. The girl was right. There is a boot at our necks, and you have been too content to suffer it. But that is done now."

Jorvik pushed himself to his feet, swaying as he tried to keep his footing. "A boot at our necks? That is what you call the blessing of the honorable Angel?"

"A blessing?" Soren's face twisted in a show of hatred like Nisha had never seen. "It is a *curse*. We have long done the Angel's bidding at the Speaker's command, and what good has that done us? We are not among the honored below. There is a reason you do not wear one of their rings. And it is not because you are incompetent. It is because we are criminals, and what good are chained criminals?"

Jorvik's laughter was bitter, erupting from his throat like acid. "Criminals, yes. But loyal ones, Soren. Something you seem to know nothing about." His voice cracked with a mixture of rage and betrayal.

Soren's expression hardened, the ethereal light from the Speaker's ring casting eerie shadows across his face. "Loyalty to tyrants is no virtue, Jorvik. It is servitude."

With a fluid motion, he raised his hand, the ring pulsing with brilliant, menacing light.

Jorvik staggered back, his face contorting in fear as the light from the ring grew, swirling around Soren.

"You would turn against your own for power?" he choked out, his voice barely audible.

"It is not power I seek," Soren replied coldly. "But freedom."

Without another word, arrows of light surged toward Jorvik and his men. Screams filled the air, brief and agonizing, as the arrows pierced their chests. Some died instantly, but Jorvik choked on his own blood. A chill ran down Nisha's spine as she watched blood bubble up and run down his chins.

She felt Laila's hand on her own. She didn't pull away.

Soren approached the throne, the seat from which Jorvik had ruled in drunken stupor, and sat down. The action was deliberately slow, ensuring all the remaining men in the chamber understood it symbolized a new era beginning as he placed his ring-laden hand on the armrest.

His gaze swept across the room, settling on Nisha and Laila before moving to his men.

"No more chains," he said, his voice solemn and heavy. The throne room, once filled with Jorvik's boisterous laughter, was now eerily silent, the only sound the death rattles of the dying men

"This is the dawn of a new Salstadir," he declared, his voice steady and commanding. "One where we are beholden to no one but ourselves."

As the chamber filled with roars of celebration, Nisha watched the crimson pool of blood creep toward her. She saw her reflection in it and felt that this was but a drop of what was to come.

CHAPTER
NINETEEN

While Soren planned the invasion of the Sanctum with his men, Nisha and her mother were escorted to a room with two plush cots and trays of food. It seemed to be Soren's way of showing his gratitude, which she appreciated. She hadn't realized how tired and hungry she was until the food appeared.

It couldn't compare to her mother's starvation though. Once she finished eating, she watched Laila continue to attack the food as if it were her last meal. Neither of them spoke, unsure how to breach the silence between them. Both were content to let the food occupy them. But that couldn't last. When Laila finished eating and settled back against her cot, she eyed Nisha.

Nisha tried to ignore it, closing her eyes and laying down, willing herself to fall asleep. But it didn't work. She still felt her mother's eyes on her.

"What?" Nisha asked, her words clipped with annoyance.

"Nothing. I'm just looking at my daughter."

Nisha dug her fingernails into her palm, and her knuckles turned white. "Don't call me that. I told you, you stopped being my mother when you left me."

Her mother chuckled then, licking her fingertips. "I know what you said, but just because you said it doesn't make it any more true."

Nisha sat up. "What're you trying to do? You think that I'm suddenly just going to forget everything that happened?"

Laila's smile slowly faded, and she sighed. "Why don't we change the topic? Tell me more about this man of yours."

"No." Nisha lay back down and closed her eyes.

"He's that special, huh?"

She hesitated, then in a small voice answered, "Yes."

"I can tell. I wouldn't have gone through all this trouble for your father."

Nisha grunted. Then, before she could stop herself, she asked, "How did you meet?"

"He sold me my first hit of emberdust. Before you say anything else, I know. Not exactly romantic. I'm not going to pretend I was a good woman or a good mother. I've got a lot to make up for, I know that."

The bed creaked as Laila lay down, folding her hands behind her head as she stared up at the ceiling. Her belly bloated with the food, and she gave a deep, satisfied sigh.

"What makes you think I'm going to let you make up for it?"

"You saved me when you didn't have to. You could've turned your back on me, like I did you."

Nisha didn't say anything. She turned on her side, facing away from her mother.

"So, did you make it out of the Glass District?" Laila asked.

She stayed quiet, doing her best to fall asleep. But her mother's voice filled every corner of her mind. There was no hiding from it.

"I'm guessing you did. You have a little meat on your bones, which is good. I like to see that."

"I didn't," Nisha said before she could stop herself.

"Oh?"

Nisha cursed under her breath. She made a mistake.

"Maybe the Glass District grew softer since I left it," her mother commented.

"It didn't."

"I'm sure it must have."

Nisha ground her teeth and turned to glare at her mother, only to see her grinning. Laila was goading her, trying to draw her into a conversation. With a frustrated sigh, Nisha sat back.

"It got worse. Especially after the Peddler died," Nisha added.

Her mother's smile disappeared.

"I ... look, I'm doing a shit job of this. I just want to know more about you. Will you tell me?"

"Why should I do that?"

Her mother thought for a moment, then a sly smile spread across her face. "Because the more you tell me about what I missed out on, the sadder I'll get?"

"If I tell you a little bit, will you let me sleep?" Nisha asked.

Nisha was tired enough to offer the trade, because if her gut feeling was right, soon enough there wouldn't be much room for sleep.

"I will," Laila agreed.

A few moments passed as Nisha thought about what to say. Then she spoke, "I'm a thief, through and through. Probably the best one you'd ever meet."

"You sound proud of that."

"I am," Nisha said, raising both her hands and waving them. "Still got both these left, don't I? If I didn't get as good as I got, then I'm not sure I'd be alive."

"Good."

"Good?"

"You did what you had to survive."

Nisha was suddenly curious about how her mother survived the Glass District. For all the memories she had of her mother being under the influence of emberdust, she could never say that she felt they were in danger of being thrown out into the sun-baked streets. What did her mother do to keep a roof over their heads? Luckily, she didn't have to ask.

"Before you, before your father, I had always made my own way, though I never had the touch for thieving. I tried once and nearly pissed myself when the merchant caught me. He had a soft heart that day and let me go. I realized then that I'd rather be hanged than watch as a blade cuts my hand from my body."

"Let me guess," Nisha said, propping herself up on her elbow. "You became a False Facer."

Laila smirked. "I'll try not to take that to heart, but no. I wasn't a False Facer either. I was a Bruiser."

Nisha gaped as she took in her thin, weak mother. She was an ant compared to every Bruiser she'd ever known. "You're lying. There's no way in the sundamned hells that *you* were a Bruiser."

"Oh, but I was."

"How?"

Laila propped herself up on her elbow to meet Nisha's incredulous stare. She held out her fist, and for the first time, Nisha saw the scars crossing the back of her knuckles.

"People misunderstand what it takes to be a good fighter. When you get into a scrap, there's three things that matter. Strength, speed, and technique. Of course, I wasn't the strongest you'd ever see. Didn't want to be either. Trying to outmuscle a man is just asking to lose. I wasn't the fastest either, but I was fast enough. No, I focused on technique."

She slowly drove her fist forward, twisting her knuckles out. It was the smooth motion of someone who'd had a lifetime of practice. "I jabbed instead of hooking. I aimed for the spots that matter, and that's not always the jaw. In the space of a second, I could fold a man with two quick punches to the liver and a kick to the calf."

She grinned. "I used to make grown men cry."

Listening to her, the tension began to unfurl, loosening the bitterness and hatred nestled in Nisha's heart. This wasn't about a mother and an abandoned daughter. This was relatable; it was the sharing of two survivors from the Glass District, and that was enough. Especially here in this awful mountain. The hour passed, and Nisha found herself laughing as Laila regaled her with stories of how she conquered giants only to lose to a one-armed man.

Soon enough, Nisha was drawn into sharing stories of her own past. It was easy to do, hearing her mother's genuine laugh.

After hours had passed, Laila regarded her knuckles again, her smile fading. "You know, when we went inside that clothing shop, I was afraid you'd become a Reaper. All that blood, and the ease you carried it with ..."

A moment of silence passed. Nisha didn't realize how easy it'd gotten. It disturbed her, thinking back to how many bodies she'd left behind.

She grimaced. "Yeah, somewhere along the line, it got easier."

Her mind turned to her first kill: another thief who tried to steal everything she had the night before she owed the tithe to the Peddler. If that was all, she might have let him go, trusted herself to stalk him and steal it back. But he'd put a blade to her neck.

She'd gotten so panicked, that everything turned into a blur. But even with her fogged memory, she could remember how surprised she'd been when she felt just how hot blood could be and how fragile life truly was. There were so many orphans in the Glass District that seemed to think themselves invincible, but the truth was, they were all just soft bags of meat, waiting for slaughter.

"Even though the Glass District wasn't kind to me, I could never become a Reaper. I've never murdered anyone that my survival didn't depend on."

That was technically a lie. The image of Zulmar chained against the wall, his eyes wide with fear and his trousers wet with piss, came to mind. She could still hear his dying screams. Only two other people knew she had murdered him: Laith, the Faithful who had handed her the relic she killed him with, and Sher, the man who broke him for her.

But was it really murder if the person you killed was a monster?

Nisha didn't think so.

She scraped her fingernail against the bedding absentmindedly. The strangest fact occurred to her out of the blue. Laila was a grandmother, and she didn't even know it.

"What is it?" Laila asked.

Nisha opened her mouth, then shut it.

"You can tell me," Laila said softly.

With a heavy sigh, Nisha lay back and stared at the ceiling. "Do you ever wish you could go back and change things?"

Out of the corner of her eye, she watched Laila lay back, folding her hands behind her head again. It felt weird to see how similar they were in mannerisms.

"You may not believe me, but no, I wouldn't."

Nisha's mouth parted in surprise. Her heart twinged with pain. "No? Why not?"

"Because if I did, you wouldn't have become the person you are. I don't want to change you, Nisha. Who you are now is incredible. You've survived the worst place I know, yet you still have a kind heart. I can tell just by looking at you. The kind of person you've become is exactly what I always hoped for—even when I wasn't there."

Nisha felt her eyes begin to water. She was speechless. All her life, she had never dared to imagine her mother saying words like these because she thought she knew the truth: her mother was just an emberdust addict who didn't carry an ounce of love in her heart. But hearing her now, it seemed she might have been wrong. Perhaps her mother was just another casualty of the Glass District.

Her mother's voice softened to a whisper. "Now I know you said I can't call myself your mother, but regardless of what you think, I am. That's the thing about being a mother. Even when your child is grown and gone from you, she is still yours, regardless of how badly you mess things up. Being a mother never stops."

She paused.

"Over the years, I always feared I'd never get my chance to show you how good I can be; that you were dead, or worse, that you had gone down the same path I had and gotten hooked on emberdust. But somehow, you've become something beyond my greatest hopes. You are better than I ever was. I know that when you have a child of your own, you'll be an even better mother. And that's all I could've ever wished for: for you to surpass me in every way."

A tear trailed down Nisha's cheek.

"I'm not so sure about that."

She turned onto her side, facing away from her mother. Blood rushed in her ears, a roar drowning out the sound of Laila saying her name. All Nisha could hear was the distant sound of her daughter's voice. The hounds of madness at the edge of her mind broke through the gate, overwhelming her with visions of Razhan slaughtering Auri for her failure to bring back the Angel's tear. She tried to fight back, but she was drowning in her fears and failures.

Then she felt Laila's hand on her shoulder, and all at once, the visions stopped. Nisha tried to draw in a breath, tried to maintain control, but she finally broke.

The tears came in earnest, and her mother pulled her into her arms. She sobbed into her mother's embrace, and she was that child once more. She clutched at her mother's arms, just as she did all those years ago when her mother abandoned her. But this time, Laila stayed and pulled her in tighter, the distinct smell of her washing over Nisha. Laila didn't say a word, but her presence comforted Nisha, anchoring her amidst the opened floodgates of all her fears, the continually mounting pressure, and the endless fight for survival.

After what felt like an eternity, the tears began to subside. Nisha's sobs turned to sniffles, and she found herself breathing more easily. The tight coil of panic constricting her heart began to unwind. She felt lighter, as if she had shed a burden she hadn't even realized she'd been carrying.

She glanced up at her mother, surprised to see that Laila's eyes were wet too. She wasn't the only one who had been crying.

Staring at each other, they suddenly began to laugh at the absurdity of it all, realizing that just days ago, the thought of crying in each other's arms would have been a madman's dream.

Nisha wiped away her tears and finally said the words that had been burning inside her.

"You're a grandmother."

Laila slipped off the bed, landing with a heavy thud. She quickly scrambled to her feet, her eyes wide with shock. "I'm what?"

"You heard right."

"But you're so young. How—" She paused, stiffening as a shadow crossed her face.

"Yeah," Nisha said simply.

Her expression changed, and Nisha could feel the torment beginning to take hold of her. "The man who hurt me, he's dead and dusted."

Laila considered this for a moment, then nodded in approval. "I hope he suffered."

"He did."

Laila sat back down next to Nisha, nervously clicking her fingernails together. Nisha could tell she had more questions, but was hesitant to ask, perhaps fearing Nisha wasn't ready to share.

"Her name is Auri," Nisha offered.

"Auri," her mother repeated softly, a tender smile forming. "It's a beautiful name."

"You want to know more?" Nisha asked, her voice equally soft.

A light bloomed in Laila's eyes.

Time slipped away as Nisha shared everything— from the day officials ripped Auri from her arms and handed her over to the Bloodlined family, to the trap laid by King Razhan, and everything about Sher, including the guilt she carried for his suffering.

Throughout it all, Laila listened without judgment. At first, Nisha shared so her mother could learn more about what she missed in the years of abandonment. But then she shared because with every spoken word, a weight lifted from her shoulders.

It was only when Soren and one of his men appeared that they realized the day had passed.

Soren's gaze swept from Laila to Nisha as his man collected the empty trays. "I thought the two of you would be getting your rest. The plan is set. We make our move in the morning."

"So soon?" Laila asked.

He nodded. "The longer we wait, the more dangerous it grows for us."

Nisha understood what he meant. By now, she imagined the Speaker would have recognized the sudden silence from the criminals, with all of his direct reports slain. That was as telling as anything else.

"Thanks. We'll get what rest we can in the meantime. We'll be ready," she said.

He gave her a rare smile. "Good. Soon, your friend will be safe, and in rescuing him, we shall deliver the Angel his reckoning."

Then he was gone. Laila drew a sharp breath and looked at Nisha, a knowing softness in her eyes. Neither of them wanted the time to end, but reality was calling. Sher was still in danger, and who knew what they were doing to him.

Laila went to her cot, but before she lay down, she

said, "It seems we are more alike than we thought, little Nisha. We both think we're terrible mothers. But we're not defined by our past. Just remember that."

With that, Laila lay down and covered herself. It wasn't long before Nisha heard her breathing deepen as she slipped into a deep sleep. Nisha closed her eyes, almost afraid to fall asleep for fear that she would wake to find this was all a dream.

It was strange, the weightlessness she felt. It was like she was floating in the darkness, and it no longer seemed as ominous as before. Instead, it embraced her with warmth.

The sleep Nisha had that night was better than any before.

CHAPTER
TWENTY

Nisha stood with Laila, each holding a wrapped bundle of Devoted clothing and looking through the hole down to the well. It didn't take two guesses to know that whatever Soren planned, he intended to launch it from here. And both of them dreaded the jump.

Before, the small chamber had been relatively empty. Now, it was packed with criminals, all holding the same bundles, waiting for Soren to appear.

It was clear that Soren had instructed everyone to wear the Devoted garb. But she found it strange. Wasn't the point of False Facing as a Devoted to blend in? With this many doing it, there was no chance of that happening.

Laila leaned in and muttered, "I need to slip some of this medicine they gave us into my pockets when this is all said and done. It'd sell for an absolute fortune."

Nisha glanced at her. Laila looked much healthier than the day before, her color having returned and the marks around her wrists already healed, leaving only a slight pink reminder of where the chains had been.

The medicine had done wonders for Nisha too. The knife wound in her shoulder had come a long way in healing, even if it still throbbed.

Nisha smiled and drew out the leftover paste stuffed into her pockets, tightly bound and wrapped. Laila grinned at the sight of it. Of course, it wasn't really for her, nor was it for smuggling back to Zareen. No, it was saved in case Sher was in bad condition when they found him. Nisha tried not to think about that too much. She didn't want to sink into worry. It was important to stay focused on what was in front of her.

"We'll get him, don't worry," Laila commented, as if she could read her mind.

Nisha nodded but didn't have a chance to respond. The echo of footsteps coming down the stairway cut through the soft chatter of the chamber. A moment later, Soren appeared.

He, too, held a wrapped bundle of Devoted clothing, except his was slightly more elaborate than everyone else's. Gold trim ran around the edge of the robe.

He took one look around, then nodded.

"We are all here then. Good. If I were Jorvik, I would give a long, drunken speech now about what a momentous day this is."

A soft undercurrent of laughter passed through the room.

Soren remained serious, sweeping his gaze across the crowd of criminals. "But I am not Jorvik. The only thing I have to say is what you already know. This is the day that we cast off our chains."

One of his men thrust his fist into the air, a loud roar ripping through the room. A breath later, it was echoed by dozens of others. The room thrummed with energy.

Nisha glanced at her mother, unsure of what to think. She'd never been part of a pre-battle speech, but where the others thrived on the energy, it only made her more nervous.

"Stay close together as we march on the Sanctum. Do not honor those you come across. Keep silent, keep your hands still, and simply march. Only attack when I command. Fail to do that, and nothing on this Earth will save you from me. So steel your resolve and prepare your jumps. Divine blood awaits."

Their feet pounded against the stone, a rhythmic beat reverberating through the mountain. It made Nisha's heart race. She could almost taste the iron tang of blood.

Soren stood next to Nisha at the edge of the hole.

"Everyone's going to know something is up if *all* of us are dressed the same," she said.

His piercing blue gaze locked with hers. "That is the plan. Have you not yet understood how you have laid the foundations of our attack?"

"Me?" Her brow furrowed. "I don't understand."

He allowed himself a small smile. "When you escaped from the Speaker's home with a body left behind and the ring in hand, they began to question every Devoted that they encountered. But you must have seen that already. The Devoted are a respectful, prideful people who dedicate their entire lives and all its bounties to the Angel. That harassment is not something they would have stood for."

"This is a protest," Nisha said, the puzzle pieces sliding into place.

"Yes, and that protest is the guise we shall wear as we make our way down to the Sanctum. By the time anyone realizes our true intentions, it will be too late."

"That's brilliant," she breathed.

Soren dipped his head in response, taking the compliment in stride. Then he turned and faced the crowd.

"Are you ready?"

They stomped and roared in response.

His smile widened, a dark gleam entering his sweeping gaze. His voice cut through the sound.

"Divine blood awaits."

He fell back through the hole.

Laila gripped Nisha's arm with a curse as they and the crowd pressed forward, watching Soren fall. Nisha closed her eyes and kept count.

Exactly thirty seconds later, the echo of a splash made its way up to them. When he surfaced, the crowd erupted into cheers, and one by one, they each jumped.

Criminals rained down into the well. Those who could swim helped others safely reach the bank of the well below. Nisha's hands quivered at the all-too-recent memory of water choking her through her mouth and nose.

Soon, the only ones that remained were Nisha and

Laila. They glanced at one another, their faces nearly as pale as the Salstadirians.

With a huff of breath, Laila said, "Oh, sundamned hells, I do miss the desert."

Before Nisha could respond, Laila jumped.

Her mother didn't scream the whole way down as Nisha had the first time she jumped. She hit with a heavier splash than Nisha had heard from the others. Worry crept through her as the seconds passed, but eventually, her mother resurfaced and scrambled through the water to one of the Salstadirians.

Nisha stepped back, shook her hands, rolled her neck. She had to agree with her mother. The desert was far better than this awful place.

Then she jumped.

She thought that it might be less terrifying the second time around, but she couldn't have been more wrong. The dread gripped her bone tight, tearing a scream from her throat as she plummeted toward the water.

All she could think about was how the water would choke her again, how it would force its way into her nose and throat and drag her down to its inky depths. So focused was she on that nightmare that she failed to realize the greater danger.

She was spinning through the air.

Soren's voice reached her. "Feet first!"

She flopped in all directions, trying to correct herself, but somehow made it even worse. She ended up upside down, the water rushing up toward her face. With just five seconds left, she knew it was too late. With her arms outstretched, she pictured her arms and neck breaking against the surface of the water.

And then she hit.

She pierced the water, and water roared in her ears, bubbles trickling up from her nose. She blinked underwater, hands clawing at her throat. Somehow, despite the ringing in her ears, she was still alive.

A pair of hands grabbed her from above and yanked her to the surface. A moment later, she breached the surface, and sweet, blessed air rushed into her lungs. She coughed out the water, cursing it to all the seven hells, resolving to never take another drink of water till the day she died.

"Are you broken yet, outsider?" Soren's silky smooth voice cut through the ringing in her ears.

Nisha coughed out water. "Not yet."

He grinned. "Good. Then get up and make yourself Devoted. We move soon."

Laila offered her a hand and pulled her to her feet. When Nisha looked around, she saw everyone changing, not caring as they stripped naked and pulled on the robes and donned the veils. They hid their daggers and blades in their sleeves and the folds of their robes.

With a heavy sigh, Nisha began to follow suit. Her mother looked away, perhaps not wanting to see all the scars that Nisha had endured over the long years she'd been abandoned. But when Laila stripped, Nisha couldn't help but notice the numerous scars lining her back, striping her from shoulder to hip. She realized with a start that Laila had been whipped, and judging by the skew of the scars, the man who'd done it took pleasure in punishing her.

Laila caught her looking and turned away.

Once they were finished dressing, they joined the crowd forming around Soren, who was doling out instructions. At the end, he left them with one last statement.

"Maintain the posture and dignity of the Devoted, but when you are offered respect, do not fold your hands over your hearts. Keep them by your sides. We shall not wish the Angel's curse on any soul today."

The crowd formed in structured lines, and with Soren leading them, they started toward the city.

It was a strange feeling, the slow march toward war. It crawled up her spine, cold and slow, until she remembered that she was responsible for kicking it off. She would have a hand in each and every death. That gave her pause. She wasn't sure of the path she had started everyone on, but there wasn't much of an option. She needed help to rescue Sher from the Speaker, and this was the only opportunity.

She leaned in and muttered to her mother, "Make sure you stay close."

"Don't want to lose me?" Laila teased.

Nisha grunted. While she wasn't sure that she and Laila were entirely on good terms yet, she was sure she at least wanted to explore what could be between them. At the very least, Auri deserved the opportunity of having a grandmother, provided Laila stuck around and stayed away from emberdust. It was one thing to make a trans-formation here, a world away from the civilization they knew. It was another to throw yourself back into the life that turned you toward emberdust in the first place.

The instant they moved into the city, they were noticed. The crowds of Salstadir parted before them in curiosity and awe, touching their hands to their foreheads. When none of Soren's crew offered their spoken blessings or folded their hands over their hearts, the people's mouths dropped open.

There were mixed reactions. Some grew angry, their backs stiffening and their pale faces turning red as they huffed. Others simply stared, as though the world had broken and they weren't sure what to do. A fair few chose to follow them, trailing behind in their wake, heads bowed as they whispered to one another.

Nisha expected to run into trouble with the honored guards at the platforms. But to her surprise, the guards simply touched their rings to the orbs and, group by group, lowered the Devoted down to the fifth level. And so it went, passing through the crowd, descending through the city of Salstadir. By the third level, so many were following them that it was impossible to see even a sliver of free space in the throng behind them. Honored guards began to take to the skies to keep watch.

Gossip must have raced far ahead of them because when they reached the first level, they found dozens of honored waiting for them.

Soren halted before them, bringing Nisha, Laila, and the rest of his crew to a stop. The chatter from the crowd trailing behind them fell silent. Nisha wasn't sure how long they stood like that—Soren and the army of Devoted staring ominously at the honored through their glowing veils. But it was long enough for several men around her to begin shifting, tension and unrest settling in.

Then came the rhythmic beat of a cane tapping against stone. One by one, the honored stepped aside, making room as the Speaker strode forward.

Hunched over his walking stick, the old man stared at them. He swept his gaze across them all without an ounce of concern. Something about him bothered Nisha. She didn't know whether it was his casual, bold stance or the fact that he somehow seemed younger in the way he eyed them. But something wasn't right.

Then she saw the ring on his finger, fitted with a black diamond. The hairs on the back of her neck stood.

"You are not Devoted," he said, his strong voice shattering the silence.

Several in the crowd gasped, as if it were sacrilegious to claim that someone was not Devoted.

Soren tore the veil from his face, revealing his slicked-back hair and the shadow of dark stubble on his jawline. His face was stoic, but his eyes were sharp.

"No, we are not," Soren said. "We are the forgotten of Salstadir. We are the ones who reside above, staring down at this beautiful city, chained to your dark commands. And we are the ones who dare to be free from them."

A murmur passed through the crowd. Several glanced upward, as if they could see the top of the cavern from where they came. The Speaker eyed the crowd to gauge their reactions, weighing his next words. When he turned his attention back to Soren, the corner of his mouth quirked.

"You mean to say that you no longer wish to follow the Angel's command?"

"I mean—"

"This great city deserves an honest answer, Soren, son of Dargam. Give them one."

Soren drew a deep breath, clearly surprised that the Speaker knew who he was. He clenched his jaw, nodded, and turned to face the crowd behind them.

"I do not."

The crowd collectively gasped. Some stepped back, but others tensed, the urge to fight and defend the Angel's honor evident in their eyes. Soren's men bristled at the growing threat, but he calmed them with a hand.

"I do not believe that the Angel, or the Speaker, has our best interests at heart any longer," he said, prompting outcries from the crowd.

"I know that many of you feel as we do. There is an outsider who has given me a glimpse of the outside world, and it is glorious. It is free from the oppression that the Speaker compels upon us."

Several in the crowd shifted from foot to foot. Nisha was surprised to see so many feeling the same way about the Speaker's rule, but it wasn't enough. For every man, woman, or child who felt that way, there were at least five others whose gazes darkened with every passing word.

"That is enough," the Speaker said, his strong voice booming across the space. The black diamond on his ring gleamed dangerously. "I will not allow you to poison Salstadir with your blasphemy any longer."

Soren grew angry, lifting his chin as he faced the old man again. He withdrew his hand from his sleeve, revealing the dark sapphire ring. It shone as his defiant voice boomed to meet the Speaker's. Another gasp passed through the people of Salstadir at the sound of Soren's voice.

"Do you see? Even now, he seeks to control me. But I cannot be controlled any longer. I stand with free men!"

Tension rippled through those around Nisha. She swallowed as she heard the slow hiss of blades being unsheathed beneath the Devoted robes. The crowd felt the tension and stepped back.

The Speaker smiled, his lips drawing so tight across his face that it seemed they would tear.

"You are not honored. You have not been blessed by the Angel, and you are undeserving of the ring," the Speaker said.

When Soren raised his voice to counter, booming across the space, something strange happened. An oppressing silence collapsed in on them, threads of crimson light spilling into the air. Soren froze, struck speechless by the power the Speaker wielded. The black diamond on his finger pulsed. When he spoke, his voice slipped into her mind.

"In the night, an outsider broke into my home. She murdered one of the honored and stole the ring from my very hand whilst I slept. And where does that ring sit now?"

He raised a bony, crooked finger and pointed it at Soren.

"Upon the finger of a criminal who used it to slaughter every poor soul who dared to disagree with him."

Soren's gaze darkened as the crowd shifted. Even those who seemed to agree with Soren's earlier statement looked wary, withdrawing unto themselves. Nisha knew what they must be thinking: the righteous did not need to murder their way to freedom. The last thing they wanted was to come out from under the rule of the Speaker straight into the rule of a blood-crazed tyrant.

"The Angel knows of the evil that stands here now, seeking to turn his blessings against us. But he has blessed me with power enough to repel it."

The old man raised his hand so all could see the black diamond ring. His gaze hardened.

"And repel it I shall."

Ethereal light burst from Soren's ring, and he roared in defiance. Nisha jumped at the sudden sound of everyone around her joining his roar, ripping the veils from their heads, and brandishing their blades.

The battle erupted into a cacophony of clashing blades and piercing cries.

The honored rushed forward to meet the criminals, blocking their path to the Speaker. Shields of light were summoned and re-summoned, protecting him from the throwing knives. They matched the criminals' brutality and rage with their own.

Hot blood spattered across Nisha's veil as she was forced forward by the wave of bodies into the throng of battle. Ethereal light clashed with blue steel, the sound ringing out over the blood-curdling screams of the injured. The air became thick with the coppery scent of blood.

Despite Nisha's best efforts to stay next to her mother, they were torn apart. She heard her mother calling for her. She tried to find her, but it was almost impossible with the rushing bodies and the blood-covered veil. She tore it off.

The closest honored guard saw her dark skin, and his face contorted with rage. He rushed toward her, only to be decapitated by a slash of light.

Nisha stumbled back from his rolling head. Soren kicked the body to the ground and shouted something to her, but it was impossible to make out his words amidst all the screams.

When she had seen the weapons the criminals were bringing to battle, she'd been skeptical they could hold their own against the magic the honored wielded. So it was a surprise to see them holding their own.

Just when she began to feel a sliver of hope, a massive rock smashed into the back of the head of the man standing next to her. The crowd of Salstadirians was turning on the criminals.

Caught between them, their fate suddenly took a turn for the worse, and Soren seemed to recognize it. But he bared his teeth, refusing to accept defeat.

A massive wall of light gleamed between the crowd and the criminals, leaving them with only one front to fight.

"Push forward!" Soren cried.

His men rallied around him, emboldened by the fact that, for the first time in their lives, they had true power on their side.

Then, everything fell silent, as though someone had wiped all sound from the world.

"Die."

Motes of light shot forward, and she watched in horror as man after man collapsed to the ground with holes in their chest. A woman next to Nisha was hit with such force that a cloud of mist erupted into the air, temporarily blinding her.

Screams of defiance turned to terror. The criminals turned back, attempting to flee the Speaker, who stood with one hand on his walking stick and the other outstretched, pointing the ring. His eyes were alight now, drunk with power.

Then, Soren stepped in.

Ethereal light clashed against crimson. Sapphire gleamed against the black diamond. But for every attempt he made to save them, another man fell.

And it fueled a growing despair within her.

She felt a hand on her shoulder.

Blood painted Laila's face and the dagger she held. Her voice was barely audible over the din. "We need to get out of this!"

Nisha nodded. She didn't need to be told twice. A thief didn't belong on the battleground. She grabbed her mother's hand and pulled her toward a narrow alleyway, hoping to escape the worst of the melee.

They followed the alleyway, but there was no escaping the sounds of the screams behind them.

Ducking under a low archway, Nisha and Laila pressed on, the clamor of battle slowly fading into a dull roar. They moved quickly, dodging debris and the occasional straggler who had also decided that survival was preferable to heroics.

After several tense minutes, they emerged back into the street. Nisha realized where they were. She led them to the platform that would take them down to the Sanctum.

"We need one of the rings to power this thing," she said, frustration evident in her voice as she gestured helplessly at the inert orb.

Laila reached into her pocket and pulled out a ring, its ruby the same shade as the bloodied band. "What kind of thief are you? These were lying everywhere."

Nisha stared at the ring in amazement, then at her mother, a surge of relief flooding her.

"You're incredible," she breathed. She took the ring from her mother and slid it over her finger before pressing it to the orb. Chains rattled as the platform hummed to life. They stepped onto the platform and slowly began to descend to the bottom level.

Nisha glanced back toward the battle, at the threads of crimson and ethereal lights streaking up into the air. She had a crushing feeling that the Speaker would win that battle. But that didn't matter. They weren't here to overthrow him or to kill the Angel like Soren wanted. They were only here to save Sher and get that sundamned Angel's tear. Then they could be gone from this forsaken place.

She turned her gaze to the Sanctum, relieved that

there were no honored standing guard. The Speaker must have ordered them all to the first level to confront Soren and his criminals.

"We've got a narrow window," she said. "We'll have to be quick."

The moment they touched down, they both took off running toward the Sanctum.

A chill ran down her spine, and it took her a moment to realize why. The sounds of the battle were already starting to soften.

They didn't have long.

CHAPTER
TWENTY-ONE

Nisha and Laila entered the Sanctum. It seemed like a lifetime ago that Fenrik had led her through the once guarded gate and guided her into the wonder of Salstadir. She had since learned the truth. Salstadir was little better than Zareen itself.

They passed through the corridors, their way lit by the glowing minerals embedded in the walls. Nisha had hoped to remember the path Fenrik had taken her through, but they quickly became hopelessly lost in the maze of corridors.

The corridors were eerily quiet. Nisha listened for the sound of other honored guards, but only heard the mocking echo of their own footsteps.

"Do you know where you're going?" Laila asked.

Nisha ground her teeth, unable to answer as tears of frustration welled up in her eyes. She knew how little time they had before the Speaker or his guards returned. Each wasted minute brought them closer to failure, adding to the failures already haunting her.

"Tell me what you're looking for. I can help."

"How are you going to help me? This is a sundamned *maze*. I don't know how anyone finds their way around this place."

Laila stopped Nisha with a gentle hand on her shoulder and smiled softly. "Just tell me what you're looking for."

Nisha met her mother's peaceful, patient gaze. A month ago, she couldn't have imagined that this day would ever come, where her *mother* of all people would be the one to put her at ease.

She sighed, "The last time I was with Sher, he walked through this glowing portal. The Speaker called it the Angel's Gate."

Laila nodded to herself, looked down one corridor, then back the way they came. "I think I know where you are talking about."

She immediately started back the way they came. Nisha blinked, then followed with hurried steps. Her mother led them through the corridors with an ease that surprised her.

"How do you know this place so well?" Nisha asked, doing her best to keep up. "With all the back alleys in Zareen, I got to be better than anyone I knew at finding my way around, but even I can't figure this place out."

"You forgot, little Nisha, how long I spent here. The Speaker brought me here more than once."

"Why?"

Laila's brows furrowed, her eyes distant. "We would spend hours walking these halls, talking about history. He told me about Salstadir and how these people were hunted by outsiders. Then they found the heart of this mountain, made a home, and defended it. It was a losing battle until the Angel found them. Under his power, they destroyed their hunters and began to thrive."

"I don't get it. Why did he talk so much about Salstadir, with you of all people?"

"To open me up."

"What do you mean?"

Laila sighed, "Isolation is a terrible brand of torture, Nisha. You spend so much time alone that you start to hear the rush of your own blood passing through your veins, and the voices in your head? You start to question if they're still in your head or if they've escaped, because they sound so real."

Nisha didn't know how to respond.

"I told him everything about the outside world: how long the sun stayed up, how hot the days grew. I told him about Zareen, the beautiful palace with its thousand pillars, the Angel's throne overshadowing it all. I described its people, the high and mighty Bloodlineds, and those of us squabbling in the slums. I even told him about you."

They turned into a side corridor. Nisha realized that things were beginning to seem more familiar.

"What did you tell him about me?"

"That you were the most beautiful girl I had ever seen. And that I left you. And that you were probably dead."

A heavy silence settled between them. Nisha was slowly starting to realize that perhaps these long years had been just as tough on her mother as they had been for her. A part of her rebelled at the thought, thinking that she deserved it for abandoning her. And perhaps she did. But another part of her ached for her.

Her mother grabbed and squeezed her hand, giving her another one of those rare smiles that Nisha had never dreamt she'd see. "Thank the Angel that didn't happen, huh?"

Nisha smiled back, but something was bothering her. "I guess I just don't get it. Why did he want to know so much about Zareen? Why not just go out there and see it for himself?"

Laila shrugged, "I used to obsess about it. I was sure that he had an ulterior motive, but the years dragged on, and I started to think less about it. I think he's just afraid, you know? Afraid we outsiders will come back and destroy Salstadir."

Nisha scoffed.

"I know. As if we could ever get our shit together enough to break this mountain open. Anyway, that's how it went. He'd free me from my chains, we'd walk and talk a bit, and then he'd leave me with a cut as a reminder of the power he holds over me."

Nisha nearly tripped. "What?"

Laila pulled back her sleeve and showed her forearm. It was covered in small cuts, like she'd been nicked with a dagger. Nisha had seen a hint of it before, when Laila was changing, but she'd thought that it was self-inflicted. She had seen more than her fair share of people from the Glass District who chose to cut themselves, chasing the small thrill of pleasure that followed. She never understood it, why you'd cut yourself when so many other people were out to cut you. But then, she supposed everyone had their vices. If she hadn't been so focused on Auri, maybe she would have fallen into the same trap.

Laila slid her sleeve back down. "Salstadir is a strange place, Nisha, full of strange people. But they're not all bad. The maid that you saw in his home, she would bring me small bits of food whenever she could. She never did say a word to me, but I would have liked to have known who she was."

Nisha was grateful then that she didn't run into the maid. She hated what she might have done to ensure her own survival.

"Enough about that," her mother said. "Now, the Speaker never took me to the Angel's Gate, but I could always tell when we were close. It should be this way."

The air grew cooler. The light from the veins running through the walls grew more pronounced. They soon reached their destination: a spiral staircase disappearing into the darkness below.

Nisha nodded, grateful that she had her mother with her. She was convinced now that she never would have found this place on her own.

As they descended, the air grew heavier with anticipation and worry. Nisha wasn't sure what she'd do if Sher was hurt. But knowing her mother had survived this sundamned place eased her worries, if only a little.

Magic buzzed in the air, raising the hairs on her arms and making her heart race.

They reached the bottom, and the golden gate stood

before them, shimmering with blinding magic. Wisps of ethereal light wafted off it in waves.

The ruby atop the worn ring glowed brighter, as if sensing the gate. The voices at the edge of her consciousness pressed on her, louder but no more distinguishable than before.

For the first time, she clasped her mother's hand. Out of the corner of her eye, she saw Laila smile. Nisha could only imagine how long she'd hoped to know what it felt like to have her daughter reach out for her.

Nisha herself wished for it even now with Auri.

She drew a deep breath. Before, the Angel had refused her an audience, turning her away from his portal like she was too unworthy for his presence. She wouldn't allow him to turn her away now. She raised the ring to the portal, as if to show that she would attempt to destroy it if it dared refuse her.

Ignoring the voices, she approached the portal.

"Here you are."

She froze.

Nisha turned and saw Fenrik at the bottom of the steps, his hands folded behind his back and a smirk playing at his lips.

"The Speaker was right about where I might find you."

Nisha squeezed her fists, her blood boiling as she remembered Fenrik's part in her near death. *He* was the one who led her to the clothing shop, straight into the ambush like a lamb to slaughter.

Laila frowned, "Do you know him?"

Nisha stepped up next to her mother, conscious that

Laila didn't have a way to defend herself against him. But she did. The ruby glowed at her hand.

"Yeah, I know him. Just a mindless rat bastard who lives to do his master's bidding."

"That is not very pleasant to hear," Fenrik said, slowly taking the final remaining steps. "I serve the Angel happily, and it is a conscious decision."

"Angel? I was talking about the old man."

His smile disappeared, his gaze narrowed. The tension in the air tightened.

His voice lowered as he responded, "You should refer to him with his honorable title. He is the Speaker."

"Eat shit, Fenrik," Nisha spat.

He blinked in surprise, and Nisha realized he might not have heard that phrase before. But she wouldn't miss this chance to catch him off guard. She raised her hand, and ethereal light shot from the ring, an arrow forming and hurtling toward him.

He gasped, but before he could dodge the arrow, it slammed into his shoulder, spinning him around. Blood spattered across the wall.

Growling, he turned to face Nisha. The peaceful mask he wore was stripped away, revealing an ugliness that showed his true character. The dark gleam in his eyes would fit right into the Glass District.

"There you are," Nisha said, grinning. She had been hoping she would get the chance to pay this bastard back for what he had done to her.

The arrow in his shoulder evaporated, wisps of light fading into nothingness. He lifted his own ring.

She took a half step forward, putting herself between

Fenrik and her mother. His gaze shifted from her to Laila, and a grim smile surfaced. He acted before Nisha could summon another construct.

Light suddenly flashed from his ruby ring, and for a heart pounding moment, she was blinded. She blinked away the spots, imagining a shield around herself and her mother and compelling it into existence.

The ring obeyed, and a half second later, a massive thud reverberated off its walls. She cursed as she tried to clear her vision. It took a moment for her to see what had nearly hit them: a massive hammer that was covered in needle points. If she hadn't summoned the shield in time, it would have killed her in one hit.

Nisha growled in frustration at how close they'd come to death. She raised the ring, but before she could do anything, a platform of light appeared beneath her feet.

Her face twisted in confusion, and a gasp escaped her lips as the platform suddenly jolted toward Fenrik. She lost her footing and landed heavily on her back with a grunt.

Laila shouted as she narrowly dodged arrow after arrow, each slamming into the wall behind her, showering her with stone chips.

Nisha scrambled to her feet, the pain from the fall throbbing through her back. Fenrik was relentless, despite the injury to his shoulder. He conjured another blast of ethereal light aimed directly at her, but Nisha rolled to the side, the light singeing the ground where she had just been.

She had to end this quickly.

Focusing all her concentration on the ring, she extended her hand towards Fenrik and summoned another construct—a spear of piercing light aimed straight for his chest. Fenrik, anticipating her move, raised his ring defensively, but this time Nisha was faster. The spear struck true, pinning him against the wall, a cry of agony escaping his lips.

But the victory was short-lived. Fenrik, with a desperate strength, pulled himself along the spear, his eyes burning with fury.

"It will take more than that to defeat me," he snarled, breaking the construct with a forceful twist of his ring. The motes of light dissolved into the air.

Nisha was ready to strike again when the platform of light suddenly slipped her feet from under her, knocking the breath from her.

Suddenly, a white-knuckled fist slammed into his jaw.

The hammer faded just as quickly as it had appeared. Nisha sat up, watching in disbelief as her mother moved with a Brawler's ferocity. Every step and jab was calculated: a sharp hit to his shoulder, an elbow to his cheekbone, a knee driven into his stomach.

Fenrik roared in pain as he stumbled back. Every attempt he made to summon some kind of defence was disrupted by a quick punch. They began to exchange blows. While she had the experience to give her the upper hand, his strength and health made it difficult for her.

His fist crashed into her nose with a sickening crunch

that turned Nisha's stomach. Laila's head snapped back, blood gushing down her face.

Before Nisha could react, light formed into a dagger that he plunged into her gut.

A wispy gasp shattered Nisha's heart, and she screamed.

Fenrik grinned at her over her mother's shoulder.

But then Laila drove her knee into Fenrik, folding him over. Seizing the opportunity, she grabbed him, twisted sharply, and with a crack that echoed through the room, broke his neck.

Laila staggered back against the wall, lifting her shirt to reveal the deep wound. Blood seeped from it. She locked eyes with Nisha. She sank to the ground.

"No!" Nisha cried, catching her mother in her arms. Panic-stricken, she pressed her hands against the wound in a futile attempt to stem the bleeding.

But both of them had seen enough stab wounds in the Glass District to know it was fatal.

Her mother removed her hands, and her life blood continued to seep from her. Nisha cradled her in her arms, grief clutching her heart with an unrelenting grip. A tear fell to mix with the blood.

"It's not fair," she whispered, struggling to breathe.

Her whole life, she had been abandoned and left to fend for herself amidst the glass sharded sands. All those years, she had wished for a version of a mother that now lay dying before her. She had only just found her, and already, she was lost.

That's what fate does. It gives. Then it takes away.

Suddenly, she understood what Sher must have felt

when he lost his mother. The thought crept into her mind that if she could get the tear back to the lamp, she could wish for her mother to come back to life. She opened her mouth to make the promise, but then her mother shook her head, as if she knew Nisha was about to say something foolish.

Her mother lifted her bloodied fingers to run through Nisha's hair. Even on the cusp of death, she smiled up at her.

"Don't be mad at how little time we had, Nisha."

Her hand ran down to cup Nisha's cheek, triggering a memory. Nisha recalled being a little girl, held by her mother on one of the rare days she wasn't hooked on emberdust, her hand cupping Nisha's cheek just like now.

Nisha clasped her hand to her mother's.

"Do you know how many nights I lay awake, wishing to the Angel that I could see you just once more? Wishing I had the chance to tell you how sorry I was?" Her mother winced, her other hand going to the wound as her face began to pale. Time was running out. "I was blessed with this. You see it as not enough, but I see it as more than enough. I got to learn who you were and had a chance to help you."

"You saved me," Nisha whispered. Once, those words would have been unthinkable to say, but now they felt so true.

"Not in the way you think."

"What do you mean?"

"I'm trying to save you from yourself," she winced again, her voice filled with pain. "We really are more alike than you know. You think you're a bad mother, like I did for all these years. But you need to know the truth. Your worth as a mother isn't defined by your past or your ability to raise your daughter. It's defined by the love you have for her and the lengths you'll go to protect her."

Nisha's chin trembled as she watched the light start to fade from her mother's eyes.

"You being here, doing this? You're already a good mother. She just doesn't know it yet," Laila said, a frown crossing her face. "I'm sorry I have to leave you again. I promised myself I wouldn't."

Nisha let out a heavy breath and pressed her forehead against her mother's. She knew these would be her mother's last moments, so every word counted. What did she want her mother to take into the deep, long night?

"You're not leaving me. You're just waiting for me," Nisha whispered.

Laila chuckled, nodding as she spoke her last words. "That's right."

Then she was gone.

Her mother went slack in her arms, her gaze staring far beyond Nisha. Nisha pulled her closer, shattering with every heaving sob.

Why did life have to be so cruel, so painful? She knew that someday, she would be grateful that she had this brief time with her mother, so that she could share what she knew of her mother to Auri. But in this moment, she could only cry and rage at not having more time.

It was hard to let her go, to rest her head against the cold stone. But she knew that even now, time was ticking down for her. It would not be long before the Speaker came.

Nisha pressed her lips to her mother's forehead, hoping she could still hear her beyond the realm of consciousness. "I love you."

She looked at her one last time, wishing she could bring her mother's body with her. But she could not.

Nisha steeled herself, stood, and turned to face the Angel's Gate.

Ethereal light crackled and wisps of light drifted around her. Nisha held up the ring and slowly approached. She flinched as the wisps drifted toward her, remembering how they had lashed out before. But this time, they embraced her, pulling her towards the gate.

She stepped through.

CHAPTER
TWENTY-TWO

Nisha wasn't sure what she expected on the other side of the gate. Perhaps a little slice of heaven as a sign that she was in the Angel's presence. But instead, all she was greeted with was more rock and stone, like she had never crossed through. She glanced back over her shoulder, finding that she couldn't even see back through the gate.

She wiped away her tears, drew a deep breath, and proceeded down the passage. The minerals glowed against the walls, guiding her deeper into the mountain. The passageway was empty, and the silence still reigned, leaving her with nothing to think about other than her mother's last words.

You're already a good mother. She just doesn't know it yet.

Their time together was short, but it was long enough for Nisha to know the truth: Laila *had* been a bad mother. But when it came to her last moments, she was everything Nisha had ever hoped she would be.

Nisha hoped that Auri would someday know all the things that she had done for her, and know all the times that Nisha had stood outside her window, come to kiss her goodnight. She hoped that Auri would not hold it against Nisha that she did not steal her back into the cruel folds of the Glass District.

As she walked, her mother's words settled into her heart. With them, the poison that had taken root, the hounds at the gates of her mind, reminding her of failure, all dissipated. She loosed a heavy breath, expelling all that was left of the tension, and a peace settled down onto her shoulders.

The path led to an empty chamber with two diverging paths, one to the left and one to the right. The indistinguishable voices at the back of her mind shifted, and she felt them pull her to the right. Another voice overpowered it: a roar of frustration from the left, a voice she knew well.

Nisha turned and sprinted toward it.

She ran towards the sound of Sher's enraged voice and the banging against steel, relief flooding her as she followed the winding path. It led her to a network of cells that looked as if they were still being constructed, making for more room at the back.

"Sher?" Nisha called out as she passed empty cell after empty cell.

The banging stopped. "Nisha?"

The voice came from the last cell. Nisha sprinted toward it to find Sher with his hands wrapped around the blue steel bars. She wasn't sure what she imagined, but it wasn't him standing in good health without so much as a bruise on him.

She rushed to the bars, and before he could say a word, she pressed her face up against the steel bars and kissed him. She didn't have words enough to express all that she felt: all the fear coiled up inside her, the pain of losing her mother, the relief she felt at the sight of him.

When the kiss ended, she stayed close, her forehead pressed against his. She breathed him in, letting the smell of him wash over her, comforting her.

"You're okay," he whispered with a trembling voice.

She looked into his golden eyes.

"You're okay," he whispered again, like he was trying to get rid of his own fear.

She didn't know how to tell him that she wasn't okay. Laila's death left her raw in a way that she hadn't felt in a long time.

"Remember the last time we had bars between us?" Nisha asked.

He froze. She could tell by the look on his face that he did. He had left her to rot, and she'd been forced to break herself out. A flicker of doubt passed through his eyes.

She forced a smile and stepped back. "The gall to call yourself the best thief after not even breaking yourself out of your own cell."

The tension melted away and he laughed, its soothing her throbbing heart. Nisha stepped back, using the ring to form a construct of ethereal light around the bars. It twisted slowly, applying leverage with every turn. The bars creaked, each twist drawing out an ear splitting screech.

She winced at the sound, hoping that there was nobody near enough to hear.

"How did you get free?"

"Free?"

"The Speaker told me he had you hostage, and that you would die if I didn't answer his questions."

Nisha frowned. The gap between the bars was nearly wide enough for Sher to squeeze through. Just a little more. The ethereal light continued to leverage the bars open.

"He didn't keep me hostage. He tried to have me killed."

Sher cursed beneath his breath. "He lied."

"What questions did he have?"

"Stuff about the outside world. Stuff about Zareen. He wanted to know about the Bloodlined."

"What about the Angel?" Nisha asked, doing her best to keep focus. The last thing she needed was to lose her chance at saving Auri too. "Did you see him?"

"The Speaker never took me to him. The second I went through the gate, he knocked me out. I woke up here."

"Nearly there," she said. A moment later, the gap between the bars widened enough for Sher to squeeze through.

He didn't waste a second. With a grunt, he pushed himself through and pulled her into his arms. She buried her face into his shoulder. They stayed like that for a while, warm breaths spilling across each other.

Then he pressed his head against hers and kissed her once more.

"I love you."

The words were so softly spoken that she wasn't sure she heard him right. She looked at him.

He leaned in, and his whisper brushed across her lips. "My soul was made for you, and you alone."

"Why are you saying this now?"

"Because I've been a sundamned fool. I was afraid to love you, afraid of the pain I'd feel if I lost you." His fingers dug into her back, as though he could feel the pain even now. "But I cannot live like this. We are thieves, through and through. So if I must someday lose you, then I will steal every second I can with you."

She stared into those golden eyes, and saw that he meant it with every fiber of his being. She didn't know what to say, except to kiss him again. Fire burned in her as she tasted his lips.

A thought passed through her mind. Perhaps fate had never freely given her time with her mother. Maybe she'd stolen them, as Sher said. Whatever the case was, she knew that she would carry the few moments they had together for the rest of her life.

Still ... as thieves always do, she wished she had stolen more.

Sher must have seen the sadness in her as he pulled back, because he asked, "What's wrong?"

The words were hard to say, as unbelievable as they were. "I ... I met my mother."

His mouth parted in surprise. "Your mother? *Here*?"

She nodded quietly. Then softly added, "She died protecting me."

She could tell that he had so many questions. How did she tell him that despite everything that had happened to her, Laila was everything she wished her mother could be? That in just this short time she had with her, her mother had redeemed herself in ways that Nisha had been too afraid to ever hope and dream for?

Thankfully, he saw she was grieving, even though she had no more tears to spill. He pulled her into his chest and held her.

"We'll make them pay," he said, squeezing her tighter, comforting her with his certainty.

A line of red drew her attention to his forearm. He had the same cut her mother had shown her.

"What's that?" she asked.

He glanced down at his forearm. "That? He was just intimidating me. Cut me with a dagger to make it clear that he could kill me anytime he wanted."

Nisha shook her head. Something was deeply wrong. "My mother had that same cut."

He frowned. "You think there's something to it?"

She studied the cut, trying to imagine what it could mean. Unfortunately, it looked like any other cut she'd seen. With a frustrated sigh, she let go of his arm.

"I don't know. Maybe we'll find answers when we find the Angel."

"Then let's find him, get that tear, and get the hell out of this damned place. Can't believe I'm saying this, but I miss the sun."

She missed it too.

They retraced their steps, the dim glow from the

passage walls casting eerie shadows around them. With Sher by her side, the silence wasn't as thick and suffocating as before. Still, her mind churned as they passed the row of empty cells again.

It was strange and unsettling. Almost nobody was allowed into the Sanctum beyond the honored. So why were there cells behind the Angel's Gate? And why so many?

There were no answers to be found here. She could only hope they'd uncover the truth the closer they got to the Angel.

They reached the room where the passages split. Nisha felt the inexplicable pull toward the passage on the right once more, the voices more insistent now. She followed them now, Sher staying close behind.

The path was long, steeped in a strangely somber note that willed both of them into silence. It wasn't lost on either one of them how close they were to the Angel. This wasn't like meeting the Peddler. This was meeting someone *divine*, who was older than perhaps the desert itself.

She face forward, trying to figure out how she could possibly ask the Angel for a tear. She supposed it wasn't something that would be freely given, and she sure as shit wasn't in a position to go do a quest for him.

They jumped at the sound of a sudden bang. Then they heard the soft echo of footsteps and the gentle hum of a voice. Nisha glanced back at Sher nervously before continuing forward. The footsteps grew louder as they approached. When they reached the tunnel's curve, she lifted her ring, fixing in her mind the image of a dagger.

A man rounded the corner, dressed in strangely clinical outfit that resembled nothing of the styles that the rest of the Salstadirians wore. He stopped at the sight of them, his humming dying in his throat.

Nisha raised her finger to her lips. "Shh. Don't say a word. Understand?"

His eyes were wide with fear, darting between them. He nodded slowly.

She beckoned for him to come forward so he was no longer in sight of the other half of the tunnel. Sher grabbed him and slammed him against the wall. Nisha glanced down the way he came.

There was nothing and nobody, the only difference being a nondescript door at the end of the tunnel. She turned back to him.

"Who are you?" she asked.

His mouth worked, but no sound escaped his lips. Sher slammed him against the wall again, and Nisha got in his face.

"I asked you a question. Who. Are. You?"

Something trickled down his leg, staining his white clothing an off shade of yellow. Nisha glanced down in surprise, then at Sher. The man had pissed himself.

When she faced him again, he was pointing to his mouth and shaking his head.

"He's mute," Sher said.

"Of course. That's just our luck. We find the one man who can tell us something, and he's *mute*." She dug her hands into his pocket, checking him as thoroughly as only a thief could. The only thing she found was a key to the door. She pointed the key at him, "I'm going to ask you some questions. You'll answer with a nod or shake of the head. If I find out you're lying, I'll choke you with your own piss-stained pants. You get me?"

The man's alabaster skin turned even paler. He nodded emphatically.

"Good. Is there anybody else down here that we need to worry about?"

He nodded and raised two fingers.

Two more men, it seemed. Nisha frowned. She thought there would have been more people down here. What was so important that so few passed through the Angel's Gate?

"Are they armed? Do they have these?" She pointed to the ring on her finger.

He shook his head this time and tapped his finger against his own chest. More men like himself.

"Are they mute too?" Sher asked.

He hesitated, then nodded.

Nisha exchanged glances with Sher. There was something here that the Angel didn't want known.

She ran her hand through her hair. "Bring him with us. Just in case."

Sher grabbed the man's collar and shoved him forward. When they reached the door, Nisha fit the key to the lock and instructed the man to open it. He hesitated until Sher leaned in and hissed something in his ear. The man's alabaster skin turned even paler. A moment later, he unlocked and pushed the door open.

In her mind, the voices grew louder, pressing against the confines of her skull. She realized they weren't as incomprehensible as before.

Nisha entered ahead of Sher and the other man, her ring outstretched in case they'd been lied to. But to her surprise, they were met with two other men, just as they'd been told.

They put their hands up just as quickly as he did. Nisha pointed to the side wall, ordering them against it. She shoved the third man in line with them.

He searched each of them, but came up empty.

"What is this?" Sher asked, returning to her.

"I don't have a sundamned clue," she said. "It doesn't make sense, does it?"

"You want to keep an eye on them while I check the rest of the place?"

She agreed, and Sher stepped further into the chamber.

The men shifted from foot to foot, eyeing each other nervously. There was something here they didn't want them to see. Several minutes passed before Sher returned. When he did, he stalked toward the three men with murder in his eyes.

"What is it?" She asked, but he didn't stop.

The men's mouths opened in silent screams as he descended upon them. She watched as he brutalized them, smashing their skulls against the walls and shattering their limbs when they tried to flee. She wasn't sure what made him so furious, but he gave them no mercy. Only once they were bloodied and unconscious did he stop, just short of taking their lives.

He turned to her, heaving and panting, but it didn't seem to be from exertion. It seemed to be from something else.

"What was that about?" she asked.

"They deserve worse," he breathed.

"What do you mean?"

He led her deeper into the chamber. The room was dimly lit, casting long shadows across several workstations. Each station was cluttered with tools and materials that seemed out of place in Salstadir. In fact, they looked like items from the outside world.

Nisha moved closer to one of the stations, running her fingers over a device that looked like it was used for shaping stone and metal—specifically, the type of materials used in crafting rings. Beside it lay several uncut gems resembling the one on her ring. The sight sent a chill through her.

"They're making them," Sher said, disbelief lacing his voice.

Nisha stepped over to another workstation, her heart sinking as she pieced things together. The stations were setups for artificers.

"I don't understand. They're making the rings?" She held up the ruby ring she wore. "But what about the power behind them?"

The atmosphere in the chamber grew heavier, a palpable tension filling the air as Sher declined to answer. Instead, he moved from the artificer stations to a door at the back of the hall.

She felt a knot form in her stomach as she followed him. The voices at the back of her mind grew louder with every approaching step, until all of a sudden, they fell dead silent. The emptiness of her mind disturbed her, frightening her more than anything else up to that point.

Nisha stepped through the door.

She gasped.

They stood on a platform that ringed a small pit. Chains hooked to the walls ran down to bind the divine being at its center.

She imagined the Angel must have been beautiful once. But now, her heart ached at the sight of him. His wings had been stripped of their feathers, and were bent and misshapen. Beneath a forcibly shaven skull, a pair of tired, broken eyes stared back at them. Every breath he took rustled her hair, bringing with it the shuddering effort it took to breathe.

Nisha could not help but see how he had been tormented, from the scars and wounds running the length of his body, healing before her eyes. She'd heard stories and legends of how his skin had once basked people alight in its beautiful glow, like the great sun itself. But if that were ever true, now it did not. It only shone with a dim, dying light.

Free me.

Kill me.

End me.

The voices at the back of her mind sharpened with clarity in the silence.

For once in her life, she was speechless.

Nisha moved closer to the edge of the platform, her eyes locked on the divine figure. The torment etched into every inch of the Angel's form was more profound than she could have imagined. It wasn't just physical; it was a deep, existential suffering that seemed to emanate from his very essence. The chains that bound him rattled softly as he shifted, a quiet, desperate movement that spoke volumes of his pain.

"The voices," Nisha said slowly, turning to Sher, her voice trembling with realization. "All this time, the voices from the ring ... they were his. He's been calling out to anyone who wore the rings, begging for release."

Sher nodded, his jaw clenched tight. "But why couldn't you understand him before?"

"It's got to be the proximity," she guessed, her gaze returning to the pit.

As they stood there, the Angel's eyes found Nisha's. There was a depth of sadness and madness there, a turbulent storm of emotions that had been brewing for centuries. His lips moved again, the words forming a silent plea that echoed directly into her mind.

Free me.

Kill me.

End me.

Mercy.

Her heart ached with a heavy burden.

"How could this happen?" she whispered. "Why would they do this? They're supposed to be believers."

Sher reached out, taking her hand and squeezing it gently, offering a silent comfort that she barely felt through the shock.

Then she noticed the strange bloodstained tubes at the bottom of the pit. They ran up the back, straight into a massive vial, as if they were farming his blood. Next to the vial were their weapons of torture, all with handles three times the length of her body and sharp edges that gleamed with dark promise.

She shook her head in disbelief. "We've got to cut him loose."

KILL ME!

She staggered back under the weight of the Angel's voice, his rage nearly forcing her to her knees.

"What is it?" Sher asked, his face etched with concern.

"He wants us to kill him," she said softly.

He frowned. "Why?"

"I don't know."

Mercy ...

The Angel's voice came across differently this time, almost as if he was keening in despair. It was heart-breaking to hear. Nisha wished she could understand.

The voice in her mind stilled, and a presence washed through her, compelling her to step closer. She gave in to it and approached the hand bound to the edge of the platform.

"Nisha," Sher said, his voice echoing a note of caution.

But she didn't hear him. She had eyes only for the Angel suffering in front of her. Something about it touched her at her core. For years, she had suffered under the shadow of his throne. She remembered the night she'd been broken by Zulmar, left pregnant with his child. Madness had touched her mind for a moment, and she had screamed out to the empty throne. Like him, she wanted death. Like him, she wanted release.

And now, he was begging her for the same.

Nisha reached for his hand, unafraid. The Angel watched her, and she locked gazes with him. It was strange. She thought there was something recognizable in his gaze—specks of gold that reminded her of Sher.

"Help me understand," she whispered.

Then she touched him.

Light consumed her.

CHAPTER
TWENTY-THREE

Nisha squinted as the light slowly faded, the dimness of the Sanctum replaced by an open blue sky. The sun beat down on her with a warming familiarity. She knew where they were.

As she turned, she was greeted by the beautiful expanse of the desert, its golden sands stretching to the horizon with their rolling dunes. And far below, nestled in the shadow of the red flat-topped mountain she stood on, was the city of Zareen.

But it wasn't the same city she knew. There was no palace with a thousand golden spires stabbing into the sky. There were no sprawling, beautiful mansions of harvested white marble. And the Glass District was nonexistent. About the only thing that remained the same was the shouting echoing up from the Market District.

Nisha turned and saw the Angel resting in his throne, staring down at the city. He looked different too: his skin glowed with beautiful light, his massive wings folded behind him, feathered and strong, and perhaps most different of all, he wore a smile.

She realized this had to have been long ago, in the times when he ruled the city she loved.

She tried to say something to him, but she couldn't make a sound. She held her hand to the sky and saw she was almost transparent, like she wasn't real. This was a memory of his, and all she could do was watch.

The Angel stood then, sighing with a breath that swept across the desert. His beautiful wings unfolded, his powerful form towering and casting a shadow over where the palace would someday be.

The Angel walked slowly to the side of the flat-topped mountain. The memory must have attached her to his presence because, though she didn't move, she found herself drifting alongside him.

He threw himself off the side.

Nisha let out a silent scream as they plummeted towards the earth, only to experience the abrupt halt as the air caught beneath the Angel's wings. They began to soar through the air. She breathed in awe.

The desert looked so small, and yet so massive from up in the sky. The sensation of peace washed over her, blew through her hair. She glanced up at the Angel and saw he felt the same. Even after a millennium, he still loved to fly.

They descended toward the city, heading for where the Glass District would someday be. When they touched down, men and women pressed forward, reaching for the Angel, calling out to him. The women's eyes gleamed with something that transcended desire as their hands brushed over his outstretched arms.

Once, she questioned why so many Bloodlined existed; why so many women had let themselves be fool enough to lie with the Angel. She thought perhaps it was because he demanded it of them, and as the Angel, they must have been helpless to refuse.

She could not have been more wrong. Staring at him now, it was easy to see how he could win over any woman's heart for a night. He was powerful, beautiful, and ... he had wings; wings that even Nisha wondered what it would feel like to touch.

As Nisha drifted after him, she allowed her attention to stray. She took in her surroundings. It was strange. She recognized the area, the view of the city above her, but to not have that ever-present danger in the back of her mind at the glass sharded sands that should have been cutting across her feet ... she didn't know what to make of it.

She wondered what happened to this place. The people here were kind-hearted, without a flicker of darkness shadowing their hearts. They probably did not even know what it meant to starve or feel the need to steal. How did this become the Glass District that she knew?

A woman with a baby shouted as she pushed her way through the crowd, the Angel's glow reflecting in her eyes.

"Please!" she called. "Bless my child!"

It wasn't the first time that a request had been made of the Angel. Even now, others clamored against one another to draw his attention, hoping he might gift them with magic that would elevate their lives forever. He seemed to ignore them all. But when he saw the woman with the child, he paused.

He raised his hand and beckoned the woman forward.

The crowd hushed and backed away to witness greatness. The woman fell into stunned awe, as though she hadn't expected the Angel to really stop and honor *her* of all people. She obeyed, tentatively stepping forward and uncovering her child's face.

The pale little thing squealed as soon as the sun touched its face. It wailed even as the Angel took it into his arms. He reached for the amulet hanging around the mother's neck.

He held the amulet to the sun with one hand, and with the other, he regarded the crying child. The crowd and Nisha both held their breath in anticipation.

Then the Angel spoke.

His voice was like a whisper of wind, sweeping across the world and brushing itself against their very souls. "For you, I give the gift of a long life, so you may witness all the beauty the world has to offer."

Ethereal light streamed from his fingertips, washing over the amulet. It was a simple little thing, more brass than gold. But when his magic was finished with it, it had transformed into something priceless. It shone with gold as pure as the desert itself, with a small bead of light reflecting at its heart.

He passed the amulet around the child's neck. It was comically big for him, Nisha thought, as the child's fingers clamped down over the edge of the amulet, his big eyes taking it in and his mouth opening in a pure, joyful smile. Someday he would grow into it, and it wouldn't be so big then.

The Angel passed the child back to the mother, slowly dipping his head in acknowledgment of the mother's gratitude. Nisha watched the mother stumble away in awe, holding her child close to her chest. She shook her head. The Angel couldn't know it now, but he had cursed that child, and every poor soul who carried that amulet.

In the Zareen she knew, men and women fought tooth and nail for each second of their lives. They greeted death with bitterness and spite. To have a relic that would delay that for them, that would give them a taste of immortality ... oh, there would come a day when they came for that child and spilled his blood all across his doorstep. Of that, she had no doubt.

The crowd continued to follow the Angel in hopes he might bless one of them too. Nisha sighed, her heart heavy as she was forced along in his wake.

They continued walking until they were close to the edge of Zareen, and then suddenly, a wall of light came into existence. The Angel passed through it as though it didn't exist, but the crowd of people came to a halt.

Nisha watched curiously as the Angel approached a simple home with tall walls and wide doors. It wasn't a sprawling mansion like the ones she had seen in the Peak District, but seemed only just big enough to consist of two or three rooms.

Nisha wondered if this was his home. Just when she thought he would enter, he stopped at the door, his grin growing in an almost boyish way that stripped him of his divinity. Instead of knocking, he sent a small wisp of ethereal light through the slit under the door.

A few moments later, the door swung open. A woman stood in the doorway, looking up at him. She had a plain face, without any noticeable features that would make her stand out in a crowd. Her hair was jet black, her eyes a mundane shade of green, and her shape didn't exactly spur the imagination.

The Angel raised his hands and began to sign to her. A soft gasp escaped Nisha as she watched the woman smile, and hells, it was as beautiful as sunset skies. The woman signed back, her hands moving so fast that Nisha could only wonder how the Angel understood her. After a few moments, the Angel laughed and stepped forward, bending down to kiss her.

Nisha drew a sharp breath. This was not a normal kiss. It was too gentle, from the touch of his lips to the hand that ran down her back. This was love, as true as one could ever hope to find.

The woman interlaced her fingers with the Angel's and pulled him into the home. Nisha felt uneasy following in their wake. It didn't feel right stepping into the woman's home, invading her privacy. But she didn't have a choice. The Angel dragged Nisha along in his presence.

The walls of the woman's home were covered with paintings, all masterfully made. She saw the rolling dunes touched by the morning light, the night skies with their glittering stars, and portraits of the people of Zareen. Her eye caught on one of a child playing in the sand with his friends. She got closer to the painting, and it felt as though she should have heard the child's laughter. There was something distinct about the paintings, something almost familiar in the way they were painted. But Nisha couldn't put her finger on what exactly it was.

A chair scraped against the floor, drawing her attention to where the woman was pulling a chair away from her workstation. The Angel stood over her desk, as still as when Nisha had first seen him.

Curious, Nisha joined him at his side.

A painting that was all too familiar rested on the desk: ocean waves rising and crashing and rolling in a blend of blues that ran deeper than the soft sky above. But unlike the last time Nisha had seen it, these waves did not move. There was no cool, salty breeze brushing against her skin. There was no subtle tang of salt in the air.

Nisha eyed the woman with awe. *She* painted this? This wasn't done from pure imagination. Nisha turned and ran her eyes over all the paintings on the walls, realizing they were all memories; times when the Angel had flown her across the skies, showing her a world the likes of which she had never seen, the likes of which she *had* to paint.

"It's beautiful," he whispered, his voice so soft it touched Nisha's very soul. He turned and signed something to the woman, and she beamed with pride.

He looked back at the painting and ran his fingers over it, a smile spreading across his face. Nisha gasped as she watched a tear slip from his eyes. It fell like a glittering diamond toward the painting. She knew this was just a memory, that this tear was not one that could save Auri. But even so, she reached to catch the tear, dismay gripping her heart as it passed through her hand to splash against the painting.

She watched as the tear seeped into the ocean waves, as ethereal light wove itself into the grooves of the painting. The painting came to life, the gentle whoosh of the ocean waves spilling across the silence. She could taste the tang of salt now.

The woman's mouth opened in a silent gasp as her hands rushed to her mouth. She stared at the painting in complete and utter awe. The Angel held her, and she looked up into his eyes. They kissed again, their touch gentle. But the gentleness did not last. They pressed against one another in feverish desire. Nisha's face burned as she turned away, choosing instead to study the painting.

She knew now that this painting was not just a simple relic. It was the deepest expression of their love for one another, infinitely more valuable than all the other relics Nisha had ever seen.

Light pressed against the edges of the memory, like it was all coming to a close. She still didn't understand why the Angel wanted her to kill him, why he wanted to be put out of his misery. With a grimace, she began to prepare herself for the harshness of reality. But it seemed the Angel had other plans.

The world suddenly jolted forward, the skies and the curve of the earth blurring as they rushed past quickly enough that Nisha felt close to throwing up. When it came to a stop, she was greeted by the sound of shouting.

They were still inside the woman's home, but it was darker now. Torches mounted in the corners of the room cast their light across the space, shadows dancing with the flickering of the flame. The woman lay on a bed against the back wall, surrounded by two midwives. She was drenched in sweat, her skin worryingly pale, and her legs sprawled apart.

Holding her hand, the Angel knelt at her side. He was worried, that much was evident in his tight expression. He signed to the woman with his free hand, doing his best to comfort her, but the woman was caught in silent scream after silent scream.

Then, after what seemed like an age, the shouting was interrupted by a mewling cry. A baby was passed to the woman, its eyes glowing a stunning shade of gold that struck at Nisha's heart. With a heavy sigh of relief, the woman held her child close to her chest, skin against skin. She smiled and ran her hand over her child's head, too tired to do anything else.

But the Angel … he studied the child with such awe. Nisha knew he must have had other children before. She had seen them when soaring over the city of Zareen: Bloodlined all across the city, with all their varying eye colors. But there was something different about this girl of his. She could see it in his expression.

Perhaps it was the fact that this was not simply a child but a product of his love. Maybe it was that the daughter already resembled her mother so much. Whatever it was, the Angel gingerly touched his child, leaning in to whisper her name.

"Yara, you are most loved."

He and the woman he loved shared a smile.

The world jolted forward again, racing with an aggressiveness that hadn't been there before. When it came to an abrupt halt, an oasis waited for her. Nisha recognized this too. It was the very same one that she and Sher had shared when that pale bastard Kaelum had nearly killed her. But it wasn't sunny anymore. It was storming, the clouds overhead angry and violent. Lightning ripped across the sky, thunder following to shake the earth.

A keening tore through it all.

The sound came from the direction of the pool where Sher had held her. She ran toward it, knowing something was grievously wrong. When she reached it, she found the Angel on his knees, holding a body in his arms.

She watched breathlessly as the Angel continued to cry, his tears falling to the earth around him. They ran into the pool, glowing as they mixed with its waters. His wings hung from heaving shoulders, as lifeless as the body he held.

Nisha didn't have to see the body to know it was the woman he loved.

She turned away, half out of respect and half because she couldn't bear the sight of his pain. The world jolted forward again, this time gentler. They were back in Zareen, and the stormy skies were replaced by the sun once again.

They were in the Peak District now. A mansion rose

behind the Angel. He sat atop a small stool, his expression thoughtful as he watched a grown woman play with her child. It was only when the grown woman glanced up with golden eyes that Nisha realized they had gone into the future again. This was Yara, and she looked every bit the part of her mother.

Nisha wondered if that was what the Angel was thinking too.

A man came out of the mansion, carrying a tray of food and drink. He offered it first to the Angel, his head bowing out of respect, before he carried the tray to his wife and child. He said something to Yara, prompting a laugh from her that made the Angel's mouth quirk into a soft smile.

This memory lasted a while, nothing happening other than Yara chasing her child around the small yard. But the longer they watched, the more a bad feeling began to grow in the pit of Nisha's stomach. It didn't feel like he was showing her something here anymore. It felt like he was reminiscing in the joy of this moment.

Then a deep sigh spread across her consciousness. The sun fell. The sky darkened. And the world jolted forward once more, roaring as it passed Nisha. It raced and raced until they came to a violent stop.

A body lay in the street.

The Angel stood over it, his shoulders bowed, but his wings spread.

A crowd formed along the edges of the street. Their terror was evident in their faces and how they clutched one another.

"Who did this?" the Angel asked, his voice nothing

like before. Now his voice scraped across their very bones, like he came not from the heavens above, but from the hells below. "Who killed my Yara?"

He was met with silence. Nisha could only stare in horror, knowing the silence must remind him of the woman he loved, and now their daughter murdered. Those beautiful, golden eyes stared up at nothing, empty and lifeless.

His hands curled into fists. An earth-rattling boom shattered the silence, and magic spewed across the space, forcing every man, woman, and child to their knees. The Angel spun slowly, his gaze burning with the need for revenge.

"Please, my Angel, we are your children!"

The Angel turned toward the Bloodlined man who had spoken. His lips curled as he approached him. "I have had thousands of you over the ages. You think I care about you?"

The man trembled before the Angel. "Then why are you so upset by her death?"

"BECAUSE SHE WAS THE DAUGHTER OF THE ONE I LOVED."

The man moaned in fear, falling to his back and holding up his arm as though it would protect him from the Angel's wrath.

The Angel backed away, turning slowly as he regarded the crowd. "Where is the one who spilt her blood?"

No man came forward.

The silence was heavy and grim as the Angel's gaze narrowed.

"So be it."

He gingerly picked up Yara's corpse. His wings lifted him into the air. He stared down at the crowd. A pillar of ethereal light erupted around the edges of the area, trapping every unfortunate soul inside.

"Burn."

With one spoken word, the sun came down to earth. Men, women, and children all burned in its flame, their chilling screams scraping across Nisha's consciousness. She watched as this part of Zareen burned, as the people turned to ash and as the sands calcified and shattered, shards of heated glass burying themselves deep into the sands, there to stay for an eternity.

The Angel flew away with Yara in his arms, leaving behind a ruin of the Glass District. All the people of Zareen cried for him to return, except for two: the husband and child who too felt the pain of Yara's loss.

Finally, she understood.

They were not immortal. Their pain would only last the rest of their lives, until they died and found peace in that everlasting darkness. But the Angel would live for an eternity, forever cursed by the memories of loved ones lost.

That was what he begged her for.

Not mercy from the Speaker's torture, but mercy from the eternity he's lived. All he wanted was to join the only people he ever loved.

Free me.

The memories fell to darkness.

CHAPTER
TWENTY-FOUR

Nisha came out of the vision, numb with sadness. She could still feel the Angel's pain even now.

"Nisha?" Sher said. His face was etched with concern, his golden eyes reminding her of Yara. He stepped closer, took her hand. "What is it?"

"That painting of yours, the one you gave me. Your ancestor painted it, didn't she?"

"How do you know that?"

She glanced toward the Angel. In a soft voice, she answered, "Because I saw it. I saw the woman he loved, the daughter they had. Yara. She had eyes like yours."

Sher breathed in disbelief, studying her for a moment. Then he said, "The woman he loved, my ancestor, her name was Humayra."

The Angel stirred at the sound of Humayra's name. Nisha and Sher stepped back as the chains rattled and the Angel lifted his head, his gaze landing on Sher.

Son of Sons, Sons of Daughters, Daughters of Yara, beloved of my Humayra.

Sher gasped as he heard the Angel's voice in his head. Nisha swallowed as she listened.

Free me.

He glanced at Nisha. "He wants us to kill him?"

She nodded.

"What about the tear? We can't save Auri without it."

Nisha looked away. After seeing what the Angel had gone through, after seeing him now, she couldn't bring herself to beg for his tears. She could hardly breathe as she answered, her voice tight with dismay. "We'll find another way."

He drew a heavy breath, as if he was battling with the decision too. She couldn't imagine what he was thinking. This was his *ancestor*. The reason he existed. He clenched his teeth, the muscles of his jaw flexing. "Okay."

She squeezed his hand. It was a stupid thing to think that would be any sort of comfort after agreeing to kill a divine being responsible for your own bloodline, but she didn't know what else to do.

He squeezed her hand back, as if he knew what she risked by giving the Angel the death he sought.

"The wounds those bastards gave him, they're starting to heal even now. Can you see?"

He was right. The Angel's wounds were slowly pulling back together, his new skin pink and fresh. She cursed, realizing that this was not the beginning of the torture the Angel had experienced at the hands of the Salstadirians. This was only what was recent.

"If mortal weapons won't do anything lasting, I'm not sure how we do this," he said.

"We—"

The air before them shimmered. Reality seemed to warp and fold.

Then the Speaker appeared, materializing with a chilling smile. Soren was on his knees next to him. Half his face was demolished, with bits of his bare skull visible through the bleeding flesh.

Soren's wheezing echoed into the silence. He seemed half dead already, completely unaware of his surroundings.

"Ah, Nisha," the Speaker said, his voice dripping with venomous pleasure. He tossed the orb he used to appear aside. It rolled off the platform and down to the bottom of the Angel's pit. "I see that you have found my guest."

She cursed.

"Where is Fenrik?" he asked, glancing behind them as if he expected the honored to appear at any moment.

"Fenrik? That bastard is busy burning in the seven hells."

He frowned. "Is that so? And your mother?"

Nisha glowered in the ensuing silence. Her knuckles cracked as fists formed at her side.

To her surprise, the Speaker actually seemed sad. "That is unfortunate. I had come to enjoy her company over the years."

"You *bastard*," Sher spat, stepping forward and drawing the Speaker's attention. "Do the people of Salstadir know what you're doing to the Angel?"

He raised a brow as he considered Sher. "You are out of your cell, Bloodlined."

"Answer me!"

He smiled. "Of course not. But rarely do people know what is done in the name of the greater good."

The greater good ... Nisha thought about the artificer workstations in the other room, the blood being collected here, and all the ruby rings that the honored wore. The thought that came to her mind was unthinkable, but ...

"You're farming the Angel's blood for his power, aren't you?" she whispered in horror. Then another thought came to mind, and her gaze swiveled to where the sapphire ring should have sat on Soren's hand. It wasn't there.

The Speaker smiled. "You *are* sharp, just as your mother always said you would be."

Her heart twisted inside her chest.

He lifted his chin, opened his hand, and revealed the sapphire ring resting in his palm. "This contains the only tear that the Angel ever shed in our presence."

Sher's hand tightened over hers.

"My forefather was wise enough to catch it and mold it into something that could benefit our people. The power within this was enough to shape our history, to carve out a home from the cruel outsiders who sought to put us in chains. The problem with singular power, though, is that it cannot be shared. My forefather sought more of the Angel's tears, but he refused to appease us, saying they were meant only for one lost soul."

He closed his hand over the ring.

"But in his wisdom, my forefather came to the realization that if a tear worked, then so should a droplet of blood. He trapped the Angel here, made himself into the first Speaker, and brought our people into an age of light that the Angel refused to share. What we have found, though, is that the Angel's blood was too *pure* for our souls to resonate. Over time, the ruby rings cease to work."

He smiled again, his gaze shifting to Sher.

"But never did we imagine that the Angel would sully his blood with mere mortals."

All the empty cells that were being built ...

"Oh, sundamned hells. That's why you're so interested in the Bloodlined," Nisha said, dread creeping up her neck. "That's why you sent Kaelum."

"Oh yes," the Speaker said, raising the black diamond ring and considering it. "Bloodlined blood fixes everything. And there is a city full of it."

Crimson wisps of light emerged from the ring. They wrapped around Soren's neck and pulled him to his feet. Only half aware, he clawed at his neck for air.

"Your newfound friend wanted to see the Angel's death. With no need for the Angel now, I can give him that before I show him to an early grave. I offer you the same choice."

"You're a sundamned fool, old man."

The Speaker smirked, an odd expression on the face of a man so ancient.

"Do tell me, outsider. How am I the fool?"

"You'd *actually* kill the Angel before you've really tested the Bloodlined ring? I thought wisdom was supposed to come with your years. Looks like I was wrong."

"You are trying to goad me into giving you a fighting

chance." The Speaker shook his head, clearly amused. "Very well. I will give you that. Let us see what kind of fight an outsider gives me."

The crimson light loosened its hold on Soren so he didn't choke to death. It dragged him and tossed him against the wall, his head rolling forward to rest against his chest.

The Speaker stood with a smirk, both hands on his cane, waiting for Nisha to make her move.

Nisha exchanged a glance with Sher, worried he would try to stop her, that he would try to intervene and demand the ring from her to protect her. But to her surprise, he did not.

She opened her mouth to say something, but he silenced her with a touch of his hand. He leaned in and whispered against her ear.

"Remember where you came from. You are greater than any threat this life has to give you, including this wrinkled old bastard. It's long past time he met his end."

Nisha grinned at Sher. He stepped back, his fists curling at his side. She could tell he dreaded the thought of her getting hurt, but he trusted her. And that was enough.

She faced the old man. Raising the ruby ring, she focused her mind. The Speaker was all that stood between her and rescuing her daughter from King Razhan. She would not fall to him. She would not fail again.

The Angel's voice that used to be at the back of her mind was silent. Hoping he could hear her thoughts, she sent him a message.

Help me defeat him, help me save my daughter, and I will give you the mercy you seek.

Disappointment sank through her with the following silence. The Angel continued to watch him, but his gaze seemed to pass into the far distance. She feared Sher might have it right. The Angel had lost his touch on reality in the wake of the Speaker's torture.

"Come, outsider," the Speaker said. "Make your m—"

Ethereal light flew forth from her ring, shaping itself into an arrow that shot through the air toward him. A crimson wall appeared in front of the Speaker, and the arrow shattered against it. The motes of light disappeared into thin air.

But Nisha was already on the move.

She knew she would lose if she went against the Speaker head-to-head. He had more experience with the magic, not to mention his own confidence that the strength behind his black diamond ring would overpower the ruby's. She didn't feel confident enough to test that theory.

Her mother had told her she was a great Brawler not because of brute strength, but because of the technique she fought with. And Nisha had a technique that she was sure the Speaker wouldn't be ready for, a technique honed over a lifetime of living in the Glass District.

She would fight dirty.

She sent a wall of light toward him, hoping that in the Speaker's old age, his vision had worsened enough that the bright light might obscure her just enough.

His lip curled in distaste as he waved his hand, cleaving through the wall with a crimson blade. As Nisha slid beneath it, she was confronted with the strangest smell: saffron, leather, and amber.

She didn't have time to think about that as she slid straight into the Speaker's walking stick. He gave a startled shout as he stepped aside, his stick rolling off the platform. Hobbling away, his face twisted in rage.

Whips emerged from thin air, lashing toward Nisha. She dodged between them, only to see a massive hammer swinging down on her. She summoned a shield of light.

The hammer smashed into her.

The shield held, barely, the impact sending tremors through her body. She could feel the strain, the Speaker's desire to crush her, but she held firm. The hammer rebounded, and Nisha seized her chance. She lunged forward with the raw desperation of a Glass District survivor that the Speaker could never know.

Her fist connected with the old man's jaw, a satisfying crack echoing against the stone walls.

Dazed, he stumbled back. Shock registered on his face for the first time.

Nisha grinned as she panted.

His thin lips pursed. A pillar of light erupted around Nisha, trapping her and squeezing in on her. She shouted, summoning her own walls around her.

She grimaced, holding her hands against her own constructs as if it could keep the Speaker's magic from crushing her. Sweat beaded along her brow and the back of her neck.

A loud roar drew her attention to Sher, where the Speaker had him in chains.

The Speaker stared at Nisha with pure hatred, a thin line of blood running down from his cracked lip. "Watch your beloved die."

A spear of crimson light the length of Nisha's body appeared over the Speaker's shoulder.

She screamed.

It hurtled toward Sher.

Time slowed as crimson reflected off the light of Sher's golden eyes. He met her gaze, and knowing that he was powerless against the Speaker, he accepted his death. He began to whisper his final words to her.

But she refused to hear them, refused to accept them. In her mind, she screamed to the Angel.

If he dies, so does the last of Humayra's blood!

The Angel's eyes sharpened at the mention of her name, and his gaze pivoted to Sher. The look in his eyes reminded Nisha of the Angel in the memories.

The dim glow of his skin brightened, and his power crept along the chains attempting to restrain him. Cracks formed as he overloaded them with power. A bubble of light, pure and untainted, formed a barrier around Sher.

The spear shattered against it.

The Speaker gaped at the sudden display of power. His face paled as he spun toward the Angel, fearing the Angel's power returning. But the glow of the Angel's skin had already dimmed.

He had returned to his madness and memories.

Distracted by the Angel, the Speaker's assault on Nisha weakened. She managed to break through his walls. She attacked before he could recover.

Her fist slammed into his stomach, a heavy gasp of

air escaping his lips. The old man shoved her back. He was stronger than she anticipated. Faster too, as the black diamond at his finger gleamed. A sword appeared in his hand.

Again, the smell of Sher washed over her. But it wasn't just the smell of him. It was his essence, his very presence. A thought passed through her mind.

With a glance toward Sher, she knew it was worth taking a gamble on.

She summoned a blade of her own and ran toward the Speaker. He smiled as he plunged the sword toward her chest.

Sher's voice tore through the air, "No!"

A deep grunt echoed in the ensuing silence.

The Speaker looked into her eyes, his triumph fading first to confusion, then to pain. Blood gushed from where she'd plunged her dagger into his chest, while crimson motes of light danced around them.

Just as the sword tip reached her chest, it faltered, dissolving away before it could pierce her skin. The Bloodlined ring couldn't harm her.

She listened to his death rattle, watched as his lifeblood bubbled up from his lips. He died before he could understand how he lost.

She let go of him, letting his body drop to the ground like a sack full of sand. She stood over him, breathing heavily, the fight draining out of her as the adrenaline faded. It was only when she retrieved the sapphire ring from his pocket and stripped the Blood-lined ring from his finger that she breathed a sigh of relief.

Sher rushed forward and pulled her into his arms. "How? I thought he had you."

She shook her head. "That ring was made with your blood, your essence."

In a very real way, their souls were intertwined.

He breathed a sigh of relief and understanding. "And no part of me could ever hurt you."

She nodded against his chest.

"It's over, then," Sher said.

Mercy ...

She swallowed, shaking her head. "Not yet."

The Angel watched them with distant eyes. He was quiet now, like the magic he'd summoned to save Sher had taken everything out of him.

"Do you want me to do it?" Sher asked.

"No. I made the promise to him."

Sher seemed to accept that readily enough. Nisha could tell that still, despite the fact that the Angel sought his own death, he was uncomfortable with the thought of it. She could understand. The Angel was the father of his bloodline, the very reason he even existed.

"What about him?" Sher asked.

Soren seemed lifeless against the wall, his head hanging against an unmoving chest. Nisha looked away quickly. His injuries were too gruesome even for the likes of her.

"He's got to be dead," she grimaced.

Sher knelt before Soren, pressing his fingers to the man's neck. He closed Soren's eyes. That was confirmation enough. With a heavy sigh, Nisha grabbed one of the torture weapons and walked to where the chains were linked to the wall. She swung it at the link, a loud clang echoing through the space as the blade met the blue steel.

Perhaps the Angel deserved to die in chains for all the terror his magic wrought upon the world, perhaps not. But for some reason, she could not stand the idea of the Angel dying clad in chains. She wanted him free as he met his end.

Sher helped her hack away at the chains.

Nisha had a feeling that if the Angel's power had not cracked them, she wouldn't have had a sundamned chance in breaking them. With one final swing, the chains finally broke, the links clattering loudly against the stone as they slid to the bottom of the pit.

The Angel was not truly free yet, because though the chains were gone, he was still imprisoned by grief. He had lived his life through, and now it was time to give him the mercy he so desired.

Nisha rounded the pit until she stood right in front of him, staring into his eyes.

She lifted the sapphire ring, turning it so that the light danced off it. "You should know that the tear you shed because you weren't there to save your daughter is going to be what saves mine. I can't tell you what that means, except that she's my world."

She paused, glancing back where Sher waited. "And when Sher's life was in danger, you saved him too. Him? I think you understand when I say he's the only man I'll ever love."

She turned back to the Angel.

"There's not much more I can say other than..." she

touched a hand to her heart, "thank you, for being my guardian angel."

She shook her head with a rueful grin. "I'm sure that your Faithful will be out to hang me by the neck if they ever find out what I've done here. But you deserve this. You deserve an ending."

She lifted her gaze to the Angel's. Her grin fell away. He still looked lost. With a heavy sigh, she replaced the ruby ring with the sapphire one. She summoned a blade of ethereal light.

"Goodbye, my Angel. Your family waits for you."

The blade shot forward and pierced his heart.

He gasped, a sound so faint yet so profound it seemed to echo through the cavern and beyond, rippling through the fabric of the world itself. It was like the sigh of the wind over a barren desert, carrying with it the weight of millennia.

The ground beneath their feet trembled, a soft rumbling that grew in intensity as if the earth itself was mourning the Angel's passing.

As the Angel's form began to dissolve into motes of light, drifting upward and fading into the ether, the atmosphere in the cavern shifted.

Sher stepped up beside Nisha, his hand finding hers, squeezing it gently in silent support. They stood together, watching as the last remnants of the Angel disappeared.

"Everything's going to be different now," Sher said, his voice so soft, as though he was afraid to disturb the ensuing silence.

Nisha nodded, her eyes wet with unshed tears. "Let's hope it'll be better."

"Let's get out of here before the Salstadirians find all of this."

Nisha nodded, but as they turned to leave, a whisper caressed her mind.

Your mother sends her love, and she wishes upon you a final gift.

Nisha froze and glanced back to where the Angel had vanished, her eyes widening as motes of light reappeared, swirling around them. The motes multiplied, enveloping them in a luminous whirlwind.

"What's happening?" Sher shouted, his voice almost lost in the growing storm.

"I don't—"

Suddenly, the world seemed to lurch forward, wrenching a scream from her. Her surroundings spun wildly, a dizzying blur of motion that snatched the breath from her lungs. Then, just as suddenly, everything came to a jarring stop.

The abrupt halt mixed with the intense heat of the sun overhead overwhelmed her; she turned and vomited.

As the last echoes of her retching faded, a distant laugh—genuine and joyful—resonated in her mind before fading into silence.

Then the Angel was gone.

"Nisha."

Sher's voice anchored her back to the moment. He swayed on his feet, visibly disoriented. Nisha gathered her strength and moved to support him. Following his gaze, she caught sight of what had captured his attention.

Below them stretched the three districts of Zareen, sprawling under the watchful eyes of the great palace. Its golden dome and thousand spires shone with the light of the harsh desert sun, overshadowed only by the throne to their side.

The familiar sounds of the Market District drifted up to them, the voices of merchants screaming as they hawked their wares. Nisha turned to Sher, a smile spreading across her face.

They were home.

CHAPTER
TWENTY-FIVE

Every step Nisha took through the sifting sands fanned the flames of her rage. Something had happened to her out in the desert and in the heart of that mountain. She had grown so distant from this place that she could not feel the heat of the King's threat. But here now, she could not push it from her mind.

King Razhan had threatened her daughter.

She knew that if she and Sher wanted, they could have marched on the palace, blown down the gates, slaughtered every guard, and demanded that the King hand over her daughter.

However, she also knew that if they did that, the King would most likely make good on his threat. Auri would suffer at the hands of his bodyguards, Malzor and Azaroth, and as powerful as Nisha and Sher were with the rings, they could not fight invisible enemies.

There was no choice except to play the King's game. But Nisha intended to play it her way.

"It's surreal," Sher muttered to her as they walked through the Glass District.

She knew what he meant. So much had happened since they'd left that she expected the city to be different too. And yet, the Glass District seemed exactly the same. There were still men standing in shadowed doorways. The homes that had been burned in Zulmar's violent takeover before his *untimely* death were still damaged. And the rats still skittered through the streets.

It seemed the only different thing about the Glass District was that *they* were walking through it, dressed in foreign clothing. Nisha was made all too aware of that when they entered deeper into the district, encountering more and more residents outside, each openly staring at them as they passed.

Nisha kept an eye out for Fatima's doorstep, hoping to see that she was still alive and well. While Nisha didn't see her, she did see the orphans crowding her doorstep. They talked with one another like it was peacetime, knowing full well that the moment they were away from her doorstep, the war to keep their coins in their pockets was back on.

Nisha drew a deep sigh. It felt only a short time ago that she was that age, thinking that there could be no greater concern than keeping her coin in her pocket. She was naive. But then, how could she have known at that age that soon her greatest concern would be keeping her daughter alive and safe?

They approached the gate between the Glass District and the Market District. More than a few guards stood armed, their narrowed eyes locked onto them as they approached, like they posed a serious threat to the city.

Then Nisha and Sher drew close enough for the captain to see Sher's golden eyes glowing from under his jet-black hair.

He cleared his throat. "Halt!"

"You would dare obstruct a Bloodlined from entering his own city?" Sher asked, his voice low and dangerous.

Nisha glanced at him. It had been a while since she heard him like that, but then, he was back in his element now. This was his city, just as much as these were her alleys.

"On the King's own orders, yes," the captain said. He shifted from one foot to the other. It was clear that he wasn't used to standing up to the Bloodlined. "He has ordered us to keep an eye out for a pair of travelers, one a Bloodlined lord and the other a uh..."

His eyes looked Nisha up and down.

"A Commonborn thief."

"And what makes you think that's us?" Nisha asked, straightening her back and slipping into the role of a Silk Rider. It didn't quite feel natural after so long. She gave him her best dazzling smile. "Do I look as though I am simply *Commonborn*?"

Something about him seemed familiar.

He winced. "Ah..."

Nisha realized how rough she looked after her fight with the Speaker.

The captain pointed to Sher. "Well, he fits the description at least."

Sher rolled his eyes, glancing toward Nisha. "Who

would have thought that I would be the one they suspect?" He turned back to the guard. "And what is that you were commanded to do if you found the... suspects?"

Just as the captain was about to answer, it clicked.

"*You're* the bastard who tackled me in the Market District," she said.

The captain recognized her then, too. His snarl returned. "Your hair's grown longer."

"And you're still just as ugly as you were then. Got a promotion, did you?"

"I did, no thanks to you. Somehow I got blamed that you escaped. Had to dig shitting holes for a solid month after that."

That put a smile on Nisha's face. She missed the city. She felt a sudden pang in her heart. If only she had been able to bring her mother back here with her. Instead, she would be buried in that Angel-damned mountain. She forced the thought to the back of her mind. It was crucial that she stay focused. Auri needed her now. There would be time for grieving later.

"Captain," Sher said, drawing the guard's attention back to him before he could do anything foolish. "What are your orders?"

"Simply to take the two of you straight to the palace gates," he said.

The other guards stepped forward, eyes flicking to each other nervously. It seemed that none of them were too eager to take them by force.

The captain must have had the same opinion. "Will you come peacefully?"

The ring weighed in her pocket. The thief in her

itched to draw it out and protect herself from these men who had endangered her all her life. It was intoxicating, knowing that she had the power to finally rebel and impose her will on them. But Auri's life was at stake. She was so close to saving her daughter. Now was not the time to screw it up.

She forced a smile. "I will."

"I was speaking to the Bloodlined lord," he said. He glanced down at a note at his side. "Lord Vasir?"

Her smile soured. Sher chuckled darkly, no doubt thinking about the danger she posed to them. He had seen what she had done to the Speaker. To do that, and nearly straight after face such humiliation...

"Yes, we will."

The captain breathed a sigh of relief. He signaled to the guards around them, and a tight circle formed around them.

"Darius, run ahead. Give the news."

One of the men sprinted ahead, his sheathed sword clattering against his belt as he shouted for the crowd to part.

The captain motioned for them to start off, leaving two guards to man the gate between the Market and Glass Districts. As they passed the Tarnished Trades, she made eye contact with Zarvo.

His three-toothed smile faltered at the sight of her and the remaining strands of his hair slipped down out of place. He plastered a smile back onto his pockmarked face and called out to her with that voice that sounded like he'd smoked emberdust since the moment his mother had shat him out.

"Nisha, you're looking quite the part of a coin-abled buyer! Why don't you step this way for but a moment, and I'll show you the best of my wares."

She shook her head, her mind turning back to the time he turned her away from the sky whirl she wanted to buy.

"Surely you must be interested in my—"

"Quiet, Zarvo, or I'll plant a fist into that ugly face of yours," the captain barked.

Zarvo's smile disappeared. "Come now, Nader. Is that any way to treat me?"

She had no doubt he was insinuating the fact that his coin graced the captain's pocket.

"It is when we're on the King's business."

Zarvo fell into a stunned silence, his beady eyes following them as they carried on.

Nisha noticed that as they moved further into the Market District, things weren't quite as loud as she remembered. There was less shouting from the merchants about their wares and more whispers. They grouped in tight huddles, men, women, and children flitting from one to the other.

Nisha turned to the nearest guard to ask him what had happened. Her gaze lingered on him as they walked. "Wait, don't I know you too? Arash, right? You were the one who needed me to clear a favor at the Matchmaker."

He shushed her, his gaze flicking nervously to the captain. "You remember me, huh? That's good, but let's keep that quiet, yeah?"

"Sure, so long as you tell me what's going on here."

He looked at her. "You didn't feel it?"

"Feel what?"

"The earth shaking? It was like nothing I'd ever seen. Watched the very dunes shift with my own eyes."

He was probably exaggerating, given that she knew he couldn't see much of the desert from where he had to have been stationed at the gate. But that was a moot point. She knew what he was talking about.

"There was this awful silence that came with it, until the whisper... That's what everybody's talking about. Nearly pissed myself."

"A whisper?" she asked. She'd felt that silence that came with the Angel's death, but she hadn't heard anything more until he spoke to her of his final gift. It would surprise her to know that his voice had made its way across the Sundaran desert.

"What did it say?"

Arash shrugged. "Don't know. That's what everybody's talking about. Everyone's saying something different."

"What about you?" she asked.

"You want my honest answer?"

She nodded.

He sighed. "I didn't make out any words. Just sounded a bit like the wind to me, except in my head. Anybody that's saying they understood it is probably full of shit."

Eyes caught onto Nisha and Sher and their strange outfits as they were being escorted through the Market District. A wave of fresh gossip rolled through the crowd. Several began to follow them, excited to see what happened. But the guards at the rear warned them off with a simple unsheathing of their swords.

Nisha glanced to the side, spotting a young thief working his way through the crowd. She smiled when she saw him slipping his fingers into several pockets as he leaned into the huddles, pretending to listen to the gossip.

Smart boy.

This was easy pickings right now, with everyone distracted by the sight of her and Sher.

Then she saw Azim. His brow furrowed in confusion as he looked her over. She could see the rage setting in, as he saw that she was alive and well.

Speak later, she signaled to him, using the same street signs she learned while she trained with Seraphina. The Silk Riders had a number of motions they used when they were in danger, ways to signal to each other.

His gaze narrowed in suspicion, but he nodded.

They passed him and the last parts of the Market District and entered the Peak District. Several of the guards breathed a sigh of relief, worried that the crowd would stop them and demand answers from Nisha and Sher. It was easy enough to understand why. Some among the Market District crowds would think the timing of their arrival, the strange foreign outfits they wore, and the shaking earth were all connected. It would sound crazy to Nisha, if it weren't true.

They garnered considerably less attention as they passed through the Peak District. The Bloodlined seemed less concerned about the earthquake. But Nisha knew they would be saving their gossip for the next ball. She had no doubt that in those same conversations, they would discuss the return of Lord Vasir after so long and the strange Commonborn he associated himself with.

Sher's mansion came into view. Perched atop a gentle sand dune, it cast its shadow over them as they passed. The white marble shone brilliantly in the light of the dying sun. It was beautiful, to say the least. And it made her heart ache.

She reached out and squeezed Sher's hand, knowing that he had to have been thinking about his mother. Judging by the slight misting of his eyes, she was right.

He gave her a sad smile and looked away from his home, choosing instead to focus on King Razhan's palace. As they approached, the imposing silhouette of his palace rose up around them, its thousand spires piercing the sky.

"Sundamned hells, what a sight," one of the guards muttered.

As much as she hated the man that ruled within, she could only agree. The palace was a masterpiece, its walls adorned with elaborate swirling designs. In the distance, gilded steps led to a pair of massive doors made from dark wood and inlaid with yet more gold.

The last time she had visited, music spilled out from the opened doors. This time, though, they were closed, and a gargantuan pair of men guarded the doors.

When the paved pathway finally gave way to the gold-specked sand, they came to a stop. Nisha bumped into the back of the guard in front of her.

"Why have we stopped?" Nisha asked.

"Instructions. Someone should be—"

Malzor and Azaroth stepped out of thin air, drawing a startled shout from the captain. Several guards stepped back at the sight of them. It was easy enough to understand why.

Dressed and masked in grey cloth, with curved relic swords at their sides and black smoke trailing from where their eyes should've been, they made for a terrifying sight.

The captain composed himself and cleared his throat. "I—"

Malzor—or Azaroth, Nisha didn't know which was which—stepped forward and dropped a gold coin into the captain's hand. The captain's eyes instantly lit up with unbridled glee. He cleared his throat again.

"Right. Time to piss off now, boys. Back the way we came."

The guards wasted no time in obeying their orders. Arash threw Nisha a final, sympathizing glance as he left with the rest of them. But Nisha was not nearly as afraid of the pair of assassins as she used to be. Her steely gaze was as hard as stone. Now that they had made their appearance, she was confident enough that she could slip the relic ring on and bury the bastards before they could lay a finger on her.

Sher squeezed her hand once more before he let go, as if he knew what she was thinking. He was right. It wasn't time to act *yet*.

"Is there something you are waiting for?" Sher asked.

Malzor circled them, his movement unnaturally fluid. Azaroth's voice whispered in her mind.

Do you have the tear?

The first time she had heard his voice in her head, she'd been terrified. But now she realized that it was a pale imitation of the Angel's own voice.

"We do," she said.

Give it to us.

"No chance."

He unsheathed the ominous sword at his side. She could feel the energy thrumming off it.

"Do you really want to test if you can kill me faster than I break the vial your master gave me?" she asked with a raised brow. "Because I'd be willing to take that bet."

Malzor paused. Azaroth's voice slipped into her mind, his tone just slightly deeper than Malzor's.

Your daughter would die.

"I'd be too dead to be concerned by that," she lied.

A growl permeated the air. She had them, and they didn't like that. A moment later, the sword was sheathed. Malzor withdrew a small relic orb that reminded Nisha of the ones in Salstadir. A portal materialized.

Enter.

The two thieves stepped through the portal.

Nisha and Sher emerged through the portal. She thought she might see the grand ballroom again, with its master-piece of a ceiling painted like a night sky. After all, it was there that she had seen the King lounging on his throne for the first time.

But to her surprise, the room they entered was far smaller. The walls were dark, with flames rippling against them from mounted torches that cast shadows into the corners. A dark throne made from what looked like blackened marble rested at its center. She couldn't fathom what that must have cost.

The portal snapped shut behind them, revealing an old door at the back of the room made from hardened steel.

Malzor's smoky gaze locked onto her, as if he could sense her impatience.

Wait.

Nisha scowled at him.

The minutes ticked by until a set of footsteps began

to echo outside the door. Then it opened with a soft creak that reverberated off the walls.

King Razhan entered, his piercing maroon eyes falling on her. He wore a tunic that matched the glow of his eyes. Again, she was struck by how young he appeared. His head shaved, his beard closely trimmed, and his back straight and firm, he made for a striking figure.

"Ah, my pair of lovely thieves," he said as the door swung shut behind him. He rounded them and took a seat on his throne, settling in with a familiarity that suggested this was where he was used to ruling from, not the ballroom throne.

His gaze swung from Nisha to Sher and back.

"Something strange happened today. The thread of magic that ties me to the Angel, that pulled me to the west, it suddenly... disappeared. I spent my day worrying about what it could mean. But I could only come up with one conclusion."

His gaze sharpened. He leaned forward, and the shadows deepened over his face, making the glow of his maroon eyes more prominent.

"The Angel is dead, isn't he?"

Neither Nisha nor Sher said a word.

His hand closed into a fist. Azaroth unsheathed his sword and had it against Sher's throat in an instant.

"Do not tell me you failed to retrieve the tear. That you somehow pushed the Angel beyond the realms of this world before I could have my *wish*."

Something about the phrase triggered a hidden

memory in Nisha's mind. She frowned as she began to pull on it, trying to draw it out.

"We have it," she said. Her voice felt so small in the chamber.

King Razhan's breath caught. Surprised, he sat back, as if he expected them to fail. "Show me."

Nisha withdrew the sapphire ring from her pocket and lifted it, the gem reflecting blue light against the walls. "This sapphire holds the Angel's final tear."

He leaned forward and held his hand out, his eyes gleaming with greed. "Give it to me."

She drew her hand back, nervousness setting in as Azaroth nicked Sher's throat in response. Sher hissed in rage but kept quiet.

"Where is Auri?"

"She is safe. Now hand me the ring."

"*Where* is my daughter?"

His brows furrowed. "Make me ask again, and I will have your lover's lifeblood spilt."

With a resigned sigh, Nisha slowly approached the King and placed the ring in his palm. The moment her finger brushed against his skin, her memories unfolded.

She stared at him, her eyes widening in shock as she suddenly remembered it all: how the legendary thief that Fatima had told her about had played them, the three wishes that he'd made of wealth, power, and immortality, only to come to regret them, and his ultimate desire to return to Fatima, the woman he loved.

"Ilyas," she whispered.

Ilyas sat back, fixed his gaze on the ring, and gave a deep, satisfied sigh.

"I do love to hear my own name after all these years."

He turned the ring over in the light, studying it with a careful eye.

"I wouldn't suggest putting it on," Nisha said.

He paused. "Why is that?"

"The ring has had an ... unfortunate effect on the people who used it."

He nodded, holding the ring with a more careful hand. "More souls tortured by the magic the Angel had to offer. I hope they found their redemption with the Angel's death. Me, I look forward to mine." He closed his hand over the ring. "Malzor, fetch the lamp."

Malzor bowed to him before stepping through a portal.

"Where is my daughter?" Nisha asked again, frustration slipping into her voice.

A moment of silence passed as Ilyas regarded her with a scrutinizing gaze. "It seems that I underestimated you."

He pointed a finger at her.

"I thought you to be a simple thief. To murder a human soul stains the soul, but to claim that of the divine?" He chuckled, his low and smooth voice echoing around them. "That is something else."

A shadow crept over Nisha's soul. "Did you hurt her?"

A moment of silence passed, each second dragging the sheer fear and rage from her.

Then, he answered. "I did not."

She breathed a quiet sigh of relief.

"The truth is this. Your daughter was never in

danger. She has been safe with her Bloodlined parents all this time."

Nisha froze.

"I wondered how much you had listened to my Fatima's stories, if you would uncover the lie I had spun before you forgot who I was. It was a gamble I made; a gamble that paid off."

She stammered, "I don't understand."

A wide, youthful grin came to his face, as though the one thing he still managed to find joy in was getting the better of others.

"I am a thief, Nisha. Not a monster. I would never harm a child."

Her knuckles cracked as fists formed at her side. This whole time, they had been risking their lives on a journey through the cruel, endless desert. They had sparked a war that cost countless lives in Salstadir over a lie.

Her mother, Laila, had died over a *lie*.

Nisha snarled, "It's time."

His grin disappeared.

A loud roar erupted from behind her, as Sher withdrew his hand from his pocket. The black diamond ring gleamed as crimson light struck Azaroth in the chest. A wheezing, mortal gasp escaped the assassin, and he collapsed to the ground. The relic sword clattered against the floor.

Ilyas surged forward, seeking to wrap his hands around her throat, but Nisha had moved first. His nose cracked as she pummeled his face, screaming for all the world to hear her rage. Even as he fell out of his throne and sheltered his face, she continued to beat him.

A portal appeared behind them. Malzor strode through, smug and arrogant, only to freeze at the sight of his twin brother's body and the blood pooling beneath it. An arrow of crimson light buried itself in his chest.

The lamp slid across the floor, coming to a halt against Nisha's boot. She stood over the beaten King, heaving and growling with unbridled fury. She retrieved the sapphire ring from where it fell out of his hands.

Sher came to stand next to her, his own rage equal to her own. He summoned a crimson blade to his hand and kicked Ilyas back against his throne. He held the edge of the blade to his neck.

"Say the word, and I'll end him forever," he said.

With blood streaming from his broken nose and a cut in his brow, Ilyas looked from the pair of thieves to the bodies of his bodyguards. Then he began to chuckle. His chuckle was low and soft at first, but it grew into a hearty laughter that filled the room.

When it came to an end, he drew a deep breath and let it out all at once. "I underestimated the both of you."

Nisha crouched before him, lifted the sapphire ring, and held it in front of his face.

"You have no idea what I lost to get this. This is not some game. This is my sundamned *life*."

He surged forward and stuck his face into hers, not caring that Sher's blade nicked his neck. "You think I don't know that? I will live an eternity, forgotten by the *only* person that matters in this forsaken world. I do not *care* what you have lost."

Nisha stared into his maroon eyes, a storm of

emotions raging within her. The turmoil turned over within her.

Ilyas leaned back, rested his head against the foot of the throne, and stared back at them. His eyes misted over with tears even as he clenched his jaw.

"So go on. Drop your tear into the lamp, and make your wish. I hope it curses you, just as it did me."

She picked up the lamp, the metal cool to the touch, and its shine long lost to the passing of time. Even with the Angel dead, there was still an aura radiating from it. She could feel it in her bones. She swallowed, remembering the lengths she had gone to steal it, and the sacrifices that she and Sher had paid along the way.

"Make the wish," Sher said. His voice was soft, and his golden eyes softer still when she met them. "You can have all the years back that you lost with your daughter."

She glanced down at the lamp, her rage suddenly forgotten as she realized the significance of this moment. She breathed, knowing that now she could wish to have her daughter back and raise her as she had always dreamt.

But if she did that, would Sher still be hers? The opportunity for them to have met would never have happened if she didn't have a reason to steal the lamp for herself. While there was pain in that thought, there was joy too, knowing that if she had not been in Sher's life, he never would have suffered as he did; he would have had the chance to be with his mother in her last moments, and Nisha knew what a mother's final words meant to a child.

"Do it."

Her heart cracked. Her chin trembled.

"I love you," he said.

She nodded, too choked with emotion to manage a response. But she knew that he could see it in her eyes. She knew that he had heard her back before she killed the Angel; he was the only man she would ever love.

She slid the lid to the side and held the sapphire ring over it. Light slowly drifted upward, its drifting threads wrapping slowly around the gem. A crack formed in the sapphire, and a moment later, it shattered.

The sound echoed deep into the silence. The three thieves watched in awe as a blue tear fell from the gemstone like it was weightless. The power in the lamp doubled, then tripled, vibrating in Nisha's hand. Light spilled out from the spout of the lamp. It was warm now.

A tear ran down Ilyas's face as he watched.

She made eye contact with Sher once more, her heart crying out for him to stop her. But he wouldn't. He knew what her daughter meant to her, and because he loved her more than his own desires, he would let her go. She closed her eyes, unable to bear the simultaneous joy and torment in his gaze.

Then with a shuddering breath, she lifted the lamp closer, set her hand against the brass, and made her wish.

"I wish to destroy the lamp."

TWENTY-SEVEN

As the words left her lips, a surge of energy pulsed through the lamp, a fierce tempest summoning itself around them. The pure light swelled until it enveloped everything around them in a brilliant, searing glow.

The world seemed to pause, holding its breath as the light reached its zenith. Then the lamp began to crack, fine lines webbing across its surface. The light intensified until it was as bright as the desert sun. Nisha forced her eyes shut.

She could hear the glassy tinkling of the lamp's body fracturing, each snap a gunshot in the silence.

When she dared to open her eyes again, she saw the light receding like the tides of Humarya's painted ocean.

The lamp lay in pieces, fragments scattered across the ground, twinkling dimly in the fading echoes of the wish.

A soft moan pulled her attention up to where Ilyas slumped back against the foot of the throne. His face had aged decades in moments, his worn crown lying beside him, like he was no longer king.

His eyes met hers, exhausted and disbelieving. His wish for eternal life had been undone. She had a feeling that if she went and looked in the vaults now, she would find nothing.

"Why?" Ilyas croaked, his voice nothing at all like it had been mere moments ago.

Nisha tossed the remaining fragments of the lamp in her hand aside. "Don't ask me why. Go spend your last years with Fatima, and hope that she passes before you, because if not, I'll come to put you in the ground. I promise you that."

Ilyas smiled sadly, "You say that like I wouldn't die from heartbreak."

She shook her head. "Just... go."

Ilyas struggled to rise, his body too frail to obey. A laugh, joyous and disbelieving, escaped him.

"Would you help an old man to his feet?" he asked.

Sher muttered a curse but gently assisted Ilyas to stand. They watched as he hobbled to the door, pausing as if to speak. After a moment's hesitation, however, he simply shook his head and exited without a word.

Nisha faced Sher, noting his expression of disbelief.

"Why did you do that?" he asked, his voice tinged with confusion. "You had everything. You could have gone back and not missed a single moment of Auri's life. You could have had everything you ever wanted."

"Not everything. Not you."

Sher's lips parted, his breath caught, and he pulled her into his arms. She melted into him, her tears running down into their kiss. She clung to him, finding comfort in the smell of him.

"I've seen how much Auri is loved by... by her parents," Nisha murmured, clutching at Sher's shirt as if it anchored her to reality. "But I've seen Fatima too. She's spent her entire life waiting for Ilyas to come back. And despite how much of a bastard he is, she loves him. I don't want to be her, wishing every night that we'd find our way to each other. I can't be her."

Sher held her close, his arms a safe haven against that fear.

There was no telling how long they stood there, embracing each other, realizing that it was all over. When she finally drew back, she took a seat in the throne, exhaustion sweeping through every muscle of hers. These were the first breaths she could take without a threat hanging over her head.

She bent over and picked up the crown. "What now?"

He took a seat on the arm of the throne, like he was every bit as exhausted as she was. "What do you mean?"

She passed him the crown, "Well, the king is no more. Someone's got to step up into his place."

He nodded quietly for a moment before his brows furrowed. "You don't mean me, do you?"

"You're Lord Vasir, the most famous Bloodlined lord in all of Sundara. Who else would it be?"

"I have no Angel-damned clue, but it won't be me."

"Why not?"

"Because I don't want it. You think I want to be the face of a kingdom that's been suddenly emptied of all its treasure? There's not a chance in the seven hells."

A moment passed as she turned the crown over in her hands. Then she added, "It's important that the next king loves the city, you know. And I mean *all* of it, not just the Bloodlined."

"Would be great to have a Commonborn sitting on the throne," he commented.

She agreed, "Would be nice, yeah."

He cleared his throat. She looked up at him and realized that she was sitting in the throne just now.

She burst out in laughter, "That's a good joke."

"Try on the crown. Let's see how it looks on you."

It was foolish, but when would a street rat like her ever get a chance to wear the king's crown again? She had paid for the opportunity with blood and sacrifice. With a grin, she fit the crown to her head. Surprisingly, it fit snug against her.

She grinned at him, "What do you think?"

Sher's eyes lit up, his admiration clear as he gazed down at her.

"It suits you," he said seriously, his voice carrying a weight that contrasted with his earlier humor. "And not just because it fits."

She raised an eyebrow, the weight of the crown feeling more significant now. "Are you saying what I think you're saying?"

"Yes, I am." Sher said, leaning in to adjust the crown. "It's time a Commonborn sat on that throne. And who better than you? You know every corner of this city, not just the Glass District. You love this city more than any Bloodlined ever could."

Nisha bit her lip, uncertainty swirling within her. The

idea of ruling, of being responsible for the whole of Sundara—it was overwhelming.

"But if not you, then who?" Sher pressed. "You know as well as I do that without a strong claim, there'll be a power struggle among the Bloodlined. And who suffers then? It won't be those in the Peak District. It'll be *your* people."

She knew he was right. If the change in power over the Glass District had been bloody for its residents, then that was nothing compared to what it would be for the throne of Sundara. Whatever new king came to power after the struggle would search for easy wins to satisfy the people, and it didn't take a guess to know that meant eradicating the thieves and the poor that put a stain on this great city.

Then Sher hammered in the final nail. "You will finally have the power to make sure Auri stays safe."

"Fine," she finally said, her voice firm. "I'll agree, but only on one condition."

His face paled.

"Don't look like you're about to piss yourself. It's not that bad."

"I know what you're going to say."

She gave him a toothy grin. "You serve as the Queen's consort."

He winced, but this time, it was her who pressed him.

"I need you to stand by me in rule. It'll legitimize the throne and make any of those Bloodlined bastards think twice about trying to overthrow me. But that's not the only reason why."

"No?"

Suddenly nervous, her fingers dug into her leg as she added, "I uh ... I want you to be my partner."

She thought that he would laugh, joke, tease her even. But to her surprise, his expression softened. He took her hand.

"I could think of no greater honor."

A massive weight lifted off her shoulder at his words. She didn't have to worry about handling everything herself. He would be there.

"Oh, sundamned hells, did you have to say the word honor? After everything we've been through in Salstadir?"

They began to laugh together, and for the first time, Nisha felt... happy. It was a temporary happiness, she knew, as she still felt the grief of her mother's death and the grief of a long-lived dream gone to ashes. But still, she leaned into the happiness for now.

A thief deserved to enjoy what they rightfully stole.

TWENTY-EIGHT

The Bloodlined had assembled in the ballroom, breaking into small circles. Sher had spent the last day giving Nisha the rundown on who might be a friend and who she should be wary of. But even among the potential allies, the pickings were slim.

Nisha wasn't a fool. She knew that her rise to power wouldn't sit well with many of the Bloodlined. Succession was always a messy business, particularly when there was no clear line to the throne. But she was ready; letting any of these bastards take control would only mean disaster for the Glass District.

She watched from the back of the ballroom as Sher moved smoothly from one group to another, his presence acknowledged with warm handshakes and cautious smiles. They were all curious about his recent disappearance. Despite his status, Sher had always been somewhat of an anomaly to them, having secluded himself away during his mother's final days and then vanishing from the city altogether, accompanied only by her, a Commonborn.

Even now, she caught several sidelong glances aimed her way, their expressions mixed with suspicion and intrigue, no doubt wondering why in the seven hells she was here.

As the minutes ticked by, the King's absence became increasingly apparent, emphasized by the empty throne that drew all eyes. Hushed whispers began to make their way through the crowd. Why would the King order them to appear, only to make a late appearance himself? Razhan was known to be late, but not this late.

"So we meet again."

A Bloodlined lord with glasses and a short, neatly trimmed beard that outlined his jawline approached. He wore the same long dark blue coat she had seen him in last, with yet another lump of a book tucked away inside his coat.

"Alaric," she said, meeting his glowing brown eyes with a genuine smile. Sher had begrudgingly admitted that while Alaric's father was someone that should be avoided at all costs, Alaric himself was someone they could trust. But Nisha already knew that.

"And here I was worried that this might be yet another boring affair," he said as he turned and stood next to her so that they could watch the crowd together. "Tell me, my friendly thief, how did it go robbing the King?"

"Terrible," she muttered.

He chuckled, his smooth voice setting her nerves at ease.

"And are you here to steal something again?"

"Something like that," she said.

He glanced at her, quirking an eyebrow. "Oh, this *will* be interesting."

"Interesting? You could call it that. One thing is for sure. I don't think you'll be needing your book tonight."

Sher began to climb the steps to the dais of the King's throne. The hushed chatter across the room fell to silence.

Before Sher had a chance to speak, Alaric leaned in, his voice quiet as a whisper, "I'm glad you're back. Warms my heart knowing a thief is here to keep us Bloodlined humbled."

Nisha grinned at that. Sher had her heart, soul, and mind, but she had a feeling that Alaric would be very easy to love.

Sher's words spilled across the ballroom.

"The King will not be coming tonight."

Several of the Bloodlined were visibly irritated and annoyed, but a handful looked at Sher with keen interest, sensing there was more to the story.

"If he isn't coming, then why did he summon us to court?"

An elderly man stepped forward, his posture rigid, a disdainful sneer marring his features.

"He was not the one who summoned you."

The old man clearly hadn't anticipated such a response. His sneer wavered as he scanned the gathered crowd for signs of comprehension or conspiracy.

"Enough of these games," a woman's voice rang out sharply. "Where is our King?"

Sher's eyes sought Nisha at the back of the room, his look seemingly asking her if she was ready for what was about to unfold. She tightened her jaw, crossed her arms, and nodded firmly. It was time.

With deliberate calm, Sher pulled the crown from his coat and raised it high. A collective intake of breath swept through the ballroom.

"As I said, it was not the King who summoned you here. He has abdicated the throne. He will not be returning."

A stunned silence held sway for a heartbeat, then the room erupted into a cacophony of rage, confusion, and most notably, greed. Sher had warned her that today would reveal the true nature of the Bloodlined as potential usurpers. And she could see that now in the eyes fixed on him with their own murderous intent, like he was all that stood between them and the throne.

Voices clamored louder, a storm of disbelief and speculation swirling around them.

"What now?" a woman shouted.

"We must have a King," another man shouted over her. "We cannot have an empty throne."

"A vote! Put this to vote!"

Nisha scoffed. She imagined very few of them would want to put themselves forward for a vote if they knew that the wealth of Sundara had disappeared. Nisha herself could hardly believe it when she had seen it for herself. She and Sher had stood in the room, and all the mountains of gold coins and relics were gone, leaving not a single thing in the room except for an empty pedestal where the lamp had once sat. It seemed that when she had wished to destroy the lamp, just as it had undone King Razhan's wish for eternal life, so had it undone his wish for wealth that would make even the greatest of Kings and Emperors envious.

If these Bloodlined knew how broke the Kingdom was, they'd be shitting their pants.

"Silence!" Sher's voice tore through it all, reining in the crowd. "There will be no vote."

A man with quivering chins stalked forward—Jamil, the man who went back on the deal to escort her into the ball. He pointed his grubby finger at Sher. "What makes you think that you get to dictate how we replace our King?"

"He *is* Lord Vasir," someone commented.

"I do not care! He has been absent from this court since his mother took ill."

Sher's face darkened at the mention of his mother. He descended another step, his rage draping itself over him like a black cloak. "Mention my mother again, and you will regret it."

Jamil snarled, but he didn't dare disrespect Sher's mother again. Instead, he turned back to the crowd. "Our King Razhan did not have children. So with no clear line of succession, why should we not put this to a vote? We will tear ourselves apart if we do not, and it is imperative that we maintain our strength as a Kingdom."

"Who said that there was no clear line of succession?" Sher called out before the crowd could respond.

Again, silence.

She felt Alaric's gaze on her. She turned to meet it. There was a questioning look behind those glasses as he considered her, like he could already anticipate what Sher had planned to say.

When Nisha gave a sly smile, his mouth parted, and a disbelieving chuckle escaped him.

"You really are something, you know."

Nisha didn't have a chance to respond. Her attention was pulled back to Sher as he withdrew a scroll from under his coat. He held it up in a display to the court, and in a held breath, they waited for him to read it.

Nisha thought back to the night before. Once they agreed she should take the throne, it didn't take long for them to realize much bloodshed could be saved if they had a letter signed and dated by Ilyas himself. Sher had caught the King before he managed to leave the palace, thankfully. From what Sher told her, Ilyas had nearly choked over his own laughter at the idea of her taking the throne.

"A thief, through and through," he had called her. But he had been far too happy to accommodate them after the mercy she had shown him.

"I have here a royal decree, marked with Razhan's own seal."

Sher unrolled it, holding it up before the crowd, his shining golden eyes sweeping across them all. Then he began to read.

"To my Bloodlined Court, I address you one last time. For reasons of my own, I have resolved to abdicate the throne, leaving it to an adopted heir that I have kept secret from the court for many years."

Adopted. Nisha wanted to laugh as hushed whispers passed through the crowd at the mention of a secret heir.

"If you are interested in the strength and prosperity of this great desert kingdom, then you will accept my choice. Else, I fear that bloodshed will bring you to ruin."

Sher paused, lifting his gaze to the Bloodlined Court to emphasize that fact. Several of them looked away, ashamed at the thought of forcibly taking the throne. The crowd began to calm, resigning itself to its new ruler.

She could hear someone mutter that this secret heir must be Lord Vasir himself. In their eyes, it made sense. He and Razhan shared the fact that they were alone on this earth, with no family to speak of.

"I name to my throne a capable woman who has done far more for the Kingdom than you will ever know, and has shown the qualities necessary to rule the desert. She has shown mercy, tenacity, the signs of a sharp mind, and most importantly, the willingness to shed blood where necessary. I name Nisha of the Glass District to the throne, where she shall be the first Commonborn Queen of Sundara."

The crowd erupted in shock and rage, screaming and howling at Sher. But next to her, Alaric laughed with tears streaming from his eyes.

As the scroll slid shut, Sher looked to her. "Long live the Queen."

Nisha steeled herself, slipping into a new version of herself that she had to become. She was no longer a Silk Rider or an orphan thief. She was the sundamned Queen of Sundara, and she wouldn't have anybody's respect unless she acted like it.

She strode forward through the crowd of screaming

Bloodlined. Despite the spittle flying from their mouths as they cursed her, none dared to touch her.

She climbed the dais, taking the crown from Sher's hands and sat in the throne like it belonged to her. With all the Bloodlined watching, she slid the crown onto her temple.

Her voice snapped through the ballroom.

"Listen up, you bastards!"

The crowd fell back into a stunned silence. She could still hear the distinct sound of Alaric chuckling at the back.

"I know I'm not what you expected when you heard the King had a secret heir. I can see it in your eyes, wondering how a street rat managed to steal the throne." Nisha leaned forward, her gaze cutting sharply across the room full of Bloodlined. "The truth is, the King chose me for a reason."

Because she asked for it after he wanted to piss off and find the love of his life, but nobody needed to know that.

A Bloodlined lord with a long beard and piercing green eyes stepped forward, his voice thick with disdain. "I'll not be ruled by someone whose blood hasn't been touched by the Angel."

The room tensed further. Nisha leaned in, commanding silence with her presence. "What is your name?"

"Lord Farhat," he replied with a sneer.

"Lord Farhat, I'm no fool. I understand the importance of tradition, of having a Bloodlined sit on the throne."

Murmurs spread through the crowd, some faces lighting up with hope, perhaps thinking she might abdicate. Others, like Farhat, seemed less hostile, perhaps believing she might choose one of them as her king. She was sure they would like that, if only for the chance to wrestle power away from her.

Maintaining eye contact with Farhat, her voice rang out, "Sher Vasir, come here."

Sher ascended the steps, stopping just below her. His eyes met hers, filled with admiration and a burning spark of desire.

"You are the best of the Bloodlined, a man whose family has earned the respect of everyone here. Will you serve as Queen's Consort, so that we can bring together the Commonborn and the Bloodlined?"

His eyes flashed as he bent the knee to her. "It would be my honor."

She grimaced at the usage of honor again, knowing he was fighting back his grin. He reached for her hand and pressed his lips to her fingertips. She could feel the heat of fire stirring in her at the sight of him kneeling before her and at the touch of his lips.

When he looked up into her eyes, she could see that he felt the same. Sundamned hells, she wanted to take him then and there. But there would be time for that later.

"Rise," she commanded.

He obeyed, and staying one step below her, stood to face the crowd.

"Are you satisfied, Lord Farhat?"

Lord Farhat snarled and shook his head. "A Queen's

Consort? That is laughable. You must take a proper king to sit the throne."

Nisha stood and stared down at him, forcing her will on the crowd. She slowly descended the steps, one by one. "Must I?"

He pursed his lips, refusing to budge from his bold statement.

Nisha stopped at the final step. "Let me make this clear, Farhat."

His brow furrowed in rage at the exclusion of his title. He opened his mouth to speak, but she spoke first.

"*I* am Queen. The throne is mine, and mine alone. There will never be a King who sits the throne, Blood-lined or Commonborn."

"You are a worthless street rat whose worth amounts to the shit-stained clothing you've worn your entire life."

The tension wound tighter.

"You think that you would deserve this throne?"

"I do."

She could feel Sher's rage over her back, could feel the urge he had to come down the steps and break this Bloodlined man before her. But he could not. This was something she had to do for herself.

She descended that final step and approached him, stopping mere inches away from him. She looked up into his green eyes, filled with hatred.

"Then fight me for it."

He blinked, surprised at her challenge.

"Fight me or bend the knee. Show me who you are."

He looked away from her, looked at the others, but

none would meet his eye. This decision was for him, and him alone.

"Fight me. Or bend your sundamned knee."

He turned away. He swept through the crowd and exited the ballroom. The rest of the ballroom turned back to face her, to see how she would react.

She swept her gaze over the crowd. "You're worried that I will make you suffer because I'm Commonborn and you're Bloodlined. You're worried that I'll abuse the power that I have. But there is a lot you don't know about me."

Then she spoke a pair of names aloud.

"Rashad and Jasmine Rahimi."

The names echoed.

A woman stepped forward with glowing blue eyes, thin lips, blonde hair, and a fair complexion. Every night Nisha had visited the Peak District, she had watched as this woman tucked Auri into bed, told her a story, and kissed her goodnight.

Her hands grasped each other, her fingers clicking nervously. It was clear this woman knew her too, as did the man who joined her side. Rashad stared at her, not with hatred as she had expected, but with sheer fear.

She remembered that same fear driving itself into her heart close to five years ago when guards and officials stripped her daughter from her arms and passed Auri over to this Bloodlined couple to raise as their own.

Now, they were afraid she would take Auri back for herself.

Nisha gestured to them. "You don't know it, but

these Bloodlined raised my child when I was too ..." her voice caught. She lifted her chin. "When I was unable."

That was the hard truth. She did not have the food, the coin, or the safe environment that Auri needed. She could have raised her, sure, but she would have raised her inside the self-perpetuating cycle of misery that is the Glass District. And it was only just now, all these years later, that she had broken free from it. It was only now that she could change it for everybody in the Glass District.

"There is not much we have in common. But there is *one* thing," she made eye contact with the mother. She could see her lip trembling, could see that thought screaming in her mind, *please don't take her.* Nisha drew a deep breath, then sighed. "We love our daughter."

She turned and slowly climbed the steps, taking her seat on her throne once again. She spoke again, partly to the mother, but also to the wider Bloodlined court. "I'm not going to make you suffer. I'm not going to take away everything you have. Bend the knee, give me your fealty, and I promise you ... I'll make this desert a better place."

Silence.

The crowd was still. Her heart slammed against her chest. Her blood raced.

Then ...

"Move aside."

The court parted as Alaric strode through, dark brown eyes glowing with pride. He knelt before the steps.

"By the blood running through my veins, I pledge

myself to you," he said, before dipping his head. "Long live the Queen."

The crowd shifted as a palpable tension filled the air. Alaric's declaration seemed to echo endlessly. Nisha held her breath, waiting for the next move.

After a moment that stretched too long, another figure stepped forward. To Nisha's surprise, it was Rashad, his features set in a grim line. He approached the throne, his eyes meeting hers with a mix of respect and gratefulness.

He knelt before her, his voice firm as he pledged his fealty.

Then Jasmine came forward, her face a mask of composed grace. Nisha felt a twinge of the old pain—this was the woman that Auri thought was her mother.

"For the future of our daughter, and for the desert Kingdom, I too pledge the blood in my veins," she said softly as she bent the knee.

One by one, others in the crowd began to bend the knee, their voices blending into a murmuring wave of allegiance.

But as they did, murmurs of dissent grew. A number of Bloodlined turned away, their faces twisted in anger and disgust. They followed Farhat's path out.

Nisha watched them go, a cold resolve settling in her heart. They wouldn't just walk away. They would come back with their relic swords, eager to spill her blood and free up the throne for a Bloodlined ruler.

She could see it now—the war that would spill blood across the sands. But at least now, she was in a position of power. She could keep Auri safe. That was the most important thing.

Sher rested a hand on her shoulder, pulling her attention away from those leaving to those who had chosen to stay and support her.

After they had all pledged their fealty, Nisha stood and regarded the Bloodlined court.

"You may rise," she said, her voice carrying across the room, strong and clear. Then she gave her best smile. "Two nights from now, we'll have a ball here that even those in the seven heavens will be envious of."

The Bloodlined cheered and, with her final dismissal, began to file out of the ballroom. She had no idea how to even go about throwing a sundamned ball, but that was something Sher could figure out. She needed to give them *something* to talk about besides the potential onset of war.

She descended the steps and embraced Alaric. "Thank you."

She had a feeling that none of the Bloodlined would have bent the knee to her without his support.

He let her go with a smile and a wink. "Stole the throne, did we?"

She laughed, letting go of some of the tension that had wound itself tight into her shoulders. "Something like that."

Sher came down to stand beside her and extended his hand. "Lord Damaris."

Alaric raised a brow. "On good terms, are we now?"

"So long as you keep your hands off my Queen."

Nisha fought to bury her blush of embarrassment as

Alaric burst into laughter. He shook Sher's hand with a firm grip.

Then, his smile disappeared. "You should know, my father will not take this well."

"He can shove a stick up his ass with the rest of the Bloodlined," Nisha said, shrugging.

"Don't dismiss him. He's not like the rest. He's ..." Alaric ran a hand through his hair, straightened his glasses, and then finished his statement. "He's brutal."

"Brutal?"

He didn't elaborate. "I will head to Sandspire and meet with him before the other Bloodlined can get in his ear."

"I'm sure the others will tell him that you were the first to pledge your fealty. If he's really that bad, shouldn't you just stay here?"

He gave her a sad smile. "I need to see what I can do before things take a turn for the worse."

Nisha understood. With a heavy sigh, she nodded. "Be safe, Alaric. I wouldn't like to see you get hurt."

"Hurt?" Sher said. "He's too tough for that."

Alaric laughed, "He's got it right."

"Make sure you take a book with you."

Alaric patted the lump showing through his dark blue coat. "Always."

Then he was gone with the rest of the Bloodlined. Nisha was ready to leave the ballroom until she noticed that Rashad and Jasmine lingered to the side.

She motioned them forward.

Rashad was the first to speak. "Why did you not demand to take little Auri back?"

She stared at him for a long while. It would be impossible to count the number of days that had passed where she fantasized about finally having the power to tear Auri away from the thieves who had taken her. But now that the day was finally here ...

"I could never tear Auri away from the ones she loves," Nisha said, her voice soft and gentle. She thought she'd be bitter about it, but instead, she felt happy that Auri had people who loved her. And Auri *did* love them. That was easy enough to see in the way that she smiled at them, in the way that she laughed around Jasmine.

Rashad's eyes welled with tears and Jasmine openly began to cry.

"Would you like to meet her?" Jasmine asked. "Your daughter?"

This time, it was Nisha's tears that fell down her cheeks. Sher's arms wrapped around her shoulders, and she answered, feeling more vulnerable than ever before.

"I would."

Jasmine nodded and left, crossing the ballroom.

Nisha drew a shuddering breath. "Now?"

Rashad smiled at her. "She's outside in our palanquin."

Rashad's words lingered in the air, and sudden panic rushed through Nisha. She had dreamt of this day for so *long*. What if Auri didn't like her? What if she *hated* her?

Nisha glanced at Sher, seeking reassurance from his steady presence. He gently squeezed her shoulder, grounding her.

The doors at the far end of the ballroom opened again, and Jasmine reappeared. This time, she was not alone. A small figure clutched her hand, taking slow, tentative steps. Nisha's heart leaped into her throat as she caught her first glimpse of Auri. Her daughter had grown so much since she had set off into the desert with Sher to find the Angel's tear.

Auri's large, curious eyes scanned the room until they settled on Nisha. Time seemed to slow as Jasmine led Auri across the ballroom floor toward her. Every step echoed in Nisha's ears, a rhythmic thud that matched her racing heart. Rashad said something, but his voice was a distant murmur against the overwhelming sound of her heartbeat.

Auri looked up at Jasmine, seeking guidance or perhaps reassurance. Jasmine smiled down at her, nodding encouragingly.

Nisha crouched to be at eye level with Auri.

"Hi," she whispered.

Auri seemed shy, pressing her face against Jasmine's leg. "Hi."

"Do you know who I am?" Nisha asked softly.

Auri hesitated, her eyes lingering on the crown on Nisha's head. Doubt began to creep in, bringing with it the tides of despair. They threatened to drown Nisha, choking all the hope from her. Did Auri think all the gifts she left were from Jasmine?

Then, Auri spoke.

"You're my Night Mother."

FATIMA

In the Solace of These Pages,

Tonight, the stars are particularly bright. They beckon me, and yet, here I sit, writing by candlelight, listening to the sound of the man breathing behind me.

You already know of the heartache I have felt these last few decades. It is contained within these pages, stained with tears enough to fill the ocean. But this night, I feel no pain. The man I love has returned to me.

My Ilyas.

As I finished telling stories to the orphans, I looked up and there he was. He stood quietly, observing me as if it were something he'd done a thousand times. And would you believe it? He was as handsome as the day I first saw him. Time has marked us both, weathering us like old parchment, yet everything I loved about him remains.

"Ilyas," I whispered. But that whisper might as well have been a shout for how it echoed in my heart.

I've doubted over the years, questioned if the sacrifices made for this love were worth it. But if any doubts remained, they melted away by the way he looked at me.

We spent the evening together under a deep velvet sky, watching the stars come to life. There were no grand declarations, just the simple warmth of his hand in mine—reminding me of our youth spent walking through snowfields.

Now, he sleeps, his breaths (and snores) giving me more peace than the stars ever did. I'm almost afraid to sleep, because this might all be the most wonderful dream. It wouldn't be the first time it's happened. But when I glance over my shoulder, I see him there, and I know he is real.

I know that tomorrow, when I wake, he will be beside me. And we'll start our lives again. It won't be the grand adventure we once dreamed of —we are too old for that—but it will be a life lived together, which is all I ever really hoped for anyway.

This will be my final entry, as a wish so wanted has finally come true. I have another solace now, and he is waiting for me to join him. But for those who inevitably find these pages, know that love is the truest adventure, and it always finds its way home.

Fatima

ALSO BY Z.R. ABADDI

The Desert of Wishes Series

Thieves of Zareen Duet

A Wish So Lost

A Wish So Wanted

Slaves of Sandspire Duet

A Wish So Dark

A Wish So Free

Champion of Morswen Trilogy

Rage to Ruin

Curse of Midnight

Whisper of Deceit

ACKNOWLEDGMENTS

During the writing of this book, I came to be friends with a special group of authors who have helped me in countless ways.

To Luna, Rosa, Sara, and Isa — you are all so incredible, and I am so blessed to be surrounded by you.

To my readers, you have no idea how much I appreciate you. It's a special feeling knowing that all over the world, I have people reading and enjoying these stories. I can't wait to bring you so many more, including the very next in the Thieves of Zareen series.

About the Author

Z.R. Abaddi is a team of husband and wife, who write in romantic fantasy and fairy tales.

They thrive in creating vast worlds full of characters who'll make you laugh and cry.

He is Jordanian American, and she is British Pakistani, and together reside in the United Kingdom where they spend time chasing down the best bubble tea.

To get in touch, visit our website at zrabaddi.com and leave a word.